VIEWS FOR TIM LEBBON

ves me, challenges me, and makes me
rich our particular strange bent can be'
best-selling author of *The Girl Next Door*

e simply the most exciting new name in
horror in years'
SFX Magazine

BERSERK

on is a master of fantasy and horror, and his
ke for disturbing and compelling reading'
glas Clegg, author of *The Attraction*

DESOLATION

rk is infused with the contemporary realism of
ephen King and the lyricism of Ray Bradbury'
Fangoria

ive, intelligent, and absolutely enthralling…Utterly
d innovative, *Desolation* proves once again that Tim
ebbon is the Grand Master of Horror today'
Horror Web

FEARS UNNAMED

'Lebbon is a genuinely masterful writer…[with] fresh ideas,
shimmering prose, and often terrifying scenarios'
Rue Morgue

The Everlasting

The Everlasting

TIM LEBBON

This edition first published in 2008 by
Allison & Busby Limited
13 Charlotte Mews
London, W1T 4EJ
www.allisonandbusby.com

A CIP catalogue record for this book is available from
the British Library.

First published in the USA by Leisure Books,
Dorchester Publishing Co., Inc., 2007.

10 9 8 7 6 5 4 3 2 1

ISBN 978-0-7490-7908-6

Typeset in 11.5/13pt Adobe Garamond Pro by
Lara Crisp

Printed and bound in Great Britain by
CPI Bookmarque, Croydon, Surrey

Born in London, TIM LEBBON has lived in South Wales since he was nine. He has always been interested in imaginary worlds, folklore and myth, and the supernatural. He started writing at an early age, and since the publication of his first novel, *Mesmer*, in 1997, Tim has gone on to have a dozen further novels published, as well as many novellas, and several collections of his stories. Now a full-time writer, Tim's work has won the British Fantasy Award three times – twice for Best Short Fiction and, in 2007, for Best Novel – as well as several other awards. He is a *New York Times* bestseller, and he has several novels and novellas under option with film companies on both sides of the Atlantic. He now lives in Monmouthshire with his wife and two children.

www.timlebbon.net

Available from
ALLISON & BUSBY
The Everlasting
Fallen

Other titles by Tim Lebbon

In the Noreela series

Dusk
Dawn

Other novels

Mesmer • *Hush* (with Gavin Williams) • *Until She Sleeps*
The Nature of Balance • *Face* • *Desolation* • *Berserk*
Hellboy: Unnatural Selection • *30 Days of Night*
Mind the Gap

Novellas

White • *Naming of Parts* • *Changing of Faces*
Exorcising Angels (with Simon Clark) • *Dead Man's Hand*
Pieces of Hate • *A Whisper of Southern Lights*

Collections

Faith in the Flesh • *As the Sun Goes Down*
White and Other Tales of Ruin
Fears Unnamed • *After the War* • *No Exit for the Lost*

For Granddad

'A dreamer lives for eternity'
Anon

Ghostly Intruders

Scott opened his eyes. And screamed.

The garden was full of dead people.

It was still his front garden. He recognised the plant pots in the shape of boots, the inexpertly trimmed bushes, and the gate with one broken hinge. And beyond the garden the world was still there; Mrs Hacker was in the distance now, and Scott could still see her casually wild brunette hair farther along the street, and neighbours' cars sloping into and out of the gutter.

But standing in the garden were monochrome images of people he had never known, and none of them were alive. He would have known that even if it were not for the evidence of their deaths; fractured skulls, ruptured chests, pale, drawn faces still twisted with the pain of their final moments. A few of them looked almost serene, but their eyes always bore the truth. These ghosts were haunted.

None of them was completely motionless. A few wavered in his sight, as though distorted by heat haze. One or two swayed where they stood, like drunks at the end of a long dark night of obsession and addiction.

Others were moving slowly towards the house…

CHAPTER ONE

the dread of a lost letter

The memories were most treasured when they came unannounced. Like rays of sunlight through stormy clouds, or sweet cherries in a bowl of sour grapes, they never failed to make Scott smile. He could be cooking dinner, dusting bookshelves, walking in the woods, staring from the window, or drifting into sleep, and Papa would appear.

'Nettles don't sting on Saturdays,' his grandfather says, and Scott, seven years old at the time, reaches out and is stung from palm to elbow. The old man laughs uproariously, leaning back to shout at the sky. Through the prickle of tears Scott laughs with him. Even at that tender age, before he knows anything of ghosts and damnation and the pains of death, he realises that the old man is special.

'Men were made to be inebriated,' Papa whispers, 'because that can be the best time to see the truth.'

Scott plays in the pub garden while his grandfather sits and drinks. Sometimes other men gather around and are lost within a haze of pipe smoke and profanity, but every now and then he sees his grandfather's cautious eyes peering from the miasma, bright and watchful and alert, checking that Scott is safe. He offers a secret grin, as if to say, *I may be sitting here with these wizened old men, but I'm your age at heart, Scotty.*

The last time Scott saw his grandfather, the old man opened his eyes, just a crack, and whispered, 'I'm not afraid, because I know the truth. And one day I'm going to tell you.' He never heard his grandfather speak again. The old man had already been dead for three days, and these last words were whispered from his open coffin.

Scott had been sixteen years and sixteen days old when he stared down at the body of the man he loved so much. The corpse's wrinkled face – not so wrinkled in death, as his mother pointed out, not so pained – was blurred by Scott's tears, the grey eyelids made to flicker, and that brief semblance of life made the tears feel good. He reached out and touched his grandfather's cheek, and even the cool finality of that contact could not change the way he felt. It was a shock, seeing the old man like this, a man so vital and strong, motionless and quiet at last.

There were muted sounds of conversation, some shuddery tears, a sad little laugh from his mother as her sister sighed something into the air, but the dead man was the centre of the room. Scott knew that, because Papa had always possessed such power.

Sixteen-year-old Scott had never really heard those final words, of course. Not through his ears, at least. Perhaps his tears made the man's cool white lips twitch, and the clicking in his ears as he sobbed combined with the breath shuddering in his chest to form those sounds: 'I'm not afraid, because I know the truth. And one day I'm going to tell you.'

Scott had always called his grandfather Papa, and Papa had loved him dearly.

The first time he ever hurt Scott was three decades after his death.

The letter took so long to hit the floor that Scott thought he'd been mistaken. Perhaps he had only dreamt the familiar sound of the mail slot snapping shut. He lay still, breathing softly, listening for the postman's footfalls retreating along the street. But he heard only peaceful breathing from Helen beside him, and the cheerful sound of birdsong.

He yawned, rubbed his eyes, and scratched his head, and then the letter dropped to the floor downstairs, delivered in slow motion. He felt as though he'd slept and dreamt between the snap of the mail slot and the landing of the letter. Papa's voice haunted that dream, though the words were old and decayed, like thoughts long gone. His wife grumbled something in her sleep. She sounded agitated. Scott sat up and rested wearily on the edge of the bed.

The sun was blazing behind the curtains, and the bedroom was already warm. It was going to be a lovely day.

He walked quietly out onto the landing. Scott enjoyed receiving mail. For every dozen circulars, invitations to own a credit card, and appeals for charity, there was one postcard or a letter from an old friend. He didn't even mind the bills, because they were addressed to him. *We're all just fleeting dreams,* his grandfather had once said in one of his more subdued moments. Scott wanted his dreams to be alive, to persist. Seeing his name in print fixed him to the world.

This morning, looking down from the top of the staircase to the front door, he could see that there was only one envelope lying there.

He went slowly downstairs, yawning and rubbing his eyes again, taking care as his aching, ageing knees became accustomed to moving him about for one more day. The birds chattered in the front garden, singing in the morning. The house was silent and peaceful, a home, somewhere lived in and loved in. There was no reason why today should be any different – better or worse, safer or more dangerous – from any other.

As he stepped from the final stair, Scott saw the handwriting on the front of the envelope. *Scotty,* it said. The only person who had ever called him Scotty had been Papa.

At that moment the world changed around him.

It grew stale. And he knew that this dream of his life was close to edging into nightmare.

The ghost found him days after his grandfather's funeral.

Scott loved to walk in the country – a love that had been instilled in him by Papa – and following the funeral it was the safest way he knew to mourn. His parents' house was still a sad place, as if echoes of his grandfather lying in the coffin still resided there, sucked into the walls along with decades of cigarette smoke. His mother went to sleep crying and woke up the same way. His father was ineffectual in comforting her, and had taken to spending long hours in their large garden, finding a multitude of tasks that suddenly needed attending. Both of his parents seemed more concerned with the circumstances of Papa's death than the fact that he was gone. Scott had tried to encourage light back into the house, but he had come to realise that such dark times were sometimes necessary. At sixteen he understood that he still had much to learn about life. This week, he believed he was growing up some more.

His favourite walk was straight out across the field behind their house and into the woods, and that was where he went three days after the funeral. It took him past an ancient oak tree that had been blasted by lightning in the distant past. Most of it was dead, blackened, hollowed out and rotten. Yet parts of it still gamely sprouted leaves each spring, and it dropped a handful of acorns come autumn. The tree provided a den for some of the younger kids in the village, and there was always evidence of their habitation. Scott had never made use of the space and fun the tree had to offer, because Papa had always taken him deeper into the woods to show him more wondrous and secret things. He passed it by with a casual glance. Its hollow trunk was empty but for scattered sweet wrappers and a crushed can.

A few steps beyond, with the edge of the woods still in sight, he heard the first footsteps behind him.

He spun around, expecting to see one of his friends creeping up on him. He didn't relish company right now; their sympathies would be awkward. But there was no one there. Only the tree, standing sentinel even so long dead.

The footfalls had stopped as soon as he turned his head, and he guessed it must have been the breeze in his ears, the sun on his neck, the throbbing wound he still nursed inside from Papa's violent death.

When he turned to start again towards the woods, the thing was standing before him. It raised a hand, and he fell back before he had a chance to see it properly: a vision of black, something old and scarred by time. It swept forward, and cool, dry fingers caressed Scott's throat.

'Where is the Chord of Souls?' the thing sighed.

Scott tried to cry out, but something like smoke

pressed across his open lips, and he tasted soil, tobacco, and spice.

'Where is the Chord of Souls?' the thing asked again, leaning over him now, blocking out the sun. It kneed him in the stomach and Scott gagged, winded, desperate to draw in a breath past the soft hand blocking his mouth and nose. He thumped his feet on the ground and tried to twist his head. The tightness in his chest brought panic closer, and for those few seconds the thing became quiet and still, staring down with fluid eyes, as though this act of suffocation were the answer it sought.

The shape's fingers splayed, and Scott drew in a stuttering, deep breath. 'What?' he asked. He tried to raise his arms, but they lay heavy and useless.

'Where is it? The old bastard couldn't have taken it with him. He *couldn't* have!'

Scott shook his head, and now he could see the thing above him at last. It was a man, that was all, a small, wizened old man with hair yellowed by decades of smoking, skin grizzled and creased by years in the sun or a lifetime of sorrow. His eyes held madness and sadness both: madness at what he had lost, and sadness that it would likely never be found again. Even then, Scott saw desperation in this old man's eyes.

And panic. He looked like someone for whom time had already run out.

'Don't know what you want,' Scott said.

'You tell me now, boy. You take me to it! Your

grandfather wouldn't have left it unresolved.' The man leant back, giving Scott room to breathe. He looked away across the field. His eyes seemed strange, as though they reflected nothing. 'Tell me he didn't leave things undone…'

Scott wanted to shout for help. Perhaps if he screamed at the top of his lungs his mother or father would hear him, or someone in the neighbouring houses. Or maybe the shout would simply frighten this old weirdo back into whatever hole he'd crawled from. But when Scott drew in a deep breath and readied himself – muscles tensed, hands clawing at the dried corn husks scattered across the ground beneath him – the old man changed. His age became power, not a hindrance. His eyes narrowed and filled with something so much more threatening than madness. And Scott felt heat exuding from him, like a breeze of hot air in the height of summer, an old, dry heat that had been stored and fed and nurtured for longer than Scott could hope to understand.

In that moment, Scott recognised him at last. 'No!' he said. It could not be.

'Tell me,' the man said. His breath made the air unreal. His presence here belied the safe truth of the field, the woods, the oak tree.

'You're dead,' Scott said.

The old man closed his eyes and slumped forward, drawing into himself as if searching for some deeper meaning. A bird chirped somewhere in the distance. The man glanced that way and the bird fell silent.

'You have one more chance,' he said. 'The Chord of Souls.'

What can I do? He was trapped here, restrained by this dead man. Papa's friend. The man Papa had murdered before taking his own life, and now here he was, returned to ask Scott about something Scott knew nothing about.

'He would have *shown* you,' the old man said, looking away across the fields, his expression turning desperate. 'He would have *told* you.'

And then Scott remembered those final words his grandfather had somehow relayed to him, through Scott's tears and sighs of grief. *I'm not afraid, because I know the truth. And one day I'm going to tell you.*

'Ahhh,' the dead old man said, seeing realisation dawning in Scott's eyes.

'He told me he wasn't afraid,' Scott whispered, 'but he didn't tell me why.'

For a second or two Scott believed he was going to die. This illusion would release the violence simmering beneath its leathery skin, and its fists would rain down, elbows, knees, and gnashing teeth tearing and pummelling until Scott was dead. But as certain as he was of this fate, he could do nothing to prevent it. His arms were still heavy by his sides. And even though the man had stood and was no longer touching him, Scott still felt stuck to the ground. If he attempted to stand he would fall from the world.

The dead man's shoulders sagged and his face relaxed as though relieved of some great effort. 'Well, he's afraid now,' he said. 'I don't see what else I can do but wait.'

Scott's vision throbbed with each terrified heartbeat. Between one blink and the next, the man vanished.

There was no way this letter could be good.

His first reaction was to burn it. He would hold the envelope and set it alight, perhaps catching an occasional teasing glimpse of the flaming words within, his grandfather's final communication smoking away unread, unknown, unfulfilled. He would always wonder, but the threat of what it might contain – the potential for hurt, pain, and loss – was surely enough to dictate his course of action.

And it *deserved* to be burnt. After all the nightmares it had given him through the years since Papa's death, the probable contents of this letter were like a heart attack sure to happen, death wrapped in a stained, thirty-year-old envelope. *One day I'm going to tell you*, Papa had said. 'Not today,' Scott whispered, and it was a plea.

'Scott,' his wife groaned from upstairs, waking slowly from her usual deep, peaceful sleep. She had no nightmares of dead old men springing at her from unseen shadows. 'What's in the post?'

'Nothing much,' he said, staring at the envelope. *Nothing much? A letter sent by my grandfather before he died, finding me thirty years later. Finding me even though we've lived in half a dozen houses since then? Not much?* 'Well…' he said. And that single, hesitant word was the point where decisions were made, and everything changed for ever.

'What?' Helen said. She appeared at the top of the stairs.

I should burn it. Even as Scott's thumb slipped below the sealed flap – the paper was old and brittle, the edges yellowed by time – he knew that it should be destroyed. 'Something strange,' he said, lifting the flap. The paper tore like only old paper could, shedding flakes of itself onto the hall carpet. *Bits of Papa in here*, Scott thought. *Molecules of his skin. His dried spittle. I'm touching him right now.*

A dog barked outside and Scott glanced up, expecting to see the mad old ghost staring in at him through the porch window.

'What is it, babe?' Helen came downstairs, nightdress creased and twisted around her, eyes still glazed from sleep.

Scott looked up at his wife of two decades and felt an intense rush of love. It struck him like this occasionally, a realisation of just how lucky he'd been in life and how lucky he was still, but this time it ended with the deadening comprehension that all things ended. One day, both of them would be dead.

'A letter,' he said. He withdrew his thumb and thought of lying, but that was so strange to him. Their relationship was not built on lies. And even though the truth was so unreal, it came out in a rush. 'A letter from my grandfather. He must have written it just before he died, posted it, and it's been lost all these years. Stuck to the bottom of some sorting tray, maybe. Weird. You hear of things like this happening all the time.'

Helen stood three steps above him, frowning, running a hand through her long hair. 'We've only lived here for ten years,' she said. 'How did it get here?'

Scott looked down at the envelope. He did not show her that it had only his name on the front. 'I suppose it's followed us move for move,' he said.

'What does it say?' For the first time Helen's voice contained the sense of wonder that this strange delivery warranted.

'I haven't taken it out yet.'

'Well, are you going to?'

Scott stared at his wife. He shook his head. 'Not just now. I…I'd like to open it alone. It's weird. You know what I thought of Papa.'

'You loved him a lot.'

He nodded. And even though he was certain that the letter contained much more than grandfatherly chat, somehow he managed to hide that knowledge from her. He did not lie, as such…he simply omitted the truth. It felt bad. But he comforted himself by believing he did it for her.

He often dreamt of Lewis, Papa's dead friend, and how he had sought Scott out two weeks after his own murder. Right now that dream seemed so close that it could be walking up his garden path.

'I'll make some tea,' Helen said. 'You go and read the letter. But if it's a treasure map, you bloody well take me with you!' She smiled, kissed his cheek, and walked into the kitchen.

Scott took the envelope into his study and placed it carefully, squarely on his desk. He sat and looked at it for some time. He knew that he was not mistaken; it really was from Papa. Somewhere inside he had always known that this letter would arrive, or something like it. He knew this not only because his grandfather had left things unfinished between them, but because of the visit he'd received from the mad ghost of Papa's dead friend.

Scott stood and pulled the window blinds aside, watching for shadows in the garden, shapes on the garage roof. And for a while, hating himself, hating whatever it was his grandfather had left unsaid, he listened for Helen's cry of fear.

He knew he should burn the letter. But he also knew that Papa had guided him better than that.

By the time Helen came in fifteen minutes later with a mug of tea and a plate of toast, Scott had read the letter three times.

'I think it's a set of directions.'

'Directions on a map, you mean?'

'Sort of. Instructions, but directions nonetheless. And there are some strange markings, some signs, shapes. I don't know. Here, you read it.'

'Are you sure?' Helen's eyes were wide, her brows raised, and she could see what an honour Scott was affording her. This was a personal letter, and it had travelled through the years to reach him here, now, where he sat only three decades younger than his grandfather had been at the time of his death.

Scott nodded. For a moment he considered the danger he might be placing Helen in from reading this, but only for an instant. Perhaps it was selfishness or fear, but he convinced himself it was love that made him wish her to be involved.

She took the letter and read it through, standing very still.

Scott stared from the window out into their garden. Was he out there now, that mad old thing? He had not seen him again since that first time just after the funeral, but there had often been a feeling that he was there, flitting across the background, still searching for whatever it was he claimed Scott's grandfather had yet to reveal. *Where is the Chord of Souls?* he had asked. He had haunted Scott as surely as a ghost in any film he'd seen or book he'd read, stalking his mind if not actually appearing to him. He inhabited his nightmares. He had an influence over Scott's whole life, and had probably changed it more than Scott dared admit.

On the worst of nights, he knew that he was destined to see that ghost again.

There was a slight breeze this morning, and the

shrubs and trees at the foot of the garden swayed in a random dance, shuffling light and shadow to create a thousand visions in one. There could be anything out there. The human mind was a strange place, so full of trust: trust that there would not be a deep hole in the road around the next bend; trust that the sun would rise when one awoke after a night's sleep; trust that there was not a madman hiding in the garden, staring, watching, biding his time until he visited once again.

'What the hell is this?' Helen said.

Scott blinked rapidly a few times, trying to dispel the ambiguous shapes he had started to see beyond the window. He looked up at his wife, not liking the uncertainty and nervousness in her expression. 'I've read it three times,' he said. 'And I think it's nothing more and nothing less than what it says: the truth. A set of directions towards eternal life.'

'"Everlasting"?' she quoted.

Scott shrugged. 'That's what it says.'

'You didn't tell me your grandfather was religious.'

'He wasn't.'

'But this is…'

Scott waited, but Helen could not say what it was.

In her hands she held a letter, and in that letter Scott's dying grandfather had written instructions to what he claimed to be one of the great secrets of life and death. *I know the truth*, he had said. And eventually, after thirty years, he had kept his promise to tell Scott what that elusive goal might be.

'It's what he believed,' Scott said. 'It's what made him happy, content, and unafraid at the end.'

'But he killed his friend,' Helen said. 'And then himself. How could he have been happy or content? This letter reads to me as though he was scared. And these signs, these shapes, what are they? They make me feel…' She trailed off, dropped the letter on his desk, and walked to the window.

Scott had never told her about being attacked by Lewis's ghost. He had not even told his parents. He always hoped that keeping it to himself would make it vanish, the memory rotting and fading. His secrecy had encouraged the opposite effect, but the more time passed by, the more difficult it had become to tell anyone.

Now, perhaps the time was right.

'I think maybe the two of them were looking for something,' Scott said. 'And right at the end, Papa didn't want it found.' He took the letter from the desk, folded it, and placed it back in the envelope. He looked from the window and made out crouched shapes in the bushes, an old man in the clouds. Helen seemed not to notice.

'Strange that a ghost from thirty years ago should convince me that this is true.' He told Helen everything.

Helen went to work that morning confused, and angry at her confusion. She had called Scott foolish, gullible, an old romantic, but he knew that it was because she was scared. She had seen something in his eyes that frightened her. After she left he looked in the mirror, and he saw it too.

Something had changed. The realisation dawned that he was not seeing or feeling things quite the same as ever before. The memory of the attack in that field had stayed with him and somehow become one of the defining moments of his life. And receiving this letter had given that memory a brighter sheen of truth than ever before.

'Papa,' he said, 'why didn't you tell me sooner?' If he and Helen had been able to have children he may well have been a grandfather himself by now, but still he felt like a young boy when he even glanced at that letter. He felt like the teenager he'd been when his grandfather had died. It had opened up his mind and fogged his horizons, dimming truths he thought he relied upon and turning them into ambiguous things at best, ideas subject to pressures he still did not understand.

How the hell did that letter get here? Helen had asked. Scott had spoken of redirected mail, told her tales he had heard of letters stuck to the bottoms of sorting trays, finding their destination decades late, and mail that for unknown reasons just became lost. But he could not escape the fact that the envelope was old, original, and there was only his name on its front face. He had not shown her that, and he was thankful she had not asked to see.

Someone had hand-delivered this letter.

Perhaps it was best not to think about it too deeply.

The contents of the letter – twenty-two lines, that was all – echoed at him whatever he did around the house that morning. And those strange shapes and sigils were shouts within the echo. He had called in sick to work, needing time to digest and absorb what he thought this letter might mean. Time also to disabuse himself of the idea that he and Helen were now in danger.

The threat had hung like a shadow from the moment the letter arrived.

The truth, Papa had written, was simple, and easily found. And reading it was to experience it as well. The words made a spell, and the unknown symbols somehow added to its potency. Scott could not recall them without looking at the letter, and when he did look its contents imbued him with a different feeling every time. The first time he read it, he felt safe and warm and cosseted. The second time, a distance had opened up around him, pulling everything back so that there was nothing that could do him harm, but also nothing to touch or love. The third time he had slipped into a fugue; it must have lasted for mere seconds, but the dreams it contained had continued for hours, whole worlds in there, whole existences that screamed to be lived, and lived again. They faded away but left their mark.

Now, he was too afraid to read the letter again.

Helen read it too, he thought. What did she feel?

What did she see? They should talk about it. But her concern had been for him, not the letter. That made him more afraid than ever. Had she felt anything other than confusion at an old man's final words?

Scott walked into the garden and strolled around the perimeter. It was a fine spring day, clear skies promising to burn away the morning chill. A soft breeze blew into the garden through the boundary hedge, setting leaves shivering, fresh buds dipping and rising as if nodding in appreciation of their burgeoning life. He paused where he had imagined seeing a shape in the leaves and probed the bushes with his foot. There was nothing strange inside. He glanced up at the drifting clouds and saw no one watching him from there.

'Papa,' he said, 'what have you given me?' He knew that he would have to read the letter again. It had changed him. His blood pumped differently; his heart was older by the length of time it had taken him to view those thirty-year-old words. And the most confusing aspect of this was that he did not know why.

As he entered his teens, Scott had become aware that Papa was more than just an old man waiting to die. Scott's parents – his father in particular – viewed the old man as an eccentric, someone to smile at and humour, and sometimes to laugh at behind his back. He visited his friend Lewis regularly, and each time Scott asked about these meetings Papa would tap the side of his nose and wink, then stare off seriously into the distance.

In the weeks before he had taken Lewis's life and his own, Papa had grown quiet and withdrawn. Scott saw him more than ever, and afterward he thought it must have been Papa trying to cram in as many visits with his only grandson as possible. He left no note, no clue as to why he did it. Lewis had been his good friend since they fought together during the war. Nobody understood why an old man would kill his friend and then himself. Most put it down to madness, and Papa's name had become mud.

Scott had always known that there was more to it than that.

'You weren't mad, Papa,' he said to his quiet garden. The small willow tree whispered in agreement.

He went back into the house, closed the back door, and made a cup of tea. The letter sat on the desk in his study. He'd half expected it to have vanished as mysteriously as it had arrived, but it was still there, inviting him to read it one more time. *And what will I feel this time?* he thought. *What will Papa tell me when I next read the letter? Something different…or is it all the same, and I just have to find a way to accept it for what it is?*

He left the room and went to run a bath.

The phone rang. It was Helen, just arrived at work and concerned about Scott.

'Really, I'm fine,' he said. 'Are you all right?'

'Yeah. But that letter creeped me out.'

'Why?'

'It's just weird. Those signs. Don't you think?'

Oh, very, Scott thought. 'A bit strange, maybe,' he said. 'So what did you think of it?'

'Just a bit of a ramble, really, wasn't it? Maybe he wrote it when he decided to…do what he did. He wasn't right in his mind, Scott.'

'Well—'

'Baby, don't take that the wrong way. I know you loved your grandfather. But it's just one of those weird things, that's all. Put it away, forget about it.'

'But what I told you this morning. The ghost. Lewis.'

Helen was silent for some time, gathering her thoughts or waiting for a work colleague to move out of earshot.

'Helen?'

'Scott, that was a long time ago.'

'You're saying I imagined it?'

'Not as such. Babe, it was so soon after his death.'

'You think I made it up.'

'No…'

'Well, what then?'

Helen was silent again.

'I feel something when I read his letter,' Scott said.

'Of course you do.'

He gripped the phone tight, wishing he could force his conviction down the line to his wife.

'Maybe we should talk about it when you get home,' he said.

'Yes, OK. Have a relaxing day, eh?'

'Yes, I'll relax. Just running a bath.'

'Cool. See you later, babe. Ring me if you want to, though I'm in a meeting after lunch.'

'Bye.' Scott hung up. He stared at the phone for a few seconds, willing it to ring and willing his wife to blurt out her belief, her confusion, her fear at what she had read. *I really want her to be afraid,* he thought. *At least then I'll know it's not just me.*

The bath running upstairs, tea growing cold, Scott went into his study and sat down to read the letter one more time.

'You have to name every single bird,' Papa says. 'If they come into your garden and take the food left out for them, it's because they trust you. And trust always has a name.'

Scott stares wide-eyed at his grandfather. He's nine years old, and even though he thinks he can see the truth from the games in the old man's stories, still there's always that element of doubt. That's what he finds so magical about Papa: an element of doubt. It's almost as if he's from somewhere else.

'Are you from space, Papa?'

The old man does not laugh. He frowns. 'Well, I have some memories of flying through the asteroid belt, but…they're fading fast.' *Then* he smiles.

'Papa!' Scott says.

'So, the birds. That siskin over there I'll call Cyril.'

'Sparrow… Arthur.'

'Arthur?'

Scott nods.

'A good name. Strong. Over there, see that wren jumping in and out of the bushes? Smallest bird in Britain. I'll call it Tiny.'

Scott goes on, pointing and naming, laughing and enjoying the heat of the sun and the weight of Papa's love. And there the memory usually ends.

But not this time.

'Reggie,' Scott says, and his grandfather is staring at him.

'What, Papa?'

Papa looks around furtively, then leans close so that he can whisper in Scott's ear. 'This world's just a veil, and there's so much more to see,' he says. 'One day I'll tell you how. Just make sure you believe.' The words carry a weight all their own, and they sink slowly into Scott's mind, echoing, implanting themselves deep, burrowing down until they're drowning beneath a young boy's minor concerns and random musings.

'Papa, what do you mean?'

But Papa laughs and points at two blue tits fighting around a cage of nuts. 'Tweedledum and Tweedledee!' he says. He leans back in his chair, the laughter turning almost manic, and a tear squeezes from the corner of one eye.

* * *

Scott closed his eyes and tried to grab onto the memory. It clung there, and he opened his eyes and reached for a notebook. He wrote down what Papa had told him before he could forget. *This world's just a veil, and there's so much more to see.*

'I've never remembered that before.' He looked at the letter open on his desk, taking in the scrawl without making out individual words. Could that have planted a false recollection? Or had it uncovered a memory hidden away for so long? That had sounded so much like Papa, but the words and their delivery were much more serious than anything Scott normally remembered.

He folded the letter again, slipped it into its crumbling envelope, and placed it in his desk drawer. He locked the drawer and pocketed the key. Glanced from the window. Saw the bushes at the bottom of the garden, waving against the breeze and projecting secret signals as their shiny new leaves caught and reflected the sun.

Scott went upstairs, stripped, and sank into the bath. He sighed with pleasure. The warm water closed over his stomach and chest and he stared up at the ceiling, counting cracks and watching a small spider exploring possible sites for a new web. He thought back to when he was young, and wondered whether he would capture that innocence, naivety, and willingness to believe ever again.

* * *

Downstairs, something groaned.

Scott's eyes snapped open and he sat up, water sloshing from the bath and splashing on the tiled floor. He held his breath and froze. The water settled, though he could not silence the popping of a thousand tiny bubbles. He strained to hear the noise again, hoping that he would not.

A groan…a moan…like branches in a tree shifting against one another.

He turned his head left and right, cupping his ears. Water pipes creaked and ticked beneath the floorboards. Perhaps in his half-sleeping state he'd heard that, and assigned it a much more sinister source.

Him? he thought. *Lewis?* Maybe he had been quizzed by a ghost all those years ago, maybe not. Perhaps, as Helen suggested, the death of his grandfather had pressed close around him, inviting in all his other fears and coalescing in this figure that sought knowledge with the intimation of violence.

Scott almost called out to ask who was there, but even the thought of that made him smile. He was not in a bad horror movie right now. Instead he reached for the towel and began to dry himself off.

That noise again, louder and more definite.

Scott wrapped the towel around his waist and stepped from the bath. He knew all the creaking floorboards and managed to avoid most of them, but standing at the head of the stairs he stepped on a loose board, wincing as it echoed down the stairwell.

The groan had stopped.

He thought of calling the police, but realised he had nothing to tell them.

Scott picked up a heavy barometer set in granite from the shelf beside the stairwell and started down, stepping on the edges of the treads. A car pulled up outside his neighbour's house and honked its horn, and he used the opportunity to dash down the final few stairs.

He turned and faced along the hallway. Three doors headed off from there, all of them half-open. He exhaled and grew still.

Then he started moving forward, and it was his study he went to first.

There was no sign of any intruders. The patio doors that led into the garden were still closed, as was the window. Nothing seemed out of place. But Scott suddenly thought he'd recognised that sound – or at least could place its possible cause – and when he went to his desk he saw that he was right.

The drawer had been forced. The lock still held, though the wood around it had splintered. One more heave with whatever had been used to do this and the drawer would have sprung open.

He tried to look through the crack between drawer and desk, but it was too dark inside to see whether the letter was still there.

Someone did this! Scott thought suddenly. He placed the barometer on the desk and picked up his brass letter opener. He was about to move back into the hallway when something caught his attention in the garden. From the corner of his eye he saw a shape down by the bushes, a tall, grey form standing motionless and watching the house. He turned to look, blinked, and the garden was empty.

'Fuck!' He exhaled. He panted a few quick breaths, scanned the lawn, the shrub borders, tried to see beneath the willow tree, but he could see no one out there.

The house suddenly felt very empty. Scott realised that before now it had felt occupied, holding its breath as though awaiting some event to come and go. Now it was just him.

He touched the desk where the wood was splintered. It spiked at his fingertips, and he relished the sensation because it was so real. Could a ghost do this? He was not sure. He knew nothing about ghosts, other than what he thought he had experienced when he was sixteen. He wasn't even sure he believed in them.

He shoved at the drawer, but the lock was bent and deformed, allowing no movement either way.

'Papa, what have you *given* me?'

The phone rang, startling Scott. The towel fell from around his waist, and he uttered a nervous giggle. He sat in the swivel chair behind his desk and picked up the receiver.

'Hi, babe. Wondering how you are.'

'I'm not too bad,' Scott said, amazed at the ease of his lie. 'You?'

'Fine. Well, Jess is bad-mouthing me to Alex again, so I'm taking her out to lunch to find out what the fuck the problem is. Other than that... hunky-dory.'

'Good.' He stared at the open study door, expecting it to darken at any moment.

'Sure you're OK? Did you have your bath?'

'Just got out. Sitting here naked right now, in fact.' He listened for footsteps out in the hallway, the living room, upstairs.

Helen laughed quietly. 'Well, I'll be home earlyish tonight,' she said. 'We can sort that out then, if you like.'

And even though Scott was scared, and he felt eyes upon him, and something about the garden just wasn't right whichever way he looked at it, he managed to muster a gentle laugh and say, 'Yes, I like.' Helen hung up. Scott dropped the receiver back onto his desk, and he wrapped the towel around him again as he stood.

He stared into the garden, keeping back from the patio doors. He knew that with the sun where it was in the morning, it was difficult to see into the study from outside, even with the blinds open. It was all shadows inside. He looked directly at where he'd seen the shape, turned his head, and tried to catch it from the corner of his eye, glancing left and right. The garden remained as empty as the house, and he decided to go upstairs to dress.

He glanced at the drawer as he went. *Something did that!*

Scott left the room and wandered around downstairs, checking every doorway, alcove, and cupboard. Upstairs he did the same, with no idea what he would do were he to find someone or something hiding there.

In his bedroom, as he was hauling on a pair of jeans, the enormity of what had happened suddenly hit him. He sat heavily on the bed and sighed, rubbing his hands across his scalp and enjoying the prickle of his shorn hair. It felt like a softer version of splintered wood.

He pulled on a shirt and ran back downstairs to his study. It was empty. He used the granite barometer to finish the job someone else had started, and when the drawer slipped open he breathed a sigh of relief to see the letter still there. He folded it in half – no longer mindful of its brittleness – and shoved it into his jeans pocket.

Then he turned and faced the garden, arms crossed. 'Want it now?' he asked. And against his better judgement, and in perfect tune with the bad horror film he had convinced himself he was not in, he said, 'Come and get it.'

Chapter Two

shapes in dust

Throughout that afternoon he kept returning to his study to look at the desk. He touched the bent lock and the ragged wound in the wood, trying to find a scar where a crowbar or screwdriver had been inserted to jimmy the drawer open. There was nothing. Only the torn wood, the bent metal. And each time he returned he tried to come up with some other explanation. Could he have caught his belt on the handle and ripped it open? But it was a strong oak desk, the lock old but firm. Perhaps he'd slammed it too hard that morning after depositing the letter inside, and ruptured the wood around the lock? But he thought not.

And there were those groans he'd heard when he was in the bath. Wood on wood, or the sounds of effort?

He did not go out into the garden again. Something seemed wrong out there. He could not make out what it was, but the more he looked, the more unsettled and hemmed in he began to feel. The light was fine, the trees and bushes moved in time with the subtle breeze, birds probed the lawn for worms and insects, shadows remained where they should have been, butterflies rode the air like ash from a distant fire. It was fine, yet everything felt wrong. He went from spending ten minutes staring out the window to an hour avoiding looking outside at all.

He rang Helen again. Her voicemail picked up, and he remembered her saying she had a meeting that afternoon. So he rang twice more and listened to her voice.

Around three o'clock Scott slouched down on the settee and popped a DVD into the machine. As the title sequence of *The Thing* played out, he pulled the letter from his pocket and read it one more time; the sound of the TV retreated; the feel of the settee grew increasingly personal. When he finished the letter and read the scrawled *Papa* at the end, he closed his eyes against the rosebud brushing against the living room window. Perhaps when he woke again it would have bloomed and died and it would be autumn, and the letter would be forgotten.

He and Helen were going to Rome in October for a few days. They travelled well. Having never had kids they'd saved a tidy sum through their working careers, though Scott sometimes thought the more money they had, the sadder it made them.

He shifted on the settee, listened to the men in

the Antarctic slowly growing apart, and felt the brush of something against his cheek, as though the rose had grown all the way through the glass.

Papa taps his cheek again, and Scott wakes. He's almost fourteen, and he's taken to sleeping away hot afternoons as the summer holidays blaze their way towards the autumn term.

It's a familiar memory, and Scott relives it as a viewer. It's like a waking dream that he has lived many times before. He knows what is coming next.

'Get up and shake your arse,' Papa says. 'We have to go to the woods!'

'Why?'

'We just do!' The old man is excited and animated, shifting here and there in Scott's room as the boy pulls on shoes and socks, baseball cap, jacket.

'You don't need that; it's hotter than the Sahara's arse out there, boy.'

Scott smiles and drops his jacket onto the bed. His cigarettes are in there. Papa doesn't yet know that he smokes, and Scott has already decided that he might never tell.

'Come on! Before it's too late!'

'What is it, Papa?' Scott hurries out after his grandfather, and it takes until they're through the gate and out onto the village street before the old man speaks again.

'The day's wasting away, boy, and you're letting

it pass you by. Sleeping in the day! I'm over seventy, and I still don't have an afternoon nap! So what are you, Scotty? A young baby who needs a couple of hours to see him through to bedtime? Or an old man recharging his batteries and waiting for the next meal to tick away another part of his life?'

'Neither,' Scott says. It's a familiar speech, a familiar game.

Papa stops and leans close. 'You sleep, and things might pass you by. You'll miss things. And some things are too valuable to miss. You know?' He nudges Scott in the ribs and laughs, eyes twinkling like those of a man fifty years younger.

They walk along the street until they reach the wide gate into the field. Across the field, past the old lightning-struck oak, the edge of the wood beckons with the promise of cool shadows and more stories from Papa. Scott never tires of these excursions, and any sleep residue has already been burnt away by the sun. He's excited, and he already knows what he's going to ask Papa to talk about today.

'So, the war,' Scott says, and Papa grows quiet, and all the weight of his years presses him down towards the ground. He looks at his grandson and smiles a sad, lost smile. For a second it's as though he died in the war, and this thing before Scott is the ghost of the man he used to be.

Here the memory usually ends, fading away as the two of them step out into the field. But this time the memory goes on and Scott is living it, not merely observing. Before it was like watching a movie, but now he's playing the lead role.

'You don't want to know about the war,' Papa says.

'I do.'

'I've told you everything there is to tell, three times over.' They're passing the old oak tree now, and Papa pauses to catch his breath. He leans against the side of the tree that is still sprouting.

'But there's more,' Scott says. 'I know there is. There has to be.'

'And why does there have to be?'

'There's always more with you, Papa.' Scott smiles, and revels in the smile his grandfather sends in return.

'I only hope you never have to go through the things I did,' Papa says, and then he is telling Scott about his time in Africa fighting Rommel. It's a familiar story, but Scott is content to let it flow because he senses that something else is coming. Papa is telling the story faster than usual, for a start. Almost as though he's keen to move past the battles and death to reach somewhere else.

They arrive at the edge of the woods, climb the stile, and enter the shadows with a grateful sigh. The heat is nowhere near as bad in here. Sunlight probes through the tree canopy and speckles the ground, and Scott tries to step only on shadows.

Papa leads the way, taking a different route from normal and heading beneath the pine trees. Wood ants' nests rise here and there from the forest floor, some of them as high as Scott's waist, and he can see the creepy movement of thousands of ants as they walk by. Sometimes when there's no breeze he can stand still and hear the movement of countless ants over fallen leaves and pine needles. On those occasions it's almost as if the whole forest is alive, and he is a living invader allowed passage through from one side to the other. He often wonders what would happen were he to abuse that permission.

They come to a clearing where there's a fallen tree. Papa brushes the tree off and sits, sighing as he leans forward and rests his elbows on his knees. He has told Scott about the Battle of El Alamein, the devastation at Tobruk, and now he has fallen silent. But Scott knows that there is more to say.

The forest seems to know it as well. Birds have gone quiet, and even the secretive rustle of wood ants has ceased.

'Papa?' Scott asks expectantly.

'Scott,' the old man says. 'We found something. Lewis and I, we found something out there in the desert. A munitions dump went up, and a day later we were sent to make sure nothing was left lying around. There were craters…' He drifts off again, looking between the trees.

'Papa? What did you find there?'

'I can't say,' he says. 'It's not possible, and I can't say. One day, perhaps. If you see me dead, maybe then I'll tell you.'

'I don't understand. You're scaring me.'

'There's more,' Papa says. His voice has dropped and taken total control of the scene. Everything is listening to him; even the trees seem to lean in to hear better. For the first time ever Papa is frightening Scott, unnerving him with the look of mad passion in his eyes and the stern set of his face.

'More what?'

'More than what we see, more than what we know. More than life. All around us all the time, Scotty, there's so much more. I can see.' He closes his eyes, takes in a deep breath, and opens them again. He looks around; then his eyes fix on something behind Scott. 'I can see,' he carries on, voice lower and heavier than ever. 'It's easy after the first time. Close your eyes, think of the song from the Chord of Souls, open them again, and you see everything else. The dead, where they gather. The storms of time eddying around our heads, so close and yet never known.' His eyes have not moved, and Scott turns around to see what his grandfather is watching.

'What is it?' he says. For him there are only trees, shrubs, leaves, and shadows.

'The spell, Scott.' And he mumbles a brief series of words, guttural sounds that do not sound right coming from a human mouth. There's a strange musical quality to them, but it's distasteful and eerie.

'But *what* do you see?'

'A young girl who died in these woods a long time ago,' Papa says.

Scott's blood runs cold, and the hairs on his back rise. 'What?'

Papa nods. 'Between the trees. There. I see her, because there's so much more, Scotty.'

Scott stands and backs away from where the old man is looking. 'Papa,' he says, and it must be the sound of desperation in his voice that brings Papa around.

The old man stands, shakes his head, and closes his eyes briefly once more. Then he walks towards Scott.

Scott backs away.

Papa pauses, frowns, then reaches out for his grandson. 'I would never, ever hurt you,' he says, and he hugs the boy close.

'You scared me.'

'It's right to be scared.'

'Why?'

'The world is a scary place.'

Scott sobs, only once, but enough to elicit a tighter hug from his grandfather.

'You need to know,' the old man says. 'I won't be here for ever, and you really need to know.'

'What if I don't *want* to know?'

Papa laughs briefly, then says no more. Scott cannot see the old man's face. For once he is glad.

Scott started awake, and he thought the sound he heard was his own startled shout. He sat up on the settee and rubbed his eyes. On the TV screen someone was screaming, and at the window the rosebush still caressed the glass.

What was he going to tell me? he thought. He could not remember. The fresh memory of the forest and what his grandfather had said was strong, but there was nothing beyond that hug. *Maybe we just went home. Maybe he didn't tell me anything at all.*

He stood and went upstairs to the toilet, looking through the open window as he urinated. The slice of garden he saw seemed quiet and peaceful, but he wondered whether the rest of the garden was quite so innocent. Perhaps it knew when he was watching and shifted to suit his gaze. He finished, flushed, and went into the spare bedroom, and from there the whole back garden was laid out to his view.

Still silent, still wrong. It was as though the garden were watching him. He turned to walk from the window and spun around again. Nothing changed, and he smiled nervously.

Downstairs, he went to the kitchen to switch on the kettle. The small side window opened out over the patio, and Scott stood there as the kettle bubbled and boiled behind him.

Something moved. He edged back from the window, startled and confused. Nothing had moved out in the garden, of that he was sure, but there had been a definite sense of *shifting* across his vision. He closed his eyes briefly and opened them again, wondering whether he had dust or an eyelash in there. But there was no pain, no discomfort. He turned to open the fridge, his view of the sun striking the window adjusted slightly, and then he saw.

The dust on the outside of the window was moving. It coalesced into separate islands like scum on a pond, then shifted as though pushed by an unseen current. There was no sound. It stopped moving, leaving erratic new shapes for the sun to reveal, then started again. Smeared, pushed, pulled across the glass, it was still shifting when Scott turned and fled from the kitchen.

His heart was thumping. What could do that? Sun, wind, moisture in the air, light refracting through deformed glass…He stopped in the hallway and leant against the wall. He was spooked, working himself up into a state of panic. And there was really nothing wrong.

(Apart from the broken drawer lock.)

Nothing strange outside, and only his own fear inside. Could fear change surroundings? He supposed so. Perception was a strange thing, and he knew it could be altered by moods, tiredness, and dread.

(But the lock. I saw the lock.)

He heard a car pull up on the gravel driveway and hurried to the front door. Through the vertical blinds at the side window he saw Helen's Astra shift slightly as she stepped out and closed the door behind her. It was early, but he was so glad that she was home that he did not wonder why.

Scott went to open the front door, and then saw the look on Helen's face. She was glancing around, down at the ground and up at the sky, towards the house and into the bushes bordering the driveway. She was frowning. As she remote-locked the car, her other hand waved around her head, as if to knock away a fly or a bee. Scott saw nothing there.

He opened the door, trying to reign in his relief at her return. 'Home early.'

Helen's face changed when she saw him. She smiled. It touched her eyes and went some way towards removing the worry there, but it also left some behind. She was troubled, and Scott did not like that one bit.

'I can't get that damn letter out of my head,' she said. 'And you sounded down on the phone, so I came home early.'

'Thanks.' Scott reached out and hugged his wife, kissing her on the cheek. He looked over her shoulder into the front garden. The light fell as it should, the shadows dwelt where they belonged, a few birds skittered around in their Kilmarnock tree. But everything was wrong. If he stepped out there, he could be changed for ever.

He shivered and knew that Helen had felt the movement.

'Let's go in,' she said. 'We'll cook a nice dinner and open a bottle of wine.'

'Sounds good,' Scott said. Helen moved past him into the house, and he did not turn his back on the front garden until the door was shut and bolted from the inside.

Scott did not mention the broken drawer, but he did let Helen read the letter again. She seemed troubled, but her reaction was similar to before.

'So what do you see when you read it?' he asked.

'None of it seems to make sense to me,' she said. 'It's…confused. He must have been in a very strange state of mind when he wrote it.'

'Must have.'

'What about you? When you read it?'

Scott did not answer, but he could not hide his own confusion over what he was feeling, seeing, remembering.

'Must be strange for you,' she said softly. 'Must make you quite emotional.'

'Yes, quite.'

'Well, let's forget about it for now, go and—'

'What was wrong when you got out of the car?'

Helen sat up straight on the settee, staring up at Scott where he stood before her.

'You looked worried about something. Nervous.'

'You were watching me?'

He nodded.

'That explains it. Felt like I was being watched. And I was.' Helen stood and went out to the kitchen, leaving Scott trying to figure out whether that explained anything at all.

* * *

Against all odds, Scott enjoyed their meal. They spent time in the kitchen chopping peppers, spring onions, and mushrooms, stir-frying chicken and sweet and sour sauce, boiling rice, and stirring everything into a tasty dish that went well with a glass of red wine. The kitchen filled with steam and the smells of cooking, and as they sat at the table to eat Scott noticed that the steam had condensed on the window, and the view out into the garden was now hidden. He was glad.

The wine settled his nerves and dulled his heightened senses. The food tasted good. He and his wife succeeded in not chatting about the letter all through the meal, and even though Scott felt it folded into his back pocket, he did not dwell on the broken drawer. *In denial* he thought once. But it seemed to be working, so he went with the flow.

It had turned six o'clock by the time they finished. Helen ran hot water into the sink while Scott cleared the work surfaces, and within ten minutes they had tidied the kitchen and retired to the living room. They sat close together on the settee, Scott's hand on Helen's thigh, Helen leaning against his arm. Their wine glasses were replenished, and Scott felt a comfortable buzz. It was still early, but he looked forward to an evening of wine, a DVD, and perhaps lovemaking later. It was at times like this that he appreciated the simple goodness in life.

'One phrase in that letter…' Helen began.

'Hmm?' Scott was annoyed that she'd brought it

up again, but at the same time he knew that it was inevitable. She had come home early because of the way he had sounded on the phone, and he'd sounded scared because he'd spooked himself. One last trick from Papa, perhaps. It had been intended for him almost three decades ago, but even after all these years Papa could fool him.

'Where he talks about the Chord of Souls. And surrounds that name with those symbols.'

'Yes.'

'What was that?'

The new memory from that afternoon floated back to him, where Papa mentioned the song from the Chord of Souls…and then that weird, almost animal-like series of sounds he had made. 'I'm not sure.'

Helen shifted, moving away slightly so that she could turn to look at him. 'Really?'

Scott nodded. Shrugged. 'Well…I think it was a book. But I don't know which one.'

'Why do you think it was a book?'

'Something Papa said to me once.'

'What?'

'I can't remember!' he snapped, immediately regretting it. 'Sorry. Just…something about something he'd found out in the desert. It was just a story.'

'You're sure?'

'Yes. No. Everything with Papa was strange.'

Helen was silent for a while, sipping her wine

and staring at the blank TV screen. Scott could see them both reflected in there. When he was a kid he'd believed that his reflection was another person.

'He talks about it in the letter as though it's still around,' she said.

Scott nodded. But he thought, *Is that what he really says?* And the letter was a shape in his pocket, yearning to be read once again.

The doorbell rang. Scott jumped, but Helen was on her feet before him. He followed her into the hallway, and the instant he left the living room dread clasped hold of him. *Don't answer*, he thought. *Don't go, don't go.* He was trying to speak those words, but something had happened to his mouth. He clasped the wine glass in his right hand and heard a *tink* as it cracked.

Helen unlocked the front door and drew it open.

There was no one there. Day was slipping towards dusk, and trees and bushes made familiar shadows across their front garden. The Astra sat on the drive, glinting with a few diamond spots of rain.

There was no one there, but Scott was so desperate for Helen not to move over the threshold that he stepped forward and grasped her arm.

'Ouch!' She pulled away, catching sight of the cracked wine glass spilling wine onto his right sleeve. 'What have you done?'

'Glass broke.' Scott was staring out into the garden, trying to use the failing daylight to discern just what was wrong out there. *Or is it all in here?*

he thought, not sure whether he meant the house or somewhere even deeper.

He could feel the letter creased against his buttock.

'Get to the kitchen; you'll stain the carpet!' Helen was already trying to steer him inside, and for that he was glad. She swung the door closed behind her.

'Lock it,' he said.

'Scott—'

He backed along the hall, holding his arm up so that his sleeve soaked up most of the spilling wine. 'Lock it, please.'

She locked the door, and Scott turned and hurried into the kitchen. By the time Helen stood beside him at the sink, he'd put down the glass and was dabbing at his shirt with a damp cloth. He took it off, Helen soaked it beneath the tap, and then he heard the sound of something scoring across a pane of glass.

'I fucking *hate* that!' Helen said, wincing.

'The living room.'

'That bloody rosebush of yours.'

Scott turned and went back into the living room, still topless. His belly swung over his belt, handles bulging at his hips. He hated being naked, even if it was only Helen who saw. He could have been so much better. *There's so much more to see*, Papa had said. *This world's just a veil.*

'Damn it, Papa!' Something waved beyond the window, vanishing from view as if being drawn away.

'What?' Helen called from the kitchen.

'Nothing.' Scott's heart was pummelling at his chest. He pulled out the letter, opened it, and read it again, and it mentioned the Chord of Souls, and he felt a sense of doom closing in around him, as though reading the letter was inviting in the same fate that had consumed Papa in the end. Murder and suicide. Perhaps the old man really had been mad after all.

Scott wondered whether insanity was hereditary.

Helen came in and surprised him by hugging him tight. 'That was weird,' she said. 'Maybe we need more wine?'

Scott nodded. 'Maybe we do.'

Helen went back to the kitchen to choose a new bottle, leaving him alone in the living room. He approached the window. The silhouette of a bud-heavy stem of the rosebush rose and fell in the strengthening breeze, whispering across the glass. Whispering, not scoring. *Not the rosebush*, he thought.

He cupped his hands to the glass to cut out reflection from the living room light, held his breath, and pressed his face close.

He remembered Papa sitting on that fallen tree, the whisper of wood ants hanging on his every word.

A car passed beyond their garden, and Scott grasped at the normality of the scene. Mrs Hacker from along the street was walking her dog. She was a beautiful woman who thought herself ugly, and Scott had always perceived a sense of tragedy about her.

Papa staring into the distance before lowering his head, closing his eyes, uttering those strange words.

The street scene was completely normal, but that was beyond the garden. It could have been a whole world and thirty years away. Scott closed his eyes and, as that long-ago scene played out in his memory, he matched the words and tune Papa had uttered word for word. It felt strange, twisting his lips and tongue and throat in strange shapes, making it feel as though he had something in his mouth, something alien that did not belong there, but which he himself had deigned to swallow.

He opened his eyes. And screamed.

The garden was full of dead people.

Helen shouted something, came at him with hands held out and eyes wide, but for those first few moments Scott could not hear her. Perhaps in her terror at his sudden cry she could not form words. That, or the blood pounding in his ears had stolen his hearing.

It was still his front garden. He recognised the plant pots in the shape of wellington boots, the inexpertly trimmed bushes, and the gate with one broken hinge. And beyond the garden the world was still there; Mrs Hacker was in the distance now, and Scott could still see her casually wild brunette hair farther along the street, and neighbours' cars sloping into and out of the gutter.

But standing in the garden were monochrome

images of people he had never known, and none of them were alive. He would have known that even if it were not for the evidence of their deaths: fractured skulls, ruptured chests, pale, drawn faces still twisted with the pain of their final moments. A few of them looked almost serene, but their eyes always bore the truth. These ghosts were haunted.

None of them were completely motionless. A few wavered in his sight, as though distorted by heat haze. One or two swayed where they stood, like drunks at the end of a long, dark night of obsession and addiction.

Others were moving slowly towards the house.

Scott gasped and tried to scream again, but his throat had dried and it came out as a pained rasp. Helen grabbed him and he jumped, pulling away from her and searching her eyes for life. He found it and gave in to her hug. She pulled him close, squeezed tight, and her body warmth was welcome.

'What is it?' she asked, still a whisper.

Scott could barely shift his gaze from the garden. They were all looking at him.

'Scott?' Louder this time, as though his shock were fading.

'In the garden,' he said, though that explained nothing. He tried to pull away, but Helen had him tight. 'In the garden!'

'There's nothing there,' she said.

One of them – an old woman – had raised her hand, leaning forward for support as she took hesitant steps across the lawn. She wore a shawl that should have been multicoloured, but death had greyed it. A young man was one of those shimmering in Scott's vision, features uncertain, leather clothing catching a weakened dusk, the wound on the side of his head obvious even through distortion. His eyes were wide: terrified or angry.

'Dead people,' Scott said. 'Ghosts.' But these were nothing like the time he had seen Lewis days after Papa's death. He had been solid, tactile, *there*. 'Wraiths,' he said, and that seemed to suit better.

'There's nothing out there, babe.'

Scott closed his eyes for a few seconds, hoping he could refresh his vision. When he opened them again something had changed, and it took him a few seconds to make out what: that shimmering, heat-haze effect had transferred to a few more of the wraiths.

He shut his eyes again, fighting every second to keep them closed against the idea that the wraiths were advancing, using his momentary lack of vision to close in on the house and Helen and him, and perhaps while he was not looking their bearing would change, anger overcoming lethargy, and violence born of anger—

Helen tried to pull him out of the living room, and he looked again. They were fading. Those that had been wavering to begin with were almost gone, and the others were starting to lose definition. Two that had been moving slowly forward stood directly outside the window now, pressing ahead as though leaning on the glass. Their features were blurred and confused.

He closed his eyes, whimpering and desperately grateful for Helen's clasp. When he looked again most of the wraiths were gone, and those that remained were shadows on the air.

Scott started to cry.

'What is it, babe?'

'They're almost gone,' he said, gasping through his tears.

'Good. That's good.'

Scott shook his head and started to shiver. 'I can't see them anymore,' he said, 'but they're *all still there!*'

He pulled away from Helen and she let him go, following him back into the hallway to the bottom of the staircase, where he sat and curled up and tried to remember exactly what Papa had told him about life and death.

'I want to run,' Scott said. 'I want to run away and find somewhere safe.'

'We're safe here.' Helen had barely left him untouched since he had seen the ghosts, leaving only to fetch a clean shirt. She did not believe him – that was obvious, and understandable – but she was with him, and he loved her for that.

'Maybe,' he said, but there was so much he didn't know. 'But I still want to go.'

'We can if you want. It's not midnight yet. We

can jump in the car and go for a drive, find a hotel. Book in as Mr and Mrs Smith.'

Scott managed a wan smile. Then he thought of those wraiths standing before the house, and the smile slipped away. 'They were there for a reason,' he said. 'Only in the garden, not beyond. All looking this way. All of them just—'

'That fucking letter,' Helen said. 'It's all because of that.'

'Yes!' Scott said, but that was not what she meant at all.

'You've got Papa on your mind, and you said he was always talking about stuff like this. Ghosts and death and weird stuff.'

'Death's not weird.'

Helen only shrugged.

'And maybe it is the letter,' Scott said. He sat up straight on the settee and stared at the picture above their fireplace. It was a modern painting of a seascape, blazing colours of sky and sand all converging into a deep, dark, blurry line tipped with a splash of white. A tiny white horse was just rising from the sea, and many nights Scott had sat back with a glass of wine, urging it to grow.

'We should sleep,' Helen said. 'Too much wine. And you've been dwelling on that letter all day. Just remember, babe, you should have had it when you were sixteen. Not now. You're an old man now.'

'Thanks.'

'Pleasure.' She smiled and touched his shoulder,

squeezing like a friend. Was she so angry with him that her affection now came to this? He leant back to look at her face, and saw that she was very tired.

'Let's go to bed,' he said.

She nodded and yawned. 'It'll be better in the morning.'

Sometimes things were. But not this. If Scott went to the window and pulled back the curtains he would see darkness, but those wraiths would still be out there, and perhaps they could see him even though he could not see them.

Could they enter the house? Come upstairs, push through closed doors, avoid all those loose floorboards that gave the building its voice? If in his sleep he muttered those words spoken by Papa in that clearing long ago, would he wake to see those ghosts surrounding his bed?

His heart stuttered in his chest, his breath came fast and shallow, but Scott did his best to hold himself together. Helen deserved that, at least.

He made sure every window and door was locked, all the while avoiding looking outside. He was so afraid that he would see an empty garden and imagine it full.

He dreamt of Papa, coming home from the hospital after thirty years and being cured of suicide. Scott was delighted to see him, and in the dream Scott and Helen had three children, all of whom recognised Papa instantly as their great-grandfather. But there was sadness, too. Scott told him about the ghosts, and Papa was devastated that it had come to this. 'It's just not right,' he said. 'I did everything I could, and still…'

Scott woke up, opened his eyes, and felt the dregs of his dream filtering back into sleep. He saw shapes in the room, and all of them he recognised: chair, wardrobe, pictures on the wall.

'Papa,' he whispered, but none of the shapes moved.

He remembered that he and Helen did not have children, and he was sad. It felt as though a chunk of his life had been knocked away. Then he recalled that Papa had died thirty years ago, and another slice was taken from his world.

Scott sighed and turned over, taking comfort from the warm shape of Helen beside him.

And now that what he lacked from his dream hit home, those extra things in his life began to pour in. The letter, the odd things it said, the memories of Papa unremembered before now, the broken drawer…the ghosts.

The shapes in the garden, crowding his home almost without moving.

Those words he had uttered. Papa's strange song, which had lifted the veil on his reality and shown him more of what there was to see and know.

Scott sat up and glanced quickly around the room. The familiar shadows were still there, with nothing new. Fear heightened his senses, but there was nothing out of place.

He stood from the bed, careful not to wake Helen, and moved to the window. Shifting the curtain allowed the half-moon access. It caught the hairs on his arm and hand and spilt to the floor behind him, revealing a long-forgotten coffee stain. *Moonlight makes everything clear,* he thought, though he did not know where that came from.

He looked down into the garden. Everything seemed as it should be. He closed his eyes, sang those guttural words he had remembered Papa saying, and opened his eyes again.

The shadows in the garden changed. Most were still, but some moved like thin trees in the breeze.

He was the centre of their attention.

Scott dropped the curtain and stepped away. He nudged against the bed and sat down heavily, creaking the mattress and causing Helen to stir. She rolled over, muttered something, and went back to sleep, snoring softly.

'They're still out there,' Scott whispered. He looked around the bedroom – empty. 'Only out there. Maybe.' Standing, he padded quietly from the room and stood on the landing. It was also empty. He leant around the corner and glanced downstairs, terrified of what he would see, glad when he saw only shadows that belonged. Across the landing, shifting aside the net curtain that covered the window there, looking down onto their driveway, he saw more of the shadows, and the strange shadows they cast. They seemed semi-solid, as though the moonlight could not make up its mind whether or not to pass through them.

He gasped, stepped back from the window, trying to breathe slowly and heavily to still his frantic heart.

'They'll get in,' he whispered. 'Papa, they'll get in. Unless…'

He had seen some of those wraiths moving towards the house, but as yet he was not sure that any of them had actually reached it. He had to go downstairs to find out.

'Look after me, Papa. Your words do this, so you must be with me now. *Must* be.' Scott hoped for another of those fresh memories of his grandfather – something that would perhaps explain what was happening to him right now – but as he descended into the cooler, darker downstairs, none came.

It was silent, and it felt more still and dead than upstairs. At least up there he had the knowledge of Helen sleeping in their bed, even though she was not a part of what he was doing. Down here there were only the empty rooms, and their familiar shadows, and those other things outside perhaps straining to get in even now.

He stood at the bottom of the staircase for a long time, alternately breathing softly and holding his breath completely in an attempt to hear anything amiss. Other than the usual sounds of the night – the unknown ticks and creaks of the house, a breeze playing around the eaves – there was nothing.

He wished he'd checked the time before leaving the bedroom. It suddenly seemed very important.

'Papa, make me strong.' The blinds beside the front door felt heavy, sodden with darkness. Scott pulled them aside, and a face stared in at him.

Somehow, he did not scream. He dropped the blinds and stepped back quickly, tripping over the bottom stair and falling onto his rump. Moaning softly, hands clasping his face as if to hold in his sanity, Scott stared at the blinds where they had fallen back into place.

It had been a young boy. Something was wrong with his head, his skull, its shape all deformed.

His face had almost been touching the glass. Almost.

'Papa,' Scott whined. 'Papa.'

And then a memory, shocking in its suddenness and intensity, equally startling because of its brevity.

Papa is swishing at a hedge with his walking stick. Scott has a stick as well, and he flicks the heads off stinging nettles as though it is a sword. It is a hot day, one of those long-ago summer days that seem to go on for ever, still existing and continuing in some childish, forgotten corner of his mind. They have done more than is possible to fit in one day already, and lunchtime has only just passed. It's a time full of potential. 'So how far *does* space go?' Scott asks again.

Papa shrugs. 'Who knows? No one's ever been that far.'

'But somebody must have a clue. Scientists or something.'

'They say it's for ever.'

Scott stands for a few seconds, frowning at the road but not really seeing it. 'I don't understand,' he says.

'You're not meant to.'

'What?'

Papa is staring at him now, all levity exhaled with his last breath. 'If we understand everything, what is there left to look for?'

'Papa?' Scott is only eight years old. His grandfather is scaring him.

Papa leans down towards his grandson. His face is stern; laughter lines are worry lines now, and his whole image has shifted. 'Sometimes it's sensible not to go looking for things you shouldn't know.'

Scott steps back, trips over his own heel, and falls onto his behind.

Papa laughs. He waves his walking stick at the sky, leans back, and roars, and when he looks back down at Scott he has tears in his eyes. Scott smiles, then laughs as well.

'But that,' Papa says, 'doesn't mean you shouldn't.'

Later, Papa sits by a stream while Scott dams it, and when it's time to go home Scott breaks the dam and they watch the water find its natural level once more.

Scott sat on the bottom stair and stared at the blinds across the front door. 'I can't know you,' he said. 'I can't see you. You're not to be seen or known. Fuck off.' He stood, stumbled into the living room, and picked up the single chair by the fireplace. It just fit through the doorway – he scraped his fingers but barely registered the pain – and he pushed it hard against the front door, wedging it beneath the handle.

He went back to the living room and made sure all the curtains were fully drawn. He could look outside and see them again, he knew, but he had no desire to do that. Perhaps he was imagining things, or maybe he truly was seeing them. It was the latter that seemed more likely to him. He had always believed, because Papa had instilled that belief. He had always known that there was much more to things than he could see or easily understand. But until now, he had been content not knowing.

He reached behind the curtain and tried to make sure the window latch was in the locked position. For a few seconds his arm was in sight of anything outside, but he turned his head away in case he saw beyond the glass. He fiddled for the latch, found it already locked, and withdrew his arm. Out in the hallway he did the same, then into the dining room – checking that the patio doors were shut and locked, the side window latched – and finally the kitchen.

He made another circuit, checking door locks and pinning the dining chairs beneath the door handles. He considered tipping the dining table onto its side and pushing it against the patio doors. It was a heavy table, oak inlaid with ceramic tiles, and he remembered that it usually needed the two of them to shift it. The thought of asking Helen to help dissuaded him from trying.

Certain that the house was locked as tight as it could be, Scott sat at the kitchen table, held his head in his hands, and felt the pressure of the impossible coming to bear.

For a while he lost himself. He cried, shook, shivered as the air in the house seemed to drop below freezing; then he started sweating. He tried to believe that he had seen nothing – that Papa's letter had inspired strange visions and hallucinations – but he knew in his heart that was wrong. Something had changed, and everything felt different. Something – the letter, the muttering of those strange words Papa had sung in the woods so long ago – had lifted the veil and afforded Scott a glimpse of the greater reality.

And he didn't want to know. He wanted Helen, and peace. He did not want to believe that there were ghosts, because that implied that everlasting rest was not for everyone.

Is Papa out there somewhere? he thought. He liked

to think not, but… *But someone made that letter come here, and someone tried to open the drawer.*

'Papa?' Scott muttered, his voice distorted through the tears.

There was no answer. He was not sure what he would have done if there had been.

He cried some more, crossed his arms on the table, and buried his face in them. His heart thumped. He felt it dancing in his chest, pulsing where he was pressed against the table edge. He heard it, like the sound of a distant wooden barrel being beaten.

The sound came closer. He breathed harder, faster, trying to drown the sound of his heart with his breaths, but it suddenly came from all around him, softly at first, then harsher and more urgent.

Scott sat upright and looked around, and the sound did not stop. It was no longer in rhythm with his heart.

The banging stopped and his heart raced on. He sat there for a while, wondering whether he'd imagined the sound. Perhaps he'd had his ear pressed against his arm in such a way that his heartbeat sounded like an echo. 'No,' he said. However much he tried denying all this, he knew what was really happening.

'Back door,' Helen said.

Scott jumped from the chair and turned. His wife was leaning against the kitchen doorjamb, eyes slitted against the harsh light. 'What?'

'Door. Back door. Someone's knocking on it.'

'You heard that?'

Helen nodded, then opened her eyes wider when she heard the stress in his voice. 'Was that you?' she asked.

'What do you mean?'

'Banging on the table?'

'No. Not me. Why would I?'

'Don't know,' she said. She ran her hand through her hair, frowning. 'I'm tired. Maybe we're both dreaming this.' Then she went for the back door.

'Don't.' Scott stood in her way. She stopped before him and he held her shoulders, pulling her close. 'Please don't.'

Helen shook her head and he felt her hair trailing across his face. 'I'm so tired,' she said. 'Put the kettle on, babe.'

Scott sighed and let her go, turned for the kettle, realising only as he heard the key turn that Helen had always intended opening the door. Maybe she wanted him to confront the fears she believed Papa's letter had implanted in him yesterday. Show him there was nothing out there but night. Let him see that maybe the only thing haunting him was Papa, a constant presence in his mind that had been aggravated by reading something he had written thirty years ago.

Or maybe she was so tired, she did not know what she was doing.

Scott felt the cool rush of air entering the house

as Helen swung the door open. Darkness heaved in, actually seeming to shove the kitchen light back for the space of an eyeblink before light and dark agreed upon equilibrium.

'Who's that?' Helen said. And Scott knew that she saw only one shape.

The shadows were still standing across the garden, shimmering now as the effect of his muttered spell wore off. They were obvious to Scott, and not only because he knew they were there. They were visible. Helen could not see them, and it was not only the darkness hiding them from her sight. Scott saw more.

But she *could* see one of them. The shape that seemed to emerge from the darkness at the edge of the garden, coming into being beneath the moonlight and walking quickly across the lawn.

'Who is that?' she asked again.

Scott moved to the door and went to push it shut.

'Who are you?' Helen said. 'What do you want?'

'Helen…' Scott pushed, but Helen had moved in front of the door, holding it open with her shoulder. 'Let me close it. What are you doing?'

She ignored him. 'I'll call the police,' she said.

'It's him.' Scott was certain. It had been thirty years, but he could remember the pained gait, the determined swing of the arms, and as the ghost of Papa's dead friend Lewis drew closer, Scott knew his face.

'Papa?' Helen said.

'Papa.' Lewis stopped three steps away from the door. He looked the same as when he had confronted Scott in the field with the shattered tree: old, drawn, his face lined with effort or pain. 'That's a name I've not heard spoken for a while.'

'Shut the door,' Scott said, but Helen would not – or could not – move.

'Where is it?' Lewis asked.

'What?'

'The Chord of Souls. Where?'

'I don't know what—'

'You *do* know what I'm talking about!' Lewis stepped forward, growled with effort, and grabbed hold of Helen's dressing gown. He screamed as he pulled hard, his face breaking into a smile of triumph as Scott's wife stumbled to his side.

'Helen!'

She had turned now, and he saw why she had not been able to move: she was petrified. Her eyes were wide-open, mouth agape, and a line of drool hung from her chin.

'Give me the book or your wife…' Lewis trailed off, but his gaze never left Scott's eyes.

'What?'

'I'll leave that unsaid,' the ghost said. 'You have an imagination, I know. Papa saw to that.'

'You're not real,' Scott said.

'You told me that last time we met.' Lewis turned to Helen. His movement seemed fluid, not solid, as though his image were ghosted on a bad TV screen. She struggled in his grasp, and the ghost's lips pressed together as he held her tighter. 'You know I'm real, don't you?' he asked.

'Holding her is an effort, isn't it?' Scott said.

'*Worth* the effort.'

Scott glanced past Lewis and out into the garden, searching for shadows. The spell of those strange words had worn off, but now he knew that the ghosts were still there. Always there.

'I don't know what book you're talking about,' Scott said. He realised that he had suddenly become very calm. Seeing Lewis again – and seeing Helen's fear – confirmed that he had not simply been imagining things. Reality crashed in and ebbed around the events of the past day, and, unimaginable as they were, Scott could now view the situation from a point of knowledge. This *was* a ghost standing before him, and the letter *had* arrived. The future began at that moment, and it was a very different place.

Lewis shook his head. 'Perhaps not,' he said. 'Maybe Papa really didn't show you the book. Old fool that he was, maybe he thought he'd be keeping you safe.'

'He'd never do anything to hurt me,' Scott said. He was looking directly at Helen now, trying to offer her calmness through his gaze.

'But now you've heard from him,' Lewis said. 'Now you've been told. I know that. Your wider self is richer. It's in your eyes. You've heard from him, and now there's more to life than you ever believed before.'

'Papa is dead. How could I have heard from him?'

'*I'm* dead! And at Papa's hand! But it doesn't always have to be this way.'

Helen whined and started struggling, and Lewis held her tighter.

'Good,' he said. 'It's getting easier.'

'What about the book?' Scott said. In spite of what was happening, he found himself interested.

'The Chord of Souls,' Lewis said. 'It contains the spells for eternal life. Ruling the Wide. Immortality. And more. You have to give it to me. It's... *important!*'

'You're a ghost.'

Lewis frowned, as though confused by the term. He looked at Helen, glanced back at Scott, then shook his head. 'Scott, I'm much less than a ghost. Didn't he tell you? Didn't you ever hear?'

'Hear what?'

Lewis spoke the words, and shadows filled with shadows. He gauged Scott's reaction and nodded. 'Then you *have* seen them before.'

Helen tried to break free. Scott stepped forward and Lewis tensed, the motion fluid, as though seen underwater.

'You have no idea what I can do,' the less-than-a-ghost said.

He's right, Scott thought. *I have no idea. Papa*

told me a little, but nowhere near enough. He told me enough to put me in danger, but not enough to save me.

The ghosts stood there, vague echoes of people. They watched. Some of them moved. And Scott wondered for the first time whether Lewis had any control over them at all.

'You have to find the book,' Lewis said.

Scott shook his head. 'I have no idea.'

'You heard from Papa.'

'Not really. A whisper. Maybe I was asleep.'

'That poor old bastard can't whisper.'

Scott's calmness was amazing him, and he saw confusion in Helen's eyes. 'What's the Wide?'

Lewis smiled, and it was a horrendous sight. *No dead person should ever smile*, Scott thought. It didn't become them.

'That's for you to find out, just like your grandfather and I did. It's a knowledge hard come by.'

Scott looked at Helen, saw the terror and confusion she was feeling, and made a decision. 'You're not here,' he said. 'I'm asleep. Dreaming. I thought of Papa yesterday and now he's in my dreams, and you're there too because he killed you. I love him and trust him. You must have deserved to die.'

'I deserve to live for ever, damn him! He can stay where he is and I—'

Scott shook his head and smiled. 'You're not real.

And now I'm going to wake up.' He closed his eyes, wondering for a second whether what he said was actually the truth.

Then he heard the scream. Helen, her voice telling him of her pain and fear.

Lewis muttered as Scott opened his eyes again, similar to what Papa had said in the woods but the chant longer, rising and falling, words twisting into and through one another as though they were a pile of writhing snakes. Lewis had wrapped his other arm around Helen and now he smiled triumphantly.

A storm struck the garden. Wind howled; lightning arced so close that Scott's hair stood on end.

'Meet the Wide,' Lewis said. 'She is here with me, and if you want her back…the Chord of Souls.' He shouted a final few words and the world split apart.

Reality ruptured. Scott was still at the back door of his house staring out over his garden, but his perception of things changed. The world grew. The garden expanded to make room for the hundreds of wraiths there, and he knew their individual stories, their lives and hopes, deaths and fears. He felt the pain of limbo, but beneath that the vicious jealousy with which they beheld the living. He could have dipped into any ghostly mind he wanted, but he held back because he did not wish to understand an echo. They continued to stare at him, and some of them tried to speak. He could hear them, he could answer, but he closed his ears and mouth to that impossibility.

The dark sky was larger than ever before. He could see the stars and the spaces in between, the scattered splash of the Milky Way bearing the potential of a billion new worlds, and all of them were touched by what he saw, what he felt. It was shattering. Scott tried to close his eyes, but when he did he saw and felt even more. For the first time ever he saw the spaces within his own mind, the vast gaps in his understanding surrounding the specks of knowledge that floated there, lonely and minuscule. He knew so little in an existence so vast. He opened his eyes again, but the pain of realisation remained.

Time parted around him and closed in beyond, bypassing him like a rock in a stream. The past and future flowed both ways, clashing in thunderous impacts that made the greatest lightning storm look like the flare of a match.

Around him was the present, and in realising this, he at last saw where Helen and Lewis were. Papa's dead friend was dragging Scott's wife away, hauling her across the garden. Her feet left a gleaming trail on the damp grass, and as she screamed her voice matched the volume of clashing aeons.

Scott could only watch as Lewis moved farther away. He flowed through ghosts, brushing them aside like wisps of cigarette smoke. They tumbled about the garden, elongating as a flow of time sucked them in, spinning where they crossed the paths left by Helen's trailing feet, and though they tried to scream they had no voice.

He went to shout, but the noise of the Wide meant that he could not hear himself.

Helen was fading into a false distance. She seemed to be miles away, becoming undefined as mists closed around her, though Lewis was as clear as ever. *The book*, the old ghost said, and the words made Scott's head ring.

He moved forward at last, his step uncertain, his balance thrown. He swayed on his feet but kept moving. The feel of wet grass seemed to root him in reality, and glancing down he saw the ground as it should be, untouched by hallucination.

This isn't just illusion.

He went on, aiming for Helen, only her scream drawing him onward now because he had finally lost sight of her. And even her scream was fading.

No hallucination, he thought. *It's the Wide, the truth of things; I'm seeing beyond the veil and—*

Helen was gone. No more screams, no more cries, no more strange words uttered or sung by Lewis.

'Helen!' he tried to shout loudly, but it seemed to arrive as a whisper. Ghosts milled before him and he moved to the side, stumbling over his own feet and falling to the ground. Wet grass welcomed him, startling him with cold. He gasped, looked up, and the Wide was narrowing.

For a moment he felt panicked more than ever before. He was being crushed, his senses compressed, his eyes squeezed so tightly that they felt as if they would implode. He shouted for Helen, and his voice was far too loud, so he shouted again. *Getting control back*, he thought. *I'm fighting it down, the madness.* Things calmed but the panic grew, expanding to fill the spaces left in his perception. He called for Helen again and again, looking around the dark garden, seeing only fleeting shadows where the ghosts had been. The falling silence was as shocking as what had come before. *How can any of us believe in such solitude?* he thought.

And then the silence was complete, and it shocked him so much that he could no longer shout.

He lay on the lawn, spreadeagled like a dead man and staring at the sky. Stars were out, and wisps of cloud passed across the face of the moon. The ghosts surrounded him, though they could no longer be seen. 'Helen,' he said. He stood unsteadily and ran into the house, searching all the downstairs rooms before running upstairs, dashing through their bedrooms, the bathroom, looking in cupboards and under the beds, the attic, tearing a wardrobe door from its hinges in his eagerness to search inside, but he did not find Helen anywhere. He whispered her name, as though repeating it could bring her back, and when that failed he searched the entire house again.

The Chord of Souls, Lewis had said as he retreated into the Wide.

'I don't know where it is!' he shouted, and his voice startled him to a standstill once again. Panting, gasping for air, he sat on the edge of their bed and started to weep.

A few minutes later he read Papa's letter again. And he began to understand.

Chapter Three

a time beyond belief

When Scott walked downstairs and into his study, there was a woman behind his desk. Even with her sitting down he could tell that she was tall. She was also attractive, though not beautiful. No face like that could ever be beautiful. It had seen far too much of life.

Standing in the doorway, looking at the woman and forming his first impression of her, he realised that he was not surprised, shocked, or scared.

'We've been waiting for you for a very long time,' she said.

'He took my wife.'

The woman nodded slowly. There was an easy grace about her movements, and when she stood from the chair she seemed to flow. She moved like a piece of classical music. She was dark skinned, her hair was long and tied with several metal bands, and there was a brutal mess of pink scars across the right side of her throat. It looked very old.

'She's at great risk,' she said, 'but I can help you get her back.'

'How?'

'You need to help me.'

Scott nodded. He looked down at the drawer and its broken lock, and the woman inclined her head, offering a brief smile with one corner of her mouth.

'I apologise for your desk.'

'You were looking for this?' He held up the folded letter, ready to flee if she made any movement towards him.

'I'll read it soon, but I already know what it is. I watched through the window. I saw him, and you, and both of you in the Wide.'

'Who are you?'

That smile again, a brief twitch of the lip. Everything about her was subtle and elegant. 'I don't suppose you have any real coffee?'

It felt dreamlike standing in the kitchen with this strange woman, brewing coffee as dawn smudged the shadows and his wife farther away from him than ever before. Scott tapped the spoon against a mug, hummed an unknown tune, looked up at the woman where she sat watching him from the breakfast bar. Her hands were steepled beneath her chin. Her eyes were timeless.

'Sugar?'

'No, thanks. No milk, either. Pure.'

Scott poured two coffees and added milk and

several heaped teaspoons of sugar to his own. He was shaking and weak. Perhaps a sugar rush would help.

'How do I get Helen back?'

'Do what he said: find the Chord of Souls.'

'Who are you?'

The woman took a sip of her boiling coffee and closed her eyes, luxuriating in the flavour. She was startlingly sexy, an effect exaggerated more by the fact that she seemed not to know. This was all very natural to her.

The woman opened her eyes. 'I'm immortal,' she said. 'I'm one of a dozen. We've been looking for the Chord of Souls for some time.'

'How long?'

'Ever since it went missing.'

'How long ago was that?'

'Just after we wrote it.'

'And how long ago was that?'

The woman took another sip of coffee and sighed. 'Too long for you to believe. And I need you to believe me, and trust me, if you're going to help.'

'You've just told me that you're immortal, and I'm supposed to believe and trust you?'

'Did you believe in ghosts before yesterday, Scott?'

'Yes. No. I…' Scott was angry at the doubt in his voice, but it was genuine. Papa had given him the gift of an open mind, and yet in many regards Scott had remained sceptical. In a strange way, the appearance of Lewis just after the funeral had rooted that scepticism in a strong foundation. It was a contradiction that had confused him for thirty years. He had seen a ghost; therefore, he found it difficult to believe in them. He'd tried to convince himself that it was something to do with faith, or lack of it, or the belief in something wider, but really it was rooted far deeper than that. His disbelief was a facet of the fear he had in a world where Papa no longer existed. He would never again hear Papa call hello through an open back door, never hear his laugh, never go out with him on his birthday, never see the old man's scrawl inside his birthday cards, never kiss him or disagree with him or sit and listen to old tales that sometimes may have been true.

'Do you believe in ghosts this morning?'

Scott looked out into the garden and thought about muttering those sing-song words. But maybe even they were simply a spell, something hypnotic and misleading that—

The woman sighed and Scott's world shifted sideways. The ghosts appeared and everything felt larger, more able to encompass the truth of things. She sighed again and the world returned to what he was used to.

'Of course I do,' he said. 'One of them just took my wife.'

'He's not a real ghost,' the woman said, 'but that doesn't matter. Your belief does. Belief can save your life.'

'Who *are* you?' Scott asked again.

'My name is Nina.'

Nina? Scott raised his eyebrows. Was she fooling with him? 'Strange name for someone who's been alive for so long.'

'I change it every couple of hundred years.' She sipped more coffee, and there was not an ounce of sarcasm or humour in her voice. She was simply stating a fact.

Scott continued to shake. His nose and eyes burnt, and the weakness had not been touched by sips of his sweet coffee. Tears formed and fell, and he could not hold back a sob.

Nina seemed embarrassed. She did not step around the breakfast bar to comfort him, nor did she speak. She took another drink and left him to cry.

'You say you can help,' he said. 'So fucking help!'

Nina nodded, finished her drink, and then stood from the stool. 'Pack a bag,' she said. 'We can talk while we drive.'

'Drive where?'

Nina shrugged. 'I'm sure we'll know when we get there.'

'You're taking this very well.' She sat in the passenger seat, having declined his request that she drive.

'Apart from breaking down in tears and my heart feeling as though it's ready to explode in my chest?'

'Ah, it won't do that. Strong, hearts. Resilient.'

'What?'

'I collect them.'

'What?'

'Oh. Sorry. Something for later, perhaps. But I mean it, your reaction is…strong. Not just the missing-wife thing, but—'

'That's not just a *thing*!'

'Whatever.' Nina waved her hand as if shooing a fly. 'I mean all this. Lewis, the Wide, me.'

'I have an open mind.'

'Really?' She paused, and Scott had to look across at her. He felt something heavy hanging between them that needed breaking. 'How open?' she asked. And that scared him more than anything.

Dawn arrived and the roads came alive with traffic: people driving to or from work, their expressions the same whichever way they were going. Scott drove on, awaiting directions. The woman in the seat beside him seemed unconcerned as to which way they were going. She didn't even seem to notice.

'Cardiff,' Scott said. 'Do I get on the motorway for Cardiff?'

'Could,' she said.

'Do I or don't I?'

'Do.'

'I could drive to the nearest police station. I don't know who the fuck you are, and I could drive there and tell them I found you breaking and entering.'

'If it'll make you feel better.'

'Do you have a record?'

'I don't exist. Not officially. And I'd just walk

right out the door.' She glanced at Scott and smiled, that disarmingly subtle twitch of her lip that had such great effect. 'I've learnt a lot over the years.'

'Such as?'

'Stuff from the Wide.'

'What is that?'

'The truth, of course.'

Scott eased the car into the flow of traffic on the motorway and kept to a steady sixty. Was he doing the right thing? The thought of going to the police and trying to explain just how Helen had gone missing was ridiculous, but wasn't there something else he should be doing?

Looking for the book, perhaps.

'Why are you helping me?'

'I'm not yet. We're just driving.'

'So fill the time for me. Tell me who you really are.'

Nina laughed, a real laugh for the first time. It made Scott realise just how grim she had been. She sounded like another woman, and he could not help glancing across to see how the laugh changed her face. He was shocked. It made her look like a much older woman.

'What's so funny?'

Her laughter quickly ceased. 'I told you I was immortal, and now you want to know about the real me. It's like a date. Is this a date?'

'No. We're going to get my wife back.'

'Right, right.' She sniggered, but all the humour seemed to have gone. 'Right.'

'So?'

'There are lots of Ninas I could tell you about. They weren't all called Nina, of course. They lived all over the world. They saw lots of things. They saw wars and revolutions, witnessed discoveries and things made secret for ever. Fell in love. Fell out of love. Saw love die in the rot of flesh. Sometimes – most of the time, lately – all they want to do now is rest.'

'You have all the time in the world. Take a decade on a beach somewhere.'

'I mean *rest*,' she said.

'You want to die.'

'Of course. That's only natural.'

'And you're supernatural.'

'If you say so.'

Doubts flurried around Scott's mind; fear played in his tense joints. A truck cut him off and he eased back on the accelerator, drifting into the inside lane, slowing some more so that he could concentrate. Wrapping the car around a bridge would not help at all.

'Where has he taken Helen?'

'Into the Wide. That's far enough. None of you can get through to there – very few, anyway – and there's no way she will get back.'

'None of who?'

'You people.'

'You mean normal people?'

'Yes, normal.'

'I got through.'

'You *saw* through. It's different.'

'Where are you from?'

She stared at him, but Scott looked ahead at the traffic. He wanted to know, that was all. He was interested.

'Africa. South of the Sahara, before it was named.'

'You have no accent.'

'I do; you just don't know it. I've lived all over the world, and I have the accent of humanity.'

Scott started laughing. Like the tears earlier in the kitchen, this laughter came out unforced and natural. It was tinged with panic – loss of control stalked beneath the surface – but he let it come, enjoying the sense of release. He guided the car onto the hard shoulder and switched off the engine. He laughed some more. It felt good, but it made every moment seem like the beginning of something new. The whole world was changing and he had to ride with it.

'You're so full of shit,' he said when he could speak. He wiped tears from his eyes and switched on the hazard lights. 'I don't know who you are, what you want, what you put in my tea last night, but I'll tell you now you can fuck off. Just…fuck off.' He started laughing again, gripping the steering wheel as though afraid Nina would steal it away.

'Oh, damn,' she said. 'This is going to hurt.'

Scott was still laughing when she pulled a heavy

knife from beneath her jacket, turned to face him, and sliced her throat from ear to ear.

The spray of blood splashed across the windscreen and pulsed onto the dashboard. Nina leant forward to rest her head against the air bag cover, letting more blood pour from her gashed throat to pool on the seat between her legs and in the footwell, soaking the front of her jacket and shirt.

Scott tried to shout, but it was as if his throat had been cut as well.

He was still holding on to the steering wheel. He gripped tight, unable to let go, and he was so silent that he could hear blood dripping, clicking in Nina's throat as she tried to breathe, and the bursting of tiny bubbles as air escaped the horrendous wound. She had dropped the knife and he wanted to pick it up, but he could not let go of the wheel. Try as he might, his fingers would not uncurl.

Nina turned to look at him. There was no panic in her expression, and little pain. If anything, it looked as though she were accusing him of some vast wrongdoing.

'Hospital,' Scott muttered, and Nina snorted. Twin trails of blood burst from her nose. Her mouth opened with a wet sound, lips parting and tongue squirming as though she were trying to speak. She shook her head and expelled a bloody sigh through her new mouth.

Scott's hands at last relinquished their hold on the wheel, and he reached for the door.

Something pressed against his side. He gasped and turned slowly to look down. Nina's hand held the knife pushed into his jacket, point first. One shove and it would be in him. It gleamed red. He looked at her and she shook her head, very slowly. With each shake her slashed neck pursed like kissing lips.

The bleeding had stopped and the wound was scabbing over.

Scott held his breath and stared at the cut, and when he looked up at Nina's face again a few seconds later he saw a smile in her eyes.

'Immortal,' he muttered. And he watched as the wound bound itself together. Every stage of a healing cut presented itself: blood clotting and scabbing, the rough scar, the smooth scar, the discolouration beneath the skin, and finally the virtual disappearance of any evidence of the cut having been there at all.

Scott timed the healing with the dash clock, and it took less than five minutes.

Nina coughed. Gurgled, spit out a mouthful of blood. Turned her head left and right, looked up and down, coughed harder. And then she spoke. Her voice started gruff and deep, but by the end of the sentence she was starting to sound like herself again. 'So you see, there are more things in heaven and earth. And the truth goes far wider than you can imagine.'

Scott could not speak. There was so much he wanted to say – so many questions he needed to ask – that he could not think of a single one.

'Sorry about the mess,' Nina said. She took a small handkerchief from her pocket and started wiping the windscreen, smudging the blood more than mopping it up. 'Oh, dear.'

'I'm going mad,' Scott said, but he did not believe that. It wasn't what he could see; it was what he could smell and taste: blood. Eyes could deceive, but nose and mouth were truer.

'Ah, madness. I've been mad a few times. Once, when they were building St. Etienne, I lived in a hole in the ground for almost a decade. Those building the chapel brought me fruit and live chickens, and they'd stand back and watch me slaughter the birds and eat them raw. I was an entertainment for them, and I played up to it. Enjoyed it. I asked them to build me into the floor of the place, but they declined. And things got nasty. See, I wanted to see how long I could live, trapped in a hole underground.'

'That would have been awful.'

'Yes. And therein lay my madness of the time.'

'How did it get nasty?'

Nina glanced at Scott, then away again. 'We fought. They called me a demon. I ran, and I haven't returned to France since.'

'When was this?'

'Ten seventy-five. Give or take a couple of years.'

'A thousand years ago.'

Nina gave her slight smile and nodded.

This is the madness of my time, Scott thought. *This is my insanity. Yet I know there's truth here. It's impossible that this can be true; yet it is. The world has changed. My world has changed, and I think it changed thirty years ago when Papa died. Perhaps even before... Perhaps when I was born and my parents took me home and he first saw me, I was already existing somewhere different from everyone else.*

'We need to get this blood cleaned up,' Nina said.

'Yes. Right.'

'Do you have Mr Wolf's number?'

'What?' *Wolf? What now? What is she going to tell me now?*

'Haven't you seen *Pulp Fiction*?'

Scott nodded and remembered. There was a woman in his car who had been alive more than a thousand years ago talking about *Pulp Fiction*.

'OK,' he said. 'All right. This is happening. You just killed yourself and now you're better, and this is happening.'

'Technically no, because I can't die. But close enough.'

Scott glared at the woman. 'Fine. But my wife. I need her back. And I have no idea where to start or how this will end, and you've appeared to offer your help. So if I accept everything you're telling me – if I accept without question the things you tell and show me – please say what we have to do next.'

Nina nodded, apparently satisfied. 'Next, you have to let me see your letter from Papa.'

'How do you know I called him that?'

She smiled. 'He liked everyone to call him that, didn't he?'

'You knew him?'

'Don't tell me that surprises you.'

Scott thought about it. And no, it did not surprise him one bit.

At the next service station Nina remained in the car while he went to buy some tissues. He handed her Papa's note as he left, and glancing back he saw the shadow of her head bent low as she read.

I wonder what she'll get from what he said, Scott thought. *I wonder what she'll think.*

He was not fond of service stations. They were temporary places inhabited by people he would never see again, and he did not like the idea of that. He passed a man whose story he would never know, a woman whose name he would never utter, and before today these places had made him feel so insignificant. Now, he felt only distant. He saw the eyes of people living such narrow lives, and while in a way he was jealous of their ignorance, still he wondered what they could really ever achieve.

Did Papa think this way about everyone? he thought. *Maybe Mother and Father, yes, but surely not me. He was training me. Grooming me to continue his quest. I was sixteen when he died...how much longer was he waiting before he told me so much more?*

In the shop he bought some tissues and wet wipes, along with several bottles of water and some pre-packed sandwiches. *Does an immortal get hungry?* he wondered, and then he remembered Nina relishing the coffee he'd made for her. He bought two strong coffees and went back out to the car. He passed a dozen people on the way, and only one of them nodded a brief acknowledgement. Even having seen what he'd seen these last two days, he was still just another man.

As soon as he opened the car door he knew something had changed. Nina looked up at him without smiling, waited until he'd sat in his seat and put the coffee down, then handed Papa's note back to him.

'Got some stuff to tell you,' she said.

'I was hoping you might.'

'That for me?' She took one of the cups and swigged the scorching liquid, sighing and licking her lips.

'So what was in the note?'

'You read it, Scott. What do you think?'

'Directions. It was telling me how to get somewhere, but I don't know those symbols.'

'Telling you where to find something, more like.'

'The book?'

Nina rested her head back against the headrest. 'It's much, much more than a book, Scott. It's the

Chord of Souls. It contains the original Chord of Souls, as well as many other things.'

'The Chord of Souls is the spell for immortality?'

'A large part of it.'

'So what else is in the book?'

'Stuff.' The look she gave him convinced Scott that nothing would encourage her to elaborate. Not now, at least.

And he was fine with that. For now. *Jesus, I'm starting to think just like Papa!*

'So where is it?'

'I don't know. But Papa's note illustrates where he hid the parts he and Lewis found in Africa.'

'Then let's go, let's—'

'Lewis can never have the book, you know. Nobody can.'

'My wife…'

'I'll do my best to help you, but Lewis will never have the Chord of Souls. I'll make sure of that. However I can, however I have to. Understand?'

'A threat?'

'No, not really. Just a statement of intent.'

Scott nodded. 'Why can't he have it? Papa did.'

'Papa and Lewis had only a few pages from the book. They discovered parts of the Chord of Souls, though not all. But what I think Papa *did* discover – somehow, and I have yet to work out how – is where the rest of the book is hidden. Lewis must have been close to discovering this as well…and that's why Papa killed him.' Nina glanced at Scott and then down at her bloodied hands. They fisted in her lap, unclenched, and she lifted them to stare at where blood had dried in her lifeline.

'And then Papa killed himself.'

'Yes. He had knowledge he could never lose. Lewis wasn't the only man alive who would value that knowledge.'

'But the note?'

Nina took a pack of tissues and began wiping down the windscreen. 'Lucky for me, some people can't let go of such powerful knowledge. It's like trying to un-invent the bomb.'

'Why do you want the rest of the book?'

'Because we've been looking for it for ever. And because it'll remind me how to die.' She spit on the glass to clear a patch of blood that had already dried.

'Papa died a good man,' Scott said. He had always known. Whatever people said about him – his mother and father included, at times – he had always believed that there was much more to the death of those two old men than met the eye. Some gossiped that they were old lovers and that some third party had come between them. Others said Papa had gone mad with the imminence of ageing and death, and wanted to take his best friend with him. Even at sixteen, Scott had believed that there was more than anyone could know.

Nina continued wiping. She seemed to ignore Scott's last statement. 'So, the book. Your grandfather. Lewis. I suppose I should fill you in on some stuff while we clean your car.'

'Did it hurt?'

'Cutting my throat? Of course. But it's not the first time I've had to prove myself.'

'I'm sorry.'

'Not your fault.' She took another wad of tissues from Scott, lifted her rump from the seat, and started mopping up blood. 'Papa craved immortality, Scott. You may have guessed as much.'

'He wanted to see beyond the veil.'

'And that's *why* he wanted it. To see into the Wide, to be there, to explore. His intentions were honest, though he was naive to believe it could be done.'

'But you're immortal.'

'And cursed. Let me continue.'

Scott wiped at the windscreen and wet the blood drying there. It ran again, dribbling down to the dashboard, where he mopped it with tissues. *Could be diseased*, he thought, but he smiled and shook his head. She was immortal.

'He and Lewis found the pages when they were out in the desert during the war. Some old ruins, unearthed when a munitions dump was destroyed. They went in, dug around, and found seven carved stone tablets.'

'Parts of the Chord of Souls?'

'Some of the original parts. Hidden for…a very long time.' Nina grew quiet and looked through the smeared windscreen, seeing something a long way off and a long time ago.

Scott continued cleaning, glancing at the woman every few seconds. He did not want to disturb her.

'I carved one of those tablets,' she said quietly. 'There were twelve of us. When we learnt, when we knew, we had to write it all down. Present the Chord as one continuous spell, as well as all the other stuff. If only we hadn't.'

'Who did you learn from?'

Nina shook her head. 'No one can ever know. No one. It would change everything. So, they found these tablets, and they brought them home, and Lewis and your grandfather spent the rest of their lives trying to read them.'

'They never told anyone? Never asked for help from…I don't know…the British Museum or something?'

'No. The lure of the Wide hit them early on. Perhaps even before they'd come home from Africa. Something as powerful and potent as the Chord of Souls can exude a spell…affect those around it without their even reading it.'

'Like radiation?'

Nina smiled. 'I suppose so. Radiated knowledge.'

'And how much did they learn?'

'It took them a long time, but slowly they started to discern the language of the stones. With every new word they translated, Papa became more certain that they were doing the wrong thing. He could see the wonders of the Wide, but he was also aware of how cursed it could be as well. It's not a place meant for people, Scott. Not people like you and Papa. Not people like me.'

'But Lewis?'

Nina turned to look at him, her face stern, and in her eyes he saw the trust of ages. 'No. Not for people like Lewis.'

'So why didn't Papa destroy the tablets?'

'It's not easy to destroy them once you've read them.'

Scott snorted. 'What, some protective spell? A magical defence?'

'Nothing quite so romantic. It's just that the more one reads of them, the more powerful the Chord of Souls seems…and as I said, such knowledge is not meant to be lost.'

'So instead of destroying them, Papa hid the tablets and killed Lewis to prevent him from reading more.'

'Yes.'

'So how did Lewis – who is dead – take Helen from me? How can a dead man take my wife?'

'Lewis had read some of the Chord, and he didn't want to die. He knew some of its effects, some of the minor enchantments that went to make its whole. He used them. So now, out in the Wide, his soul still wanders. He's angry at what Papa denied him.'

'But Papa has gone. Or is he still somewhere

too? Will I see him?' Suddenly the prospect of Papa visiting him in the same way Lewis had seemed very real, and it was terrifying. Lewis was a man he had barely known, but should Papa appear in such a form – there, but not there – Scott would find it awful.

'Your Papa was a good man, Scott. He *wanted* to die. He already knew too much, and he knew that. He was ready.'

'And you? How did you know him? Are you part of the reason he killed himself?'

Nina spit on a fresh tissue and wiped it across the dashboard. Another thick smear of her blood was washed away. 'Too many questions,' she said. 'Not enough action. We should go to find what we can of those seven tablets.'

'No,' Scott said. 'No, no. I know far too little. There's so much more. Where is Helen? Why can't you find these things yourself? What do you need me for? And Papa's note…why did it take so long to reach me? Just what the hell are you really, Nina?'

'Like I said, too many questions.' She nodded ahead. 'Cardiff. By the castle. There's a pub, and Papa hid some of the tablets there.'

'How do you know?'

She frowned. 'Haven't you read his letter?'

'Yes, but…'

'But you haven't got a mind as open as you claim, perhaps.'

Scott shrugged. 'Perhaps.'

'Papa loved you, Scott.'

'I know.'

'He really did. He loved you. But he wanted you to carry on what he had been doing. And that would have cursed you.'

Scott shook his head and started the engine. 'Let's go.'

Nina crumpled the tissues into a blood-sodden ball and dropped them by her feet.

Scott pointed at the windscreen. 'Missed a bit.'

Chapter Four

a book blighted by death

It took them almost an hour to get into Cardiff. He had driven this way hundreds of times before, but now everything seemed new. The row of warehouse shops – Carpetland, PC World, Mothercare – were cathedrals to lost causes. Hundreds of cars were parking in their forecourts even now, disgorging hapless couples or hassled families to be swallowed into the shops' maws, seeking goods and services that would make their lives seem less difficult and more valued. A new set of curtains might lift a couple's spirit for a few days. A fresh set of toys for their growing youngster could make them feel as though they were being good parents, the shine in their child's eyes evidence enough. They spent for comfort and shopped for peace, and all the while their bodies carried them inexorably towards a time and place where none of this would matter anymore. Because at the end of it all – past the hugs and kisses, the promises and lies, the smiles and nods and the knowing frowns, the gratitude and anger, the tears and the all-too-brief instances of clear, unhindered happiness that sometimes exploded a moment away – there was death.

And for some, that was when the real adventure began.

'Who is in the Wide?' Scott asked. He was looking around as he drove, staring into other cars, where drivers and passengers sat immersed in their own private worlds. Most of them looked glum and sad; a few talked into hands-free phones. One or two smiled, but only briefly; perhaps they were remembering yesterday or looking forward to tonight.

'It's not a place for people.'

'Are you there?'

'I have been.'

'The ghosts I saw…those things in my garden…I saw them when I said the words Papa taught me.'

'A rhyme from the Chord of Souls. It touches your vision; that's all.'

'I felt everything growing so much wider. A huge potential.'

'They were wraiths. Echoes of lost souls.'

'They seemed more than that.'

'Lewis presented them that way.'

Scott edged forward and then stopped again at a set of traffic lights. He glanced to his right and a woman looked away, embarrassed. *We're so private in these moments,* he thought. *Shouldn't we be chatting while we sit here? Windows down, talking, being a part of each other's day?* He stared at the woman until she glanced back, but then felt ashamed of making her uncomfortable. 'So Lewis is in the Wide.'

'It's the only place he can be without…'

'He was here, but it hurt him.'

Nina nodded. 'It would. It does. He's in pain.'

'He must want what you have very much.' He watched her for a reaction, but her face gave away nothing. She did not even blink.

The lights changed and they moved on, two lanes filtering into one. 'Where are we aiming for?'

Nina read Papa's note again. 'A public house close to the castle. Across the road. Down in the ground.'

'The cellar?'

'Deeper.'

'You read all that from the note?'

'It gives me a map in my mind.'

'Papa was clever.'

Nina smiled. Scott saw the expression in the rear-view mirror, which he had angled slightly to the left so that he could see her mouth, chin, scarred neck. He did not think the smile was something he was meant to see.

'He was,' she said.

'What's the name of the pub?'

'I'll know it when we're there. The language he used can't make names.'

Papa, you were such a mystery to us all. Scott thought of their walks in the countryside, those brief snatched moments newly remembered when Papa had tried to tell him something important. Somehow they had been hidden in his memory – or hidden *by* his memory – until now, when the note was here. Scott believed that Papa would have intended that. But with everything he discovered about his grandfather, he became more a stranger to Scott than ever. He was starting to respect the old man more and more, but he knew him less. That made him sad.

Scott drove them around to the castle car park. They had to climb three floors before they found a parking space, and when Scott turned off the engine he slumped back in his seat, arms and shoulders tense, neck strained. 'I don't believe any of this is happening,' he said.

'Don't tell me I have to reach for my knife again.'

'Was that humour?'

'If you like.'

'An immortal woman from before history began is telling me jokes.'

'Like I said, Nina is lots of women. I adapt to the time I'm in. The woman from back then is almost as much a stranger to me as to you. I just share some of her memories.'

'Do you remember everything?'

Nina shrugged and smiled, and this time the smile was meant for him. 'The Battle of Trafalgar is a bit hazy.'

'Hazy.' Scott closed his eyes and thought of

Helen being taken from him, the real sense that she was being dragged farther away than simple distance could allow. She had grown hazy as Lewis took her away.

He started to cry. He could not help himself. This time yesterday morning he had only just read the letter from Papa, and things were still relatively normal. Now...

'Where am I?' he said. 'I feel so lost.'

'Everyone is lost.' Nina said. 'Believe me. I've been all over, and everyone is lost. There are those who buy, those who steal, and those who pray to ground themselves, but really we're all just floating.'

'Waiting for what?'

'That's something else I won't answer for you,' she said. Something about her softened then, and Scott wondered how many men had fallen in love with those eyes. *A lot*, he thought. *Many. It would be easy.* 'We'll get your wife back,' she said. But she looked away and reached for the door handle. Scott caught sight of her face in the rear-view mirror once again.

For the first time since he saw her sitting behind the desk in his study, Nina looked truly old.

'The pub won't be open for a couple of hours yet.'

'Doesn't matter. I'll get us inside.'

'Something you learnt in the Wide?'

She reached into her pocket and pulled out a ring containing several wiry keys. 'Prison.'

They sat on the banked grass verge that skirted

the walls of Cardiff Castle, watching the traffic go by and drinking scalding coffee from cardboard cups. Nina seemed to like it almost boiling, closing her eyes and sighing as she drank her coffee with a double shot of espresso.

'What are we waiting for?'

'The right time.' She sipped again. Eyes closed. Perhaps she was listening rather than looking.

Scott watched people walking by. They all ignored him and Nina, enthralled in their own private worlds. They seemed to carry their personal space from their car and maintain it as they walked, rarely passing close enough to smell one another's perfumes or breath, and certainly not close enough to have to catch one another's eyes. *I wonder if they can see us?* he thought. *Maybe she's got us slightly removed, just a bit closer to the Wide.*

Across the road from them sat the Mason's Vaults, an old pub sandwiched between a Gap clothing store on one side and a branch of Forbidden Planet on the other. It had black oak beams, leaded windows and a heavy oak door that could well have been hundreds of years old. Beside the door a glazed framed case held a food menu, and the glass had been smashed. Someone had kicked the glass against the wall, but a few shards remained on the pavement, catching the morning sun. Scott wondered how he could see them from all the way across the road.

'Have you taken us somewhere?'

'No. You drove.'

'You know what I mean.'

'Knowledge is power. You're just seeing a little more.'

'Not sure I'm happy with it.'

Nina turned her face up to the sun. Scott took the opportunity to examine her profile once again, such a peaceful sight in so much traffic noise and bustle. Someone across the road shouted, a teenager calling to another, and though it distracted Scott briefly, Nina seemed unconcerned. She must have seen and heard so much. If all this was true, she must have seen *so much*.

'I've seen plenty,' she said.

Scott blinked. 'So you read my mind now, too?'

Nina shook her head. 'I read your silences.'

'Remind me to keep talking.'

'I've seen attack ships on fire off the shoulder of Orion.' She smiled, eyes still closed.

Scott drank some more coffee, stretching for something, some memory. A car horn tooted, brakes squealed, someone else shouted. Shoes struck concrete. Engines grumbled with impatience. Across the road, glass shards glittered on the pavement before the Mason's Vaults, and then he knew. '*Blade Runner,*' he said.

'Very good.'

'So you're a big movie buff?'

'I like the movies.' Nina's eyes were still closed, and she took another long gulp of hot coffee.

'You like coffee, too.'

'Yes. And salmon dressed in frog spawn, dog's liver fried in yak fat, and seeing the heat of a summer's day scorch paint shades lighter.'

'Weird.'

'I also collect the hearts of dead things.'

Scott said nothing, yet Nina responded to his silence.

'Because they're tough and strong. They outlast the rot of flesh. For a while, at least.'

'Some odd things,' he said.

'I've been around a long time. I've developed certain peccadilloes.'

'Is teasing mere mortals one of them?'

Nina looked at him, her face stern and so, so old once again. 'I'm not teasing you, Scott,' she said. Then she looked across the road at the pub. 'It's time to go. Stay close. *We're so close.*' She whispered the last three words, speaking to herself more than him.

'If these were the pages Papa had, you could have taken them at any time.'

'He hid them. And besides, it's not only these pages we're here for. It's the clue Papa left with them that will lead us on.'

'And that's in his letter too?'

Nina stood up and brushed grass cuttings from her rump. Her trousers were stained dark with her own blood, stiffened like cardboard, but even then she appeared the image of gracefulness. 'No. I just knew him. The clue will be here, because Papa left it for you.'

* * *

To begin with – before the blights came, and Scott fell, and things turned bad – events *flowed*.

It seemed to Scott that Nina had been waiting for a convergence of chances. She had closed her eyes and listened to the surge of the world, and somehow she knew how long it would take her and Scott to stand, walk across the pavement, reach the other side, pick the lock on the pub's front door, and go inside. There were no pauses, no wasted moments, and he tried hard to work out why wasted moments should mean so much to an immortal.

Nina stood and walked out into the road. She did not stop at the kerbside and look both ways. She did not alter her pace. And Scott followed. They walked through the traffic, gliding through gaps between vehicles. Nobody tooted their horns because they were not risking their lives. Nobody gave them the finger and leant from their window, shouting about what stupid arseholes they were, because Nina and Scott steered through the traffic as easily as a bird flying through a forest.

By the time they reached the opposite pavement Scott was sweating. He felt a mixture of elation and dread.

Nina did not pause. She stepped between a tall blond woman scratching her nose and a short black man talking into a mobile phone, knelt at the pub door, and withdrew the ring of keys from her pocket. Scott followed, so caught up in her confidence that he did not look around to see whether anyone was watching. If he had looked he knew what he would have seen: someone walking by, glancing at their watch just as they drew level; a driver trapped in the slow-moving traffic, changing a CD in his car stereo; someone else staring into the comic shop window next door to the pub, something about last night drawn in their wistful expression.

'Are you hiding us?' he asked.

'I just pick my moments well.' Nina was working on the lock with her skeleton keys, her hands moving delicately as she manipulated the tumblers inside.

Scott stood behind her, staring at her back. *Is she making them all ignore us, or can they just not see us?* He looked around at last and saw exactly what he knew he would see: the world continued, ignoring this brash crime in their midst.

'In we go.' Nina stood and shoved the door with her shoulder, glancing back and nodding Scott inside.

He went in and she closed the door. 'No alarm?'

'Hope not.'

'You mean you don't know?'

'I'm immortal, not God.'

'You believe in God?' It came naturally, but Scott suddenly realised what a significant question that might be.

Nina looked straight at him, blinking slowly. Her coffee-coloured skin looked almost too smooth to touch. 'Now that really is a question for another time,' she said.

'OK...another time. Right now we're in a closed

pub. You think Papa hid the stone tablets in here?'

'That's what it says in his note.'

'So he chose a place like this to conceal part of the Chord of Souls.'

'What better place? No one would think of looking here. And it had to be somewhere accessible for you to find.'

Scott looked around. There were still a few dirty glasses and overflowing ashtrays on tables, and there was a spray of crumbs on the floor by the bar. Glass cases held signed rugby shirts. A menu was chalked onto a wall board, offering standard pub food. A quiz machine glowed green where it had been left on, and at the shady rear of the pub a large white screen hung awaiting the next match. A basic city-centre pub, with nothing to differentiate it from a dozen others. What better place, indeed.

'So where are they?'

'Down.' Nina followed the L-shaped bar to the rear of the pub, turned the corner, and pushed through a door marked with male and female toilet signs. The light was poor back here, supplied by a rooflight covered with a decade's worth of moss and city grime. Male toilet on their right, female on their left, but Nina chose a third door with a heavy padlock locking the hasp and staple latch. She went to work with her key ring again.

'What were you in jail for?' Scott asked.

'Armed robbery.' The padlock fell to the floor and Nina opened the door.

'Great.' Scott was not sure whether or not he wanted her to elaborate. She said no more. He felt around on the wall for a light switch, and by the time he'd found it Nina was already at the bottom of the stairs. Scott went down and stood beside her.

They were in the beer cellar. It stank of spilt beer, a sickly, stale caramel stench that seemed to coat the inside of his nostrils in seconds. A dozen barrels, stacked two high, lined the wall on one side. The opposite wall was piled with boxes and crates of bottles, some of them opened and half-empty, others full. A few bottles lay smashed and disregarded on the floor, the largest glass chunks kicked to one side. The light down here was not very good, but Scott could still see the handful of rodent traps scattered beneath barrels and between boxes, a couple of them bearing dead, rotting mice. The stink of their demise was evident below that of spilt drink: old rot, dried fur.

'So where are they?' Scott asked.

'Where do you think?' Nina turned to him, a strange look on her face.

'Are you all right?'

She nodded. 'Fine. So where do you think Papa would have hidden them?'

'You're asking me? Don't you know?'

'It was you he was hiding them for. I'm just curious. Wondering whether—'

'You told me you wanted to die.'

Nina frowned. 'I'd like the knowledge of how to end my curse, yes.'

'But you're still curious. If you're tired of life, I can't imagine you being curious about anything.'

'Don't try to second-guess me, Scott. You'll never understand. Now…where do you think they are?'

'I have no idea.'

'Sure?'

'Nina – or whatever your real name is, or will be, or was – I have no fucking idea. Please stop playing games. I'm afraid. My wife has gone, I'm afraid, and I want to get her back as soon as I can.'

Nina looked down at her feet. 'Of course, I'm sorry. Truly.'

'Deeper,' Scott said. 'I think he'd have buried them deeper.'

'I think so too.' Nina did not offend him by smiling, but he could see the satisfaction in her eyes as she walked to the end of the long, narrow room.

At first glance the wall looked solid, but as Nina ran her hands across the painted surface her fingers seemed to draw the outline of something buried. Scott frowned, glanced slightly to the left and right, closed his eyes. When he opened them again a few seconds later the door was more than apparent.

Seeing more, she had said.

'We need to find something to open this,' Nina said.

'How long will it take? Someone could be here anytime.'

'Then let's hurry.'

Scott searched the few shelves on the wall beneath the stairs, feeling by touch because the light barely reached that far. He returned to Nina with a screwdriver and claw hammer, though half the hammer's handle had snapped off. 'All I could find.'

'It'll do.' Nina set to work. First she ran the screwdriver's point around the outline in the wall, clearing powdery plaster from a sunken seal. She stepped back, breathing heavily, and it was then that Scott noticed she was panting.

'What is it?'

Nina shook her head, reaching out for the hammer.

Scott stepped back. 'What's wrong?'

'I can't touch them,' she said. 'Even being near them…it's like I can taste the end of time.'

'That's why I'm here?'

She nodded.

'Well…thanks for being honest.'

'Scott—'

He moved beside Nina and pried the hammer's claws beneath the edge of the seal. It was metal, rusted into the plaster, weak, and a few wrenches on the hammer saw a foot-long section of lining pop from the wall. It brought a spread of plaster with it, filling the air with dust and exposing a timber board behind the wall. He worked around the board, breaking the seal easily enough, scoring the surface of the wood, getting closer and closer to whatever lay behind. And it felt all wrong.

He should not have been doing this. It was not his place.

'Something's wrong,' he said. Nina was standing behind him now, and he could feel her eyes on the back of his neck. He turned. 'Nina.'

She was sweating, wringing her hands together as if to squeeze out fear. 'They're so close!' she said.

'You wrote them, Nina. Why can't you touch them?'

'Just the way things are. I don't make the laws; I just follow them.'

'Does that include armed robbery?'

'I mean the *real* laws,' she scoffed.

'So what happens when we find them? How do we carry them out?'

'You can. But it's the clue that's more important. Your grandfather would have left something, some hint…'

'Maybe not. Maybe he never wanted the book found at all.'

Nina stared at him without answering.

Scott went back to work, and soon the whole metal seal was ripped away. He set to work on the wood, breathing in air heavy with dust. He wanted to cough, but he was afraid that once he started he would not be able to stop.

The board was jammed in tight. He pushed the screwdriver through between the top of the board and the wall, encountering gritty resistance that

soon crumbled when he twisted the tool from side
to side. He felt like Lord Caernarvon gaining his
first look into Tutankhamen's tomb, and he held his
breath for a few seconds lest this buried place also
carried a curse.

It's Nina who's cursed, he thought, but he
wondered whether that was entirely true. Eternal
life? Many would kill for that.

Some already had.

The wood popped out without warning, falling
against his legs and scraping his knees. He stepped
back and let it clatter to the floor.

Nina moaned behind him. He turned to see
what was wrong, and turned back when he saw that
she was looking directly into the hole in the wall.
It was totally dark in there, as though a huge space
extended back beyond the new doorway.

Scott stepped aside to allow light access, and he
reached out and touched Nina's arm, urging her
aside as well. He realised that it was the first time he
had touched her.

'I can't see anything,' he said.

'They're there. I can feel them.'

'Where?'

'Deeper.'

'We'll need a torch.' Scott left Nina in the cellar,
dashing upstairs to the pub, vaulting the bar, and
looking around for a torch. He found one behind a
row of dusty pint mugs, obviously unused. Perhaps
it had been a locals' place once, but modern city

life had bled the pub's personality.

Back past the toilets, downstairs, and when he reached the basement Nina had gone.

He paused for a moment, wondering whether he would spend the rest of his life haunted by ghosts.

Then he heard the scrambling sounds coming from the hole in the wall. He hurried to it and shined the torch inside. It illuminated a bare earth wall three feet away, the far edge of a vertical pit. *Deeper*, Nina had said. And deeper she had gone.

Scott leant in and shined the torch down. There were metal rungs set in the wall, along with the remains of timber boards still buried in the earth here and there. Others had rotted away. This was an old place.

Nina looked up. 'They're down here, Scott. Come down!'

'What if I don't want to touch them for you?'

'Then you don't want Helen back.'

Who's using who? he thought, but he shoved the idea aside. He had to believe that they were helping each other.

He climbed through the hole and started down the metal rungs, holding the torch in his left hand. The rungs were badly rusted in places, and a few had already bent beneath Nina's weight. He was heavier. He tried to avoid damaged rungs where he could, because he was very conscious that they had to climb back out this way.

'I'm down,' Nina said below him. Her voice was

strangely deadened by the walls of the pit.

Did Papa really go to these lengths? he thought. *Did he come here and dig? If not, what was this place before? Someone must have known about it. He can't have just come here and found—*

'Oh, no,' Nina said.

'What? Nina?' Scott leant sideways and shined the torch down. He could see the top of Nina's head, and around her a deeper darkness where the pit opened up into a wider room. At her feet, set into the earthen floor of this place, were seven stone slabs. He could see the carvings on their faces from here; the torch made shadows that danced in the grooves and cuts.

Nina looked up at him. 'Scott, I didn't know.'

'Didn't know what? Is that them?'

'Yes, they're here. But I had no idea how far Lewis had travelled in the Wide. I had no inkling. Scott, listen to me. We have a few heartbeats before something arrives. I feel it closing. *Don't* let them touch you. Got it? *Whatever happens, do not...let them...touch you.*' She was staring up into his eyes, her own eyes heavier and deeper than any pit could be.

Scott descended the last few rungs, stood beside Nina, and shined the torch over the walls. He looked down at the stone tablets splayed around his feet. Considering that they supposedly contained part of the secret of eternal life, they looked fairly innocuous.

'I don't see what you're talking about.'

'You're about to. They're called blights.' And then there was something else in the pit with them, and Scott's world opened up wider than ever before.

Chapter Five

broken chords

The torch flickered out and darkness vanished. The light that came from somewhere else flooded the hole. No shadows were cast, no shades of light and dark. It was as if the air itself were on fire.

Behind the fire came the blights.

They grew from an impossible distance. Scott saw them coming in, and he must have been looking into the earth, through soil and rock, old sewers and other buried things. The blights were moments of nothing in the timeline of what was happening, patches of absence – no sound, no feeling, no sight or smell. They moved closer without traversing the spaces between there and here. And yet they moved as though they had a purpose.

There were three of them. Each seemed as large as Scott's head, or perhaps they were a mile away and the size of a house.

'Don't let them touch you,' Nina said again, her voice seeming to come from very far away.

'What will they do?'

'Just don't.' He sensed her moving beside him, coming closer and holding on to his arm. 'I can't touch the tablets, so you have to turn them and find what Papa left here for you.'

The blights closed in and the hole grew larger.

'What are those things?'

'Death.'

Scott turned to look at Nina, but she was staring down at her feet, shaking, sweat dripping from her nose and splashing clean, dark spots on the ancient stone tablets. She was standing on her toes between two of them, muscles in her calves and ankles straining as she tried not to touch the stone.

What happens if she does? Scott wondered.

Something brushed past his head, a cool breath on his ear, and the hairs on the back of his neck stood up. He spun around and saw a blight fading away before him, drifting into the wall of the pit.

I can see through the walls. I can see farther. In the distances around him there was mist and sunlight, darkness and snow, and other places bathing in weather he could not really understand. Another blight closed in and hovered before him. He stared into it, seeing nothing. Not just darkness, but an absence, a void in his wider view of the world. It was as though a piece of reality had yet to be sketched in, or had been rubbed out altogether.

Nina threw a punch at the blight. Her fist disappeared and came out the other side, and the blight moved back slightly.

'*You* touched it!'

'I'm immortal.'

But Scott could see the pain on Nina's face. Her skin turned grey and her eyelids drooped, and he slapped her across the face. 'Please stay with me. I'm scared! I don't know what to do.'

'Do as I said. Search. *And try not to let them touch you.*'

Scott knelt down and felt the massiveness of space moving around him. It dizzied him for a moment, and he reached out on both sides to steady himself. His left hand met dirt, but his right hand touched stone. Even without looking he could feel the etchings of ancient words of wisdom and magic against his fingertips. *Here's immortality*, he thought. *Part of it, at least. Here it is.*

Something screamed. He looked up, terrified that it was Nina, but she was still standing astride one of the stone tablets, apparently throwing punches at the air. The scream rose in volume and pitch.

Scott looked back down at the stone tablets. He worked his fingers into the soil beside one and started to lift.

Something passed by close to his face, and Nina's knee knocked against his head. This time he did not bother looking up.

The stone lifted, and from beneath came a waft

of coolness. *Trapped breath?* Scott thought. *Papa's trapped breath?* He inhaled but smelt no tobacco or coffee.

The tablet was about the size of a road atlas, and a couple of inches thick. It was heavy, but its weight gave comfort, while all around the air seemed to be lighter than ever, the basics of distance and perspective skewed.

The scream was coming from the blights.

'They're taking form!' Nina shouted.

'I thought they were already here!'

'Not even close…those are just their shadows. Keep looking, Scott! You don't have very long.'

There was nothing beneath the stone except for soil, packed hard and smoothed over three decades. Papa was the last one to touch this, and Scott took some comfort in that as the world came apart around him. He wiped at the underside of the slab, saw nothing there, lowered it back to the ground. He crawled across it to the next tablet and blew dust from its surface.

The carvings did not resemble any sort of language he knew. There were shapes in there that could have been insectoid, swirls and curlicues that may have formed letters, and in places the stone had been raised instead of lowered, as though it was the space around the carvings that really meant something. Some of it reminded him of shapes in the letter, but much more was unseen. *I should take these*, he thought. *These are important.*

'Scott!' Nina shouted. He looked up at her and she looked so *old*. Her dark hair was grey… or perhaps the strange light was making it look that way. Shadows danced on her face and gave her wrinkles, even though the light was constant. '*Hurry!*'

He almost looked around at what was scaring her, but somehow he turned his attention back to the ground. Papa had told him about deep breathing and concentration – meditation on the move, he'd called it – and Scott tried that now. He closed his eyes for a few seconds and thought of the one safe place he had always known: the presence of his grandfather. Papa smiled at him, and Scott kept that moment in his mind, breathing deeply, opening his eyes, and feeling the old man's influence guiding his hand towards a stone tablet just out of reach.

He crawled forward, away from Nina, and stretched out to touch the stone farthest away. It felt just as cold as the first, just as old, but when he blew dust from its surface he knew that something was different. There were only three symbols carved there. And though the representation of people seemed strange – they were too tall, their limbs too long to be human – it was clear that it was a set of instructions.

'Don't concern yourself,' Nina said in his ear. 'Just find the clue.' There was no threat in her voice, yet she had bent down to shout at him. Taking her attention from the blights. Offering her back to those things that she had called death.

Scott worked the fingers of both hands beneath the stone and heaved.

The train-scream came in again, louder than before. He could not help but look up, and what he saw froze the moment and turned it into forever.

The blights had come. Their shadows were still there, attached to three tall, multilimbed things that stood swaying at the fringes of where the pit should have been. Beyond them, strange landscapes faded into infinity. Shadows floated in the distance, wraiths and the hints of wraiths. Some had faces and traces of limbs, but most were too pale and faded to resemble anything more than a shaped drift of mist.

'All those people,' Scott said, and the first of the blights came at him.

Nina stepped before it, arms raised, hands flat in a warding-off gesture. 'He's not for you,' she said. Her voice was strange, as though it had risen from her whole body, not just her mouth. She shimmered before him.

The blight's many limbs whipped at the air, but none seemed to touch Nina. She stood solid between it and Scott, and one fierce look over her shoulder told him how close he was to death.

Don't let them touch you, she had warned.

He turned the stone over, and there, pressed into the soil beneath it, was something he recognised instantly: one of his grandfather's old metal tobacco tins.

A flood of recollection hit him, and a memory of intense love as he grabbed the box. 'Papa,' he said, and smiled. Touching the tin felt like completing a small circle in the large course of his life.

'Scott!' Nina said. And there was something about her voice…

Scott let the tablet drop and stood, slipping the box into his back pocket.

'That'll be mine,' a voice said, and Scott knew him.

'Fuck you.' He backed away from Nina and the blight, glancing around to place the others, and Lewis hung above him, floating horizontally as though reclined on a bed of air.

'I'll have it, Scott. Papa would have wanted it that way.'

'Where is my wife?'

'Not far away from me,' Lewis said. He smiled a comforting old-man's smile. 'But an infinity away from you. And there she'll stay, confused and sad and afraid, until you hand over to me what is rightfully mine.'

A blight closed in on Scott's left, another on his right. Their limbs flickered at the air like tongues of negative flame, and he could not be sure how close they were, nor how far away.

'Papa killed you to keep you from this. Why would I be so keen to hand it over?'

'Because your wife is alive in a place of the dead.'

'Papa knew what he was doing.'

'Helen will not die, Scott. I'll never kill her. There's far, far worse that I can do.'

'Don't listen to him, Scott!' Nina was grappling with the blight and staring at the other two. Where its tendrils touched her, her skin was almost white, flaking, peeling away from her flesh like curled leaves. She looked at Scott and pleaded with her eyes, but he really had no idea what was happening.

'Don't listen to *her*!' Lewis said.

'Fuck you,' Scott said again. 'I'm alive, and there's nothing—'

A blight moved in, reaching for him.

Nina screamed.

There was movement all around, things clashing above and below, shadows where there should have been none, and an impression of pure violence that Scott had never before experienced. This was primal fury, not just anger. He closed his eyes and fell. He seemed to fall a very long way, and the more time passed, the less inclined he was to open his eyes. Above him he sensed the real things of the world receding, held within a small, neat box that he had come to know as life. There was waking and sleeping, walking and eating, loving and being loved, and hardly a moment spent *wondering*. There were reality TV shows, car ads and celebrity news. There were the trivial concerns of everyday life blown out of all proportion, worries over spilt milk while another hundred children died from starvation in Africa. And rarely ever any real wonder.

There went life. And the farther away it was, the more pitiful it all seemed.

Below him – the way he was falling – Scott sensed nothing. But not because there was nothing there. He knew that he was approaching some wider truth, skirting below the thin veil of his existence and discovering the first grainy visions of reality.

He sensed nothing, because as yet he had no frame of reference.

There's Nina, he thought, but she was only a woman who had lived for ever. There were greater wonders ahead.

There were the blights, but they were merely wayward stains of death drifting to and fro at Lewis's command.

There was Lewis. The half ghost of a dead old man – an evil man, if what Scott had seen and heard was to be believed.

And there were Papa and Helen, and with them came true love. Helen was alive, and he had no doubt at all that he would see her again, but...

'There's *always* Papa,' he whispered. His voice was loud, because suddenly everything else was silence.

When he hit the ground he felt the metal box in his back pocket. *I still have it. Lewis hasn't got it. I still have it.*

Something cold and final fell across his arm and chest.

Helen...

More violence, things moving too quickly for him to comprehend.

Helen...?

Scott went elsewhere. Papa came for him, an old man walking out of memory and holding his hand. Together they left a dark, dangerous place somewhere in the fields and found themselves on a country lane. All the best memories were here waiting for him. They picked blackberries until their fingers were purple, built a dam across a stream and packed it with mud, collected frog spawn and waited for the tadpoles to hatch, found empty bird eggs and placed their delicate shells in a shoe box stuffed with tissue. Papa never spoke, but Scott knew that he was there. He could feel him. Papa was always there.

Someone was panting close by. Their breath was fast and light, the result of intense physical exertion. Scott tried to open his eyes, but when he did there was nothing more to see. Darkness crowded in. He listened for other sounds – the screams of the dying, perhaps, or the lost moans of the recently dead. But there was the panting, and nothing else.

Then feeling began to return. Cool soil at his back, moisture seeping through his trousers and shirt and cooling his skin. Something pressing into him, a hard shape in his back pocket.

A hand touching his face.

'Scott, I'm so sorry.'

He opened his mouth to speak but could only utter a groan. His throat was parched, and when he coughed it felt as though he were gargling with broken glass.

That glass I saw, scattered across the pavement. Such detail. She told me it was because I was seeing more. Now I see nothing.

'Nothing,' he said.

'Scott?' The panting lessened and the voice came closer. 'Wake up, now. Come on!' Something pushed his head to one side. Again, and this time he felt the sting of the slap.

Darkness receded, replaced by a circle of weak light directly above him. Into that circle moved a face.

'Helen?'

'Nina. How do you feel?'

'Weak. Weird. Where are those things?'

'Gone. I sent them away.'

'Lewis?'

'Went with them. But…' The silhouette of her head shook slightly; then Scott felt hands beneath his arms, lifting.

He pushed with his hands. Both of them rested on cool, carved stone, and he remembered where he was.

'I still have it,' he said. 'The thing Papa left. The clue.'

'Good. But Scott…'

'I went somewhere,' he said. 'I fell. And everything felt…different.'

'Everything is.'

'Am I somewhere else? Are we in the Wide?'

'Not right now, no.' She sounded weak and sad, and neither suited her.

'What is it?' he asked.

'Let's get you out of here.' She lifted him to his feet, and he swayed there for a while, glad that Nina was still holding his arms. *Where is up and where is down?* he thought. *Which way did I fall?* He looked up at the light and realised it was the weak cellar light shining through the doorway.

'How long have we been down here?'

'Long enough. We should go up.'

'There's something you're not telling me, Nina.'

'Let's get out of this pit.'

'Is it Helen? Is it my wife?'

'Helen's fine,' she said. 'Lewis has no reason to hurt her, so long as you still have what you have. She's his insurance.'

'That's comforting.'

'Sorry. But his only interest in her is to get to you.'

'But he *did* get to me. He was there, ready to take what he wanted, and then…such *violence*. It makes me feel sick just remembering it, and I didn't even really see…' He remembered something cold touching down across his chest and arm. 'What happened?'

She nudged him towards the rungs set in the wall. 'Up. I'll climb behind you, push if you need it.'

'I feel fine.'

Nina was silent. Scott thought she looked away, but the light down here was poor, and he could not be sure.

He climbed, using the rusted rungs that bent beneath his hands because he did not trust himself to reach higher. He'd said that he felt fine, but he did not. Not at all. He felt weak and sick, and the farther he rose from the pit the more something seemed to stink. His vision swam, and the memory of that long fall was never far away. He wondered just what it was he was climbing toward.

Nina was behind him, and as he reached the hole in the wall she shoved him up and out, following with her usual grace.

Scott lay on the floor of the beer cellar, inhaling the stale fumes of spilt ale. He was breathing hard. His right arm hurt like hell, and his chest felt…light. Hollow.

'Nina…'

'Scott, one of the blights touched you. Only for a moment, but I couldn't stop it. I'm sorry.'

'What do you mean? What does that *mean*?'

'Your arm and the top right part of your chest… they're dead. The flesh there is rotting, and though blood still flows, it's slowly being poisoned.'

'I'm dying?'

'Yes.'

Scott was silent for a while. He didn't *feel* like he was dying. He was weak and dizzy, but…What was that smell? *That's me*, he thought. *That's my flesh starting to rot.*

'How long?'

Nina sat on the floor beside him and took his right hand. 'Not too long,' she said. 'But listen, Scott, there's hope. There's someone I could take you to see. Someone else like me, one of the other immortals. He took a very different path, but he *might* know how to help you. Or at least give you more time.'

'To get Helen back.'

Nina looked away. 'Yes, to do that.'

Scott sat up and took his hand from hers. 'You fought the blights?'

'I sent them back. But I wasn't ready to do it. I didn't know Lewis had gone so far into the Wide and come back, and he's much stronger than I could have believed. He's very close to what he wants. And that's why there's no way he can have the rest of the book. It's such a fine balance…If we don't find the book and destroy it, he could have it soon. If we do find it, he could get it before it is destroyed.' She sat back against the wall and closed her eyes. 'And even being so near makes me sick.'

'You want me to destroy it after you've found out how to die?'

'After, yes.'

'But I might die soon. I might be gone. I'll be

one of those things, those wraiths that Lewis seems to surround himself with.'

'I promise, Scott, that if that happens I'll make sure you go the way your Papa went. *All* the way. I'd never see you tortured.'

'Heaven?'

Nina shrugged and looked away.

Scott stared at the opposite wall, trying to see through, as he had when the Wide was upon him. 'I saw so much,' he said.

Nina nodded. 'You did. And you'll find it's a different world up there now.' She came to him and helped him up, and together they climbed the stone steps back into the pub. He sat at one of the tables and Nina went behind the bar. She poured two generous glasses of single-malt and returned to the table. By the time she sat down most of her drink had gone.

'Scott—'

'I'll go back down.'

'You don't have to.'

'We can't just leave them, can we? And you say you can't touch them.'

'You doubt me?'

'No, no.' He shook his head, but he could not convince himself that easily. *There's so much she hasn't told me.*

'You can give me what you found, if you like.'

Scott's hand went around to the box in his back pocket. He had not opened it yet, and he had no idea what was inside. 'You could run.'

'If I wanted to do that, I'd just take it off you anyway.' She stood and went to the bar to refill her drink.

Scott sipped his whiskey and relished the warmth coursing down through his body. 'You said things would be different now that I saw…whatever I saw down there.'

Nina glanced back at Scott, then nodded towards the corner of the pub.

There was an old man. He seemed completely unaware of their presence. A beer glass stood before him, half-empty, and as Scott watched he brought it to his mouth and took a long drink. When the glass touched the table again the level had not changed.

'Ghost.'

Nina nodded. 'A lost soul.'

'We're in the Wide right now.'

'At its very edge, yes. So go back down for me, Scott. Destroy what's there. Then we have to follow Papa's clue to the rest of the book.'

Scott stood and walked slowly across the pub. His arm ached, and the right side of his chest felt numb. *I'm dying*, he thought. *But she won't let me be like him.* The old man raised his drink again, looking around the pub and seeing nothing that Scott could see. Memories, perhaps. Or visions he could never touch again.

Scott took the tobacco box from his pocket and placed it carefully on the bar. 'How do you know I'll be safe down there?'

'Lewis finds it difficult coming through. He'll be weak. I sent him back weaker.'

'You fought?'

'We fought.'

Scott nodded. 'I'll be back up in a few minutes,' he said.

'Make sure they can never be put back together. Make them dust.'

He found what he wanted in the cellar: a lump hammer, used to wedge or unwedge barrels from the old racks. And he found something else he'd been hoping for as well: a pile of old invoices. They were printed on one side only, folded and shoved out of the way on a high shelf. Beside them was the stub of a pencil.

Scott took them all down.

He took a rubbing from each stone tablet. He pressed lightly on the paper, taking care not to drive the pencil right through where it passed across dips and scrapes in the stone. The light was still poor down in the pit, but good enough to see that the rubbings had been quite successful.

He and Papa had used to go to the village church with a ream of paper and a handful of charcoal. They'd take rubbings from some of the interesting headstones, and inside the church they had found an old stone column with strange markings circling it, curling anitclockwise from the floor up. They took impressions of these, too, and for a while Papa had persuaded Scott that he'd been studying them every evening, and he believed them to be the work of the Knights Templar. *The Grail could well be here*, he had told Scott, *a wonder of the world, buried beneath our feet as we're taking impressions of old headstones.* Scott had been enraptured. Papa had soon admitted that he did not really know what those strange carvings meant, and Scott had found that even more fascinating. *They could mean anything*, he said. *They probably do*, Papa had replied.

'Look what I have, Papa,' he said, holding up the final piece of paper. 'I don't know why, but something like this can't just be destroyed. There's so much I don't know about it. Maybe I'll find out, given time.'

Then he went to work breaking up the stone tablets.

With the first strike of the hammer, the first slab broke into three large pieces. He gasped and held his breath. *What have I done?* The pit remained gloomy, no strange light intruded, and the shadows did not move. Scott's shoulder was hurting, though he could barely feel his right arm. He looked at his hand and tried to move his fingers. They shifted only slightly.

'I'm dying, and I'm destroying part of the Chord of Souls. I'm shunning immortality.' But then there were the sheets of paper folded into his back pocket, replacing the feel of the metal tobacco box that had been there so briefly. And somehow, that felt right.

He smashed the other stones into smaller pieces, broke them down again, the hammer rising and falling, rising and falling. Nina must have been able to hear from where she sat up there in the bar. He wondered what she was thinking as she listened to him destroying something she had carved so many years ago. *How long, I wonder? Hundreds of years? Thousands? Tens of thousands? How old is she, really?*

When the stones were broken into shards and dust he mixed the mess together, kicking it around the base of the pit and stomping it into the soil. He smashed up the few remaining larger pieces and then had to sit down, dizziness overcoming him. He closed his eyes and dropped the hammer, and sweat ran onto his eyelids. Helen used to kiss him there like that; butterfly kisses, she called them. Tears joined the sweat on his face.

'I have no idea what's going on, angel, but I promise I'll get you back.'

On the way back up he noticed a deeper shadow hunched in the corner of the beer cellar. Looking closer, he made out the ghostly pale echo of a man. The ghost looked up at him pleadingly, but Scott did not know what it wanted, and he left it on its own.

He heard the sound of something clinking against glass as he went back into the bar. Nina looked up and offered him a weak smile.

'Is it done?'

'Yes, all done.' As he walked he could feel the paper in his pocket.

'Papa left you this. He was very clever. I assume no one else but you would know the significance.'

Nina looked down at the table, where she was gently tapping her whiskey glass with a small bronze skull key ring.

'Oh, my God!' Scott could not help blurting out. 'I'd forgotten all about that!' On the day Papa died Scott had realised that his key ring was missing. Papa had bought it for him several years before, a secret memento of one of their long, ongoing discussions. They'd spent time reading about the skulls and catching references to them in obscure TV programmes, and Scott had always found them fascinating.

Wonder what they've got to scream about so much? Papa used to say.

Perhaps now Scott would find out.

'So you know what this is,' Nina said.

'Yes,' Scott said. 'And I know where it's sending me. Shall we go?'

Nina looked desperate to sit him down and talk, but for the first time Scott began to feel some semblance of control. Ever since Helen had been taken away by Lewis, he had been stumbling blindly along, Nina leading the way as though he were an obedient dog. Now, with flesh dying on his bones and his blood turning to poison, he knew something that Nina did not.

'Where are we going?' Nina asked.

'To get Helen back.' Scott strode to the front door.

It opened onto another world.

Chapter Six

a cool, grey day

There were ghosts everywhere. On the pavement directly in front of the pub lay an old woman, arms stretched up for help that would never come. People walked on her. Through her. Scott could see pain on her face, but it was old pain.

In the road several wraiths walked, crawled, or rolled from one place to another. Once their brief movements ended they would return to their starting places again, flickering back like bad TV pictures. One of them launched high into the air, spinning and losing parts of himself to a cool, grey day long ago. He was dressed as a soldier from the Second World War. Scott wondered how terrible it must have been to survive that conflict, only to be run over on his way home to his family.

Across the road, ghosts seemed to mill at the castle walls like windblown leaves. Some of them described very defined routes, while others wandered here and there with no apparent pattern or reason.

In places several of them overlapped, existing within one another.

Nobody else saw them. A young couple was sitting on the grass verge below the castle's wall – almost exactly where he and Nina had sat before breaking into the Mason's Vaults – and as they ate their baguettes, the image of a child walked over the boy's legs and through the girl's torso and head. There was no sign that the girl felt anything at all. She smiled at what the boy was saying between mouthfuls, watched the traffic, finished her baguette, and looked up at the sun.

The child turned and walked back, emerging from the girl like her own tired soul taking leave.

'We should move from the doorway,' Nina said. She touched Scott's back and pushed gently, urging him out into the street.

'Do you see this all the time?' he asked.

'You learn to ignore it.'

'How can you ignore it?' Scott sidled sideways to avoid the old woman on the pavement. His feet crunched through the glass spilt from the pub's menu board, and he leant back against the wall.

'Do you worry about stepping on the cracks in the pavement? Stepping on shadow or sunlight?'

'No.'

'Same thing.' Nina crossed the pavement and stood inside the old woman.

Scott cringed.

'They can't feel it, Scott. Especially ones like

this, repeating the same moment again and again. She's just an old echo, a shred of a lost soul. And the others…even if they do see us, we can't interact with them, nor they us.'

'There were some in my garden,' he said.

Nina nodded and frowned. 'Yes, Lewis had guided them there. To disturb you.'

'It worked. But how can he interact with them?'

Nina stared at him without answering.

'You don't know?'

She shrugged.

'But you're immortal. You've lived for ever!'

'I've lived for a very long time, Scott. But I don't know everything. If I did…'

'You'd have no need of me.'

'Right.'

Scott looked down at his arm and chest. Both were covered, and he was suddenly terrified of opening his shirt and seeing what he had become. He touched his shirt cuff, opened the button, and rolled the sleeve slightly up his arm. His wrist was pale and he could see the veins, crossed like motorways on a road map. Farther up the skin began to turn darker, and when he reached his elbow it suddenly became dark as burnt sausage. He touched it with one fingertip. It was cold, and too soft.

Nina looked at him with what could have been sympathy.

'How long do I have?' he asked.

She shook her head. 'I don't know. But we need

to go where I said, to see the man I mentioned.'

'Another immortal. What's his name?'

'He has no name. We just call him Old Man.'
She smiled. Then, as a ghost passed between her and
Scott, she laughed.

'Old Man?'

'What, you think immortals don't need a sense of
humour?'

They walked past the castle and entered the park,
and Scott knew that he would never get used to
seeing so many ghosts. 'What must it be like on old
battlefields?' he said. 'Or in hospitals?' Nina did not
answer, and he supposed it was because the answer
was obvious.

They walked across the park and Nina guided
them towards a copse of trees. A man hung in mid-
air, swinging from a rope tied to a tree long gone
from the here and now. His face was swollen and
black, but, like a picture, his eyes seemed to follow
Scott as he walked by.

'In here,' Nina said.

'This is where Old Man lives?'

'In a park? Don't be soft. No, this is where we'll
leave to go to him.'

'Leave how?' Scott asked. But already he was
starting to feel a sense of dread.

'I'll sort that out. Just keep up with me.' Nina
was looking around with more than interest, and
that worried Scott as well. Here he was in Cardiff,
surrounded suddenly by a world he did not know,

following a woman who seemed to be immortal, to meet another immortal who might be able to save him now that he'd been touched by death…

'I think I believe all this,' he said. Nina glanced back, offering only a quirky frown. 'I shouldn't, but I do. Papa would have loved this, Nina.'

She stopped and looked back at him again. This time the frown was replaced by a smile. 'He did,' she said. 'He really did.'

Papa sits on a rock beside the stream while Scott wades into the water. He's wearing his new trainers and socks, and his mother will be mad when he goes home with them soaked. He purposely hasn't turned around in at least ten minutes, scared that he will attract Papa's attention to what he is doing. But really Scott knows that he knows. Papa, as his father so often says when the old man is not present, lets Scott get away with murder.

He wades out farther, catching his breath as he slips on a mossy stone. Something darts past his leg and disappears beneath a spread of stream glaring with sunlight. Stickleback? Scott's not sure, but he'd love to catch one. He'd put it back afterward, of course. But he really needs to catch one.

'That's far enough,' Papa says.

'It's not deep.'

'Not there, no. But farther out it is. That's far enough, Scott.'

The memory usually ends here, segueing into

an evening spent raking grass cuttings and helping his father trim a tree at the bottom of the garden. Usually. But this time the memory remains, and it's as fresh as if it is happening right now.

Scott takes another step forward in the stream. He's not sure why; he usually does what Papa says, because he knows how much freedom the old man gives him.

His foot comes down and hovers over nothing.

'Scott!' Papa's voice is thunder, shattering the tranquillity of the scene and darkening the sun. 'Get back!'

Scott turns to see why his grandfather is so angry, and he starts to dip backward into the stream. For a few seconds he balances there, two possibilities juggling and jousting to decide which path he will travel down next. The safer of the two wins. He finds his feet again and picks his way back across the stream, reaching the bank and his red-faced Papa.

'Sorry,' he says quietly, but already Papa is calming down. His hand shakes as he touches the back of Scott's neck and pulls him in for a hug.

'Death's always so close, Scotty. People have drowned in that stream.'

'How do you know?'

'I just do.' And for the briefest of moments, Scott senses that it's not only him Papa is talking to.

They walk home across a field, and Papa has a smile on his face. Scott darts here and there, picking dandelions, kicking molehills, trying to balance on the crusts of old cow patties without sinking through. He glances at Papa now and then, aware that the old man is in some other zone, enjoying being in this field in a completely different way from Scott. It's as if he is somewhere else entirely, and his face shows his joy at being there.

'In here,' Nina said. 'Sit down.'

'Why are you nervous?'

Nina sat beside him, her back against the tree. 'I don't want to be seen.'

'By Lewis?'

'Maybe. I'm not as certain of his capabilities as I once was. It's almost as if he's getting help.'

'Who would help him?'

Nina shrugged. 'But I have to help you right now. That's the priority. That's the only thing we can concentrate on so that—'

'Helen is the only thing I'm concentrating on here,' Scott said. 'Why can't you just go and find her? Why can't you take me with you, and we'll both go?'

'The Wide is endless, Scott. She could be anywhere. Anywhere.'

'She's not on your mind, is she? She's not important to you at all.'

'She is. She is. Because she's important to you.'

Scott rested his head back against the tree and looked up into the branches. It was a relief to be able to look somewhere where there were no ghosts. If he glanced around where he was sitting he could see none, but he could feel them everywhere. If he looked carefully, he was sure they would reveal themselves. In the tree's canopy birds chirped and hopped invisibly from branch to branch. A small spider lowered before him, spinning on its invisible line of silk. He reached out and touched the line, moving it left and right and setting the spider swaying.

'What are you doing?' Nina asked.

'Trying to find a moment's peace.'

'Believe me, true peace is not easy.'

He let the spider go and it crawled quickly back up into the tree. 'You've had enough time to look for it.'

'The longer you have, the more elusive it becomes. That's why…' She trailed off.

'That's why you want to know how to die.'

Nina nodded. 'Partly.'

'What is there after death, if you don't become one of those lost souls?' He waved his hand, though there were no ghosts in sight.

'The other side of the Wide.'

'And what's there?'

'That's what I want to find out.'

Scott sighed. 'So whatever you're going to do, let's do it.'

Nina edged herself closer to him, their legs touching. She was surprisingly warm. She's no ghost, he thought. But he began to wonder. If she truly was immortal, then perhaps she was some kind of ghost, a soul trapped in her own body instead of set free to wander or repeat the moment of its death. Maybe there was a lot more to being a ghost than simply being lost. Maybe it had a lot to do with being damned.

'You damned yourself,' Scott said.

Nina looked at him, surprised. 'No.'

'You look damned. You feel damned, don't you?'

She glanced past him into the infinity between drooping branches. She was silent for some time. 'No,' she said at last. 'I don't feel damned. I feel blessed. But I'm not able to accept the blessing, or use it as it should be used.'

'Are any of the other immortals able to do that?'

'That's a difficult one.' She picked a blade of grass and rolled it between her fingers. Picked another blade, tied it around the first. She concentrated hard, then cast them aside. 'Old Man has achieved a lot,' she said. 'You'll see that soon. But even he doesn't use his immortality as he could.'

'Now I'm worried.'

'Don't be. He's harmless.'

'I'm not sure whether or not you're being ironic.'

Nina smiled fleetingly. 'Right. I'll tell you what's going to happen, and you have to listen to me. Listen to me, Scott. The Wide is the path from life to what lies after. For those lost souls – the ones who can't even find the start of the path – it's endless, and has no direction. We're going to skirt the very edge of the Wide. But you have to hold on to me. I can find my way through, but you're going to be lost. Hold on to me, Scott. If you don't – if you let go, and I lose you – then you'll be lost in there for ever.'

'Helen is in there?'

'Don't think about that. Don't even consider going to find her, because you never will. Imagine dropping a penny into the Atlantic, then taking a snorkel to go and look for it. It can never be found, and you don't have the right equipment to look.'

'And you have the right equipment? The knowledge?'

'I've learnt a few small facts about the Wide since I've been alive.'

Scott stood and his knees clicked. *Getting old,* he thought. *And here I am, about to get a preview of what is yet to come.*

'But you'll help me find Helen. Once we've got the book, you'll help me get her back from Lewis. Right?'

'Maybe even before then.'

'How?'

'Lewis will be following us every step of the way.'

Following us. Scott shivered. It's almost as if he's getting help, Nina had said.

'Now come and sit back down with me,' Nina said. 'We'll link arms.'

Scott sat so that his good arm was linked through Nina's. *Not my dead arm. I won't link that one with hers. It could come off.* He felt a moment of intense giddiness, and the whole world seemed to tip in an attempt to throw him off. Initially he thought it was Nina taking them into the Wide, but then he felt her hands on his face, smelt the spicy mystery of her breath as she brought her face close to his, and he heard her shout as a whisper.

'Scott, hold on. *Fight it!*'

Fight what? he thought. But then he knew. He felt something vast and endless opening up around him, and it was the draw of the Wide.

'Not yet, Scott!'

Sound and smell returned slowly, and Nina's voice grew louder.

'That's good, that's good. *Damn it!*' It was her curse more than anything that brought him around. She lost control for a moment, and that scared Scott out of his dance with unconsciousness.

'Nina...'

'It's not your time yet, Scott. Come on. Sit up again, hold me, and we'll go to see Old Man. It's been a long time.' She hauled him up beside her, sitting with his back against the tree, and she linked her arm tightly through his.

He still felt dizzy and hazy, but even through that he found time to wonder what a long time was to an immortal.

'Don't hold your breath,' she said. 'You can breathe out there. And remember, you're not one of them. You're alive, Scott. You need yourself.'

'Need myself?'

'You'll see. Here we go.' Nina muttered a few

words that rose and fell with a sing-song lilt. Her voice became deep – almost subaudible – and the phrases so obviously held power. Scott sensed them rumbling in his chest, tickling his heart and the deeper parts of him, and he felt as though he were acting as a tuning fork for the phrase she sang again and again.

He sensed it in the distance first, places he could not see dozens or hundreds of miles away blinking from existence. The line where reality and unreality blurred closed in quickly, like reverse ripples on the pond of time. The surface was the world he inhabited, and below the surface lay the whole rounded truth of reality. And it had such hidden depths.

Cardiff began to fade. Fields and streets, homes and factories, hospitals and schools and parks, they all flickered away to nothing. He could still see through the trees to the park around them, and in the distance the castle stood defiantly, a huge, ancient edifice that could surely never be humbled or changed. He could also see several shapes wandering across the park, but from beneath the copse of trees he could not make out whether they were people or ghosts, or both.

'Almost there,' Nina whispered, and she clasped Scott's arm so tightly with hers that it began to hurt.

The distant sky began to change. It wavered with heat haze, then lost its pale colours. Grey or white, Scott could not tell, but perspective was leached away. The haze came closer. No sound accompanied it.

Reality was being purged silently and with no fanfare, and the only sound that accompanied the sight of the castle, park, and trees disappearing into a glare of nothingness was Scott's scream.

He closed his eyes. That was the only reaction he could offer. Time and space opened up around him, pulling away with frightening velocity. It was as if everything he knew and understood had expanded from nothing to the size of the universe in the blink of an eye, a big bang of personal proportions that would utterly steal away his personality if he allowed it. He was less than a speck of dust under the gaze of the universe, so insignificant that the irrelevance of his life and looming death took his breath away.

You need yourself, she had said. And she was right. Under the impression of all that was around and within, if he lost himself, then there was nothing. And no sane mind could stand that.

The endlessness of life, death, and time stretched around him, and he kept his eyes closed because it terrified him. He was conscious only of the turmoil in his mind, and the feeling of Nina's arm holding him tight.

There was no sense of movement. No time passed, and though he was breathing light and fast, there was no impression that these breaths carried him from moment to moment. He could be here for ever, and he wondered how madness would work with no time to permit its growth.

* * *

The reality of infinity abandoned him. He sat down with a bump. His eyes opened and a brief flash of pain blossomed behind them.

'Shit!' He gasped. And that grounded him. He had been through something mindless and terrifying, and his first reaction upon emerging from the other side was to curse. No expression of wonder or amazement or disbelief…just a curse.

'Indeed,' Nina said. 'That's usually my reaction.'

Scott moved his arm slightly, and when Nina lifted her own he knew it was safe for them to part. He massaged his shoulder, glad that the pain was rapidly fading. 'That place was…' He could not finish.

'The Wide,' Nina said. And that said it all.

Their immediate reality crashed in then, and it was only as it appeared around them that Scott registered its brief absence. A pale mist of nothing was replaced by cool concrete slabs beneath them, a building at their back, railings before them supporting a mass of rampant shrubs, and a road grew into the distance, spotted with parked cars and crossed here and there by dogs or foxes. It was night-time, and something howled.

It had been daytime in Cardiff.

The howl was answered from closer by. Something flapped around his head, and just as he began to panic a sound screamed in from his right. The motorcycle roared past along the street, Dopplering into the distance and carrying a splash of light with it.

'Holy shit, I thought we were somewhere else,' Scott said. 'I thought…the howls.'

'Dogs,' Nina said. She listened. 'Scottish dogs, I think.'

'You're *joking* with me?'

She nudged his arm and laughed. 'We're here! I'm just pleased, that's all. You kept your eyes closed through there, but I find I never can. It's always good to come back.'

'It was daylight when we left Cardiff.'

'And now we're in Edinburgh, and it's night-time.'

'It feels like seconds.'

'The Wide's weird with time. Who knows? We might have come out a century in the future.'

Scott's eyes went wide and he looked around. 'That motorbike looked pretty normal. And—'

'I'm fucking with you, Scott.' Nina held his left hand, helping him stand from the cold ground.

Scott brushed himself off and looked around. The row of buildings behind them was three stories high, town houses each displaying bed-and-breakfast signs. Most of them had vacancies. There were lights on at a couple of windows, but no other sign of activity.

It was dark and overcast, no moon or stars. Street lights were off, so it must have been in the early hours, but when Scott turned around and looked past the overgrown railings, his jaw dropped.

Edinburgh Castle stood before them, high and majestic on its volcanic foundation. It was illuminated from all sides, and the cliffs below were in darkness, making it appear as though the castle floated a hundred feet up in the sky. It was stunning and humbling, and Scott was profoundly grateful that a human construct still had the power to astound after what he had just been through. He would hate to find his sense of wonder stolen away by the Wide.

'Very pretty,' Nina said quietly. 'Old stone, new light. They go well together. I wonder what it would have looked like five hundred years ago.'

'Didn't you see it back then?'

'No. I haven't been to see Old Man in a long time.'

'Is he close?'

'Hopefully. He's not the sort to move around.' She was staring dreamily at the castle, and Scott saw its decorative lights reflected in her eyes.

'So let's go,' he said.

Nina turned, her expression unreadable. 'Scott, you know he's going to be very strange to you, don't you?'

'Stranger than you?'

She blinked, as though trying to decide whether or not he was joking.

'You told me you collect the hearts of dead things.'

She nodded. 'But Old Man…he doesn't move

around. Doesn't interact with people. He studies. Practises. Experiments.'

'What with?'

'Life and death. That's why we're here, with you balancing between the two.' She waved her hand. 'Just be warned. He's not with the times like I am.'

'With the times,' he repeated, and laughed. But it was a bitter sound, humourless, because his wife was still missing. 'I *need* to be fixed,' he said, and the tears came then. 'I need to be made better so I can find her. Will he do that for me? Can he?'

'We'll see. Follow me.' Nina touched him on the shoulder, a brief expression of support, and then crossed the road. Scott followed.

They walked along the railing until Nina found a gate buried beneath a fall of shrubs. She lifted the plants away and pulled at the gate. Its hinges squealed as it opened, and Scott thought of *The Secret Garden* and all those other children's books where the characters found another reality and entered into a world-changing adventure. On this side of the fence was a quiet Edinburgh road, home to sleeping tourists and dogs that wandered the streets at night. On the other side, just what would they find?

'Where are we going?' he asked.

'Old Man,' Nina said. 'He probably knows we're here already. We'll know soon enough whether or not…Ahh, there we are.' She stepped through the gate and motioned Scott to follow. When he pushed past the reaching fronds of unknown plants she pointed, and he saw.

On the sheer slopes below the stark face of Edinburgh Castle, a strange light glowed. It was not yellow or white, but grey, reminiscent of the blankness of the Wide.

'Homing light,' she said. 'He welcomes us. I wonder how much he knows?'

'About what?'

'You, the book, your wife.'

'I thought you said he never went out?'

'Doesn't mean he hasn't got his ear to the ground. Come on.'

They headed through the park, following paths where they led in the right direction, then crossing tended lawns. When they reached the foot of the cliff Nina stood back for a while, staring at the light fifty feet up the sheer slope.

'Can't walk up there,' Scott said.

'No, but we can climb.'

'What if we fall? It's OK for you; you're immortal.'

Nina offered her lopsided smile. 'Then be careful.'

'Thanks.'

'I'll climb first. Watch my hands and feet. Try to follow.'

'My arm—'

'You'll be fine. We'll get you better; then we can head off to find Helen.'

Scott nodded, but he knew that he was being played. She said all the right things and made the right moves, but Nina wanted only one thing from him. She had no concerns for Helen or even for him. And though that frightened him in part, in another way he found it comforting. She was immortal – as inhuman as a human could be – and to believe that she was concerned with anything so grounded as love would feel so unnatural.

'You're a monster,' he said, surprised that he had uttered instead of thought it.

Nina turned and started working her way up the slope. He had not seen her face. Maybe for just an instant, the monster would have shown through.

They climbed. The cliff was not as sheer as it appeared from the ground, and Scott found that he could crawl up on hands and feet. His right hand was almost useless, supported as it was by his dying arm, but he could still curl his fingers around grasses and the roots of small bushes. He followed Nina, trying to use the same handholds, but something seemed to be lifting him up that slope. When he looked behind and down it seemed a long way, but he knew he would not fall. He could not, so he would not. If he fell, Helen would be lost for ever.

The higher they went, the more of Edinburgh was laid out behind them. Without moonlight the city was a darkness speckled with street lights. Lines of them snaked around one another, and individual illuminations cast a thousand spots across the old town. A plane took off in the distance, too far away to hear but still visible. Life continuing.

I've just been to where it ends, Scott thought. *I've just felt the start of the journey to eternity. I've seen more than anyone, and now I'm climbing a cliff to meet an immortal who may be able to keep me on this side of the Wide, at least for a while longer. I'm coming for you, Helen. Don't worry. And Lewis…*

A shape fell past him, blurring lights and wailing as it bounced from a rocky outcrop six feet below his left foot. It spun out into the darkness and disappeared. Scott did not hear the thump.

He pressed himself to the ground before him, breathing in the loamy reality. Then he looked up.

Nina stared down at him. 'Lucky we've seen only one,' she said. 'It's such an old place.'

Scott closed his eyes and pressed his face farther into the moss. It smelt so good, so real, that he plucked a handful from between rocks and rolled it in his hand, getting the smell of it beneath his fingernails and into his lifeline.

It took only a minute for a shape to fall past him again, striking the rock and disappearing out into the night, trailing its haunted wail behind. He pressed his hand to his nose and inhaled the mossy tang.

When he was dead, he'd no longer be able to smell.

They climbed on. Nina moved faster, and it took her only a few minutes to reach the splash of weak grey light exuding from the cliff. She sat there on a small ledge and waited for him, waving impatiently when Scott leant back to look up.

A shape fell past again, close by, the wail distant.

Are you new or old? he thought. *Are you a tourist who fell from the walls, or someone who died building this place?*

He reached Nina; she held his arm to keep him steady, and he saw where the light was coming from. A large rock formed an overhang, protruding from the cliff like the broken nose on an ancient face. Beneath the overhang, where the nostrils would be, light leaked from the cliff like pus oozing from an old sore. It was almost as if the light were heavier than air, struggling to keep itself airborne as it probed weakly into the Scottish night.

'What is that?' Scott asked.

'Like I said, homing light. Old Man must have lit it when he knew we were close.'

'Won't anyone else see it?'

'I doubt it.' She smiled an enigmatic smile that meant there was more to this than Scott could know. He was already becoming sick of that expression.

She's cold, he thought. *A cold fish. However friendly she acts, however enthralling I find her presence, I must never forget that.*

'I've lived too long to dilly-dally over what's not important,' Nina said.

Scott looked away. Yet again, she seemed to know exactly the way he was thinking.

He lowered himself slightly and tried to see past the light. 'So where do we go?'

'Patience.' Nina leant against the rock and raised her face to the sky. She closed her eyes and breathed in deeply. 'Smells good,' she said.

'What does?'

'History.'

Scott put his hand to his nose again and breathed in the aroma of earth and moss. Smells good, he thought. Reality.

The light faded away to nothing.

'There we are,' Nina said. She lowered herself down so that she was level with Scott, leant forward, and probed the sudden darkness beneath the overhang. 'In here.'

'He's in there?'

'Come on.' She crawled into the gap in the land.

Scott watched until her feet disappeared. He heard the sound of crawling, Nina dragging herself deeper into the hole beneath the castle, and for a moment he wondered what would happen if he fled. He could climb down the steep hill, run into Edinburgh, find a guesthouse at random, and spend what was left of the night thinking things through. Helen gone. Papa dead but affecting him more than ever before. His arm and chest…his flesh dying, and the death spreading through his blood, infecting him elsewhere, killing him.

He did not really want to kill himself for the sake of independence. Like it or not, one way or another, he was tied to Nina until this was over.

He heard a whisper from the hole in the cliff, and it sounded like *Old Man*.

There was no answering voice, and no other sounds. He was alone. And the choice really was not difficult to make.

The hole was wider than it looked, hidden in the shadows of the overhang. To begin with, Scott crawled over sharp shale and angled rocks, which dug into his palms and knees. But a few feet in, when any borrowed light from the city failed to penetrate, the ground changed to something smooth. He could not easily identify what it was; it felt like grass, but was warm and fine as felt.

He leant down and took a sniff, and it smelt of nothing.

He lay still and breathed out slowly, listening for any sounds from deeper in the cave. There were none. He crawled on, enjoying the feel of the stuff beneath his hands, and within a few seconds he saw a light up ahead. It flickered and flowed, dancing in unseen currents, perhaps caused by his entry into the cave. And he could smell the smoky taint of burning oil.

'Hello!' His voice did not echo at all. 'Nina?' he called. 'Old Man?' The rock ate his words. Nothing came back.

Scott crawled on, aiming for the light. He hauled with his left hand, pushed with his feet, pulled his right hand along after him. It was getting worse. He caught a whiff of something wrong and smelt the mud on his hand. *I'm dying.*

He reached back and touched the papers folded in his pocket. They felt suddenly dangerous, evidence of some vast betrayal that he did not yet understand, and all he wanted to do was throw them away. But what if he did? What if he crawled back to the cave entrance, curled the papers into balls, and threw them from the cliff? Perhaps they would blow away on a breeze and be lost for ever. Or perhaps they would be found, an enigma, a puzzle, just as challenging to the discoverer as the original tablets had been to Papa and Lewis sixty years before.

He could not do that.

And much as they felt heavy as guilt, neither could he destroy them.

He crawled on, came to a bend, turned almost ninety degrees, and found Nina looking at him.

She was standing in a small, spherical cave. Several holes in the walls bore bluish flames, lighting the cave and giving the smell of burning oil to the air. The ceiling shone with crystal brilliance, and the floor was lined with dozens of overlapping rugs: reed, wool, and silk.

'Old Man not home?' Scott asked. He lowered himself from the crawl space and stretched straight.

'This is only his front door,' Nina said. 'He asked me to wait here for you, guide you in.'

'Guide?' Scott looked around. Other than the

way he had come, there was one exit from the cave, a round doorway behind Nina.

'There are lots of ways in, but only one way out,' she said. 'I don't want you to get lost down here.' She turned and entered the doorway, and Scott followed.

The corridor wound left and right, up and down, and the entire route was lit by burning oil reservoirs held in hollows in the wall. In places the smoke hazed the air slightly, but generally the cave was kept clear, though Scott could detect no real air movement. Other tunnels veered off from the main corridor, varying from the same size to too small for someone to pass through. They joined from above and below as well as from the sides, and Scott quickly formed the impression of a vast ants' nest below Edinburgh Castle, inhabited by just one man.

'How far?' he asked.

'Almost there. How do you feel?'

'Tired.' His chest was starting to ache as the rot ate its way inside. His muscles were turning to jelly, and his joints were so stiff that he was amazed Nina could not hear them creaking. He was much, much more than tired.

'Almost there,' she said again, glancing back at him over her shoulder. Her beautiful dark eyes… sometimes so cold, now tinged with sympathy. Was she really just playing him?

A minute later Nina stopped, glanced around as if to orient herself, and then turned back to Scott.

'He'll see you,' she said, 'but he'll seem…'

'Strange. Yes. You told me.'

'Well…' She shrugged, turned, and headed through an arched doorway.

Scott followed. Strange. And when he entered the wildly illuminated chamber beyond, he thought that had to be one of the greatest understatements ever.

Papa sits in his comfortable fishing chair and stares out across the river. He has never seriously fished – not that Scott has observed, anyway – but he seems to enjoy the tranquillity of the river. It gives his mind free rein to wonder, so Papa says, though Scott thinks that maybe he means wander as well. Its soporific flow provides a certain hush and solitude. And to underscore it all, there are sounds and sights to the river that many people seem unable to appreciate. Water flows musically across rocks, reeds hush and sigh as currents pull them this way and that, ducks paddle, pond skaters float on the surface, dragonflies speckle the air, kingfishers make a blur of blue, a heron stands still as an ornament until it darts for the kill, fish leap and make rippled patterns, and insects and birds buzz and sing, adding their own concerto. Life follows the river, Papa says, and what better place to join in?

But today things are different. Today the far side of the river has been invaded by tourists.

'There was a time when they'd never have let that

damn monster drive down this far,' Papa says. 'Let alone disgorge all those sheep to scatter their picnic waste and crush the grass with their fat arses.'

'We can move if you like, Papa,' Scott says. He's eleven years old, and he'll do anything to help his grandfather.

Papa waves his hand, shakes his head. 'Too relaxed to do that,' he says. 'For now, anyway. Look at them! Damn them. A sample of all that's annoying about humanity.'

Scott watches the tourists disembark from the coach and flow along the riverbank. They have no grace about them, and within minutes the riverbank has been polluted by their colourful clothes, picnic hampers, and the annoying chatter of conversation. He and Papa are too far away to hear what is being said, and he's glad for that.

'People have a lot to answer for,' Papa says. And here the memory normally ends, with the old man staring across the river and Scott staring at him. It's a saying that Papa used a lot in his final few years, and Scott often wondered why it sounded so weighted coming from Papa's mouth, so judged. He would mumble it while reading of a new housing estate being built on the other side of their village, but his tone implied that the builders were using dead babies as foundations.

And now the memory continues, telling Scott more than he has ever remembered before.

'People are different,' Papa says.

'From who?' Scott asks.

'One another.' Papa waves his hand, as though shooing away objections that have not yet been spoken. 'No, no, I don't just mean the differences from country to country, colour to colour, creed to creed – though there *are* differences all across there, and don't let any of these new politically correct cretins tell you otherwise. It's what makes humanity *great*, all those differences. It's what makes us so wonderful and diverse. Embrace the diversity, Scott, and you'll be great as well. No, it's not that.' He sits back in his chair, chewing a stem of grass and resting one finger on his fishing rod, testing for movement. Scott has never seen him catch anything.

'What is it, Papa?'

'It's us and them, Scott.' Papa closes his eyes.

'Us and who?'

'Us – thinkers and seekers, and explorers of places and things. And them.' He opens his eyes again and nods slightly across the river. 'Them. The flock. Ignorant of so much, and happy in their ignorance. All great people are sad people, Scotty.'

'What are you sad about, Papa?'

'They're sad because they gain a glimpse at the truth. And I'm getting there. I'm getting there.'

The memory came and went in an instant, the phrase *people are different* sticking in Scott's mind as he looked in upon Old Man. And in that same instant Scott wondered whether Papa had been referring to the people picnicking on the other side of the river, or the ghosts that dwelt among them.

The cavern was almost perfectly cuboid, and Old Man hung in one top corner. He was startlingly skinny, bald and naked, and his long limbs ended in hooked claws that found purchase in the rough walls and ceiling. He was staring directly at Scott, and for someone who appeared almost animalistic, the intelligence in his eyes was startling.

Scott glanced around the cavern. There were dozens of electric lights set in the walls and ceiling, some of them on, some off. They were a variety of colours. Two walls were taken up entirely by a range of shelves, all of them crammed with books and loose bundles of paper. Another wall was adorned with exotic-looking tapestries and weavings, all of them overlapping so that the wall behind was totally obscured. There was a cot in one corner piled with rumpled sheets and blankets, and in the centre of the room stood a chair and large desk. The desk was almost bare except for one huge, thick book, open at its midpoint, and a vast selection of pens.

The remaining wall through which Scott had entered the room was pocked with dozens of holes, each the width of his clenched fist.

'You've changed,' Nina said. 'I like what you've done with your hair.'

'Peace, Nina. Quiet, girl. Don't taunt Old Man.'

'I was teasing, not taunting. Big difference.'

Something hissed somewhere in the room and Scott looked around, panicked. Snake? Insect?

'Another secret,' Old Man said. 'Still so many. No end to secrets, Nina. Lately, all bad.' He moved down the tapestry-covered wall like a spider, crossed the floor on all fours, and climbed onto the chair. His head tilted and his eyes almost closed.

The hissing grew louder. Scott glared at Nina, but she offered him nothing.

Something spit from one of the holes behind him. Old Man raised his hand faster than Scott would have believed possible and plucked a shape from the air. He held it up before his face, sniffing it, tilting his head to listen, and before Scott could even begin to make out what he held, Old Man had opened his mouth wide and thrust it inside.

For a moment his cheeks seemed to glow with some inner light.

'Ahh,' he said. He looked at Scott and nodded. 'Secrets.'

'Old Man, I need your help.' Nina knelt beside the table, then sat cross-legged on the floor. She glanced at Scott and motioned him over, but he remained where he was.

Not just yet, he thought. *Not until I know this is safe.*

'He won't hurt you,' Nina said.

'Won't hurt human,' Old Man said, and when he smiled, the coloured lights reflected from a mouthful of sharp, white teeth.

Scott walked across the soft carpet and sat beside Nina, sighing as the weight relaxed from his frame. He wanted to close his eyes and rest, but he dared not. He was afraid that he would never open them again.

Old Man picked up a pen and wrote a few words in his book. Scott and Nina watched silently, listening to the scratch of pen on paper and Old Man's breath as he concentrated on every letter, every curl and spot of ink. He leant back when he was finished, dropped the pen, and sighed. 'Almost done, this one.'

'What are you working on right now?' Nina asked.

'Deciphering the root of Linear A,' Old Man said. 'Oldest language, still unknown. Secrets? Yes, it holds many.'

'Such as?'

Old Man glared down at Nina, and for the first time Scott noticed that his eyes were a pale milky white. 'I can't say.'

'You can tell me,' Nina said. 'You can tell me anything; you know that. Come on, old guy.'

'Talk strange,' Old Man said. He sat back in the chair and laced his hands behind his head. 'Talk like people. You, always ready to blend in. Can't live with humans. Stars don't live with rats. Gods don't eat with spiders. Order of things, Nina. Order.'

'You used to tell me all about the things you've been researching,' she said. 'There was a time we'd sit out there on the volcano's shoulder and talk for days about your latest fascinations. You'd tell me all the new secrets.'

Old Man nodded. 'Look what happened.'

Nina's smile slipped and she looked down at her hands. 'What do you expect?'

'Greed. Human conceit.'

'Aren't you human?' Scott asked.

The man smiled. It was a strange expression, both gruesome and beautiful. It made Scott distinctly uncomfortable. 'Human once. Long time back. Now I'm more…' He shrugged.

A very human gesture, Scott thought.

Nina stood and walked to one of the book-lined walls. She took a tome down and started leafing through it, and Scott realised that they were all journals. Some were larger than the one currently sitting on Old Man's desk, a few smaller, but if he squinted against the harsh light he could see that their spines all contained the same spidery handwriting.

'So let's see what you've found since we last met,' Nina said.

'Nina…care,' Old Man said, and there was a hint of warning in his voice.

Nina looked up, her skin so smooth in this light. 'I always take care, Old Man.'

'I'm ill,' Scott said. 'I've been touched by blights.' He found himself unbuttoning his shirt and showing his chest.

Nina sighed. 'I was coming to that. But yes, he has.'

'You want me to cure?' Old Man asked. He tapped the desk with one of his clawed hands.

'I know you can.'

'Used to be able to. Long time ago. Now, not sure.'

'You don't *forget* things,' Nina said.

'No, I learn. Nothing I learn is mine. I—'

Another hiss came and another object – a burst of light, a smear of something harsher – spurted from a hole in the wall. Old Man snatched it from the air and pressed it to his mouth. Scott saw his tongue snake out and curl between his fingers; then he swallowed the object whole. He closed his eyes and nodded, leaning forward for the pen even before the glow had gone from his face.

'You're blind,' Scott said, amazed.

'You see well.' Old Man wrote several more words into the massive book.

'Here,' Nina said. 'Here. Old Man has a cure for cancer.' She lifted the book she was holding as though offering it to Scott.

'You can cure it?'

Old Man only nodded.

'But…why don't you share that?'

'The cure, I stole. From…out there.' He waved his hand around his head, indicating nothing in particular. 'Perhaps never meant to be known. I give out the cure, people get better, something much worse comes along.'

'But the suffering you could end. The pain and heartache!'

'People have to die.'

'You don't,' Scott said bitterly. 'I'm here before you dying, and you tell me you have a cure for cancer, and you're so casual about it. Because you don't have to die.'

Old Man leant quickly across his table, spilling pens to the floor, reaching out and grasping Scott's neck in his strange hooked fingers.

'And there's the curse!' Old Man spit. 'Immortal? Not good. Not *natural*. We found it, should have left it. Instead…*greed*.' He let go and eased back into his chair, panting slightly and obviously surprised at his own reaction.

'Apologies,' he said.

Scott nodded. 'No problem.'

'Old Man, Scott is more than just a person,' Nina said. 'His grandfather found the Lost Pages, and Scott believes he knows where the Chord of Souls may be.'

Old Man froze in his chair. He became utterly still, and his strange cavern fell silent. Scott could hear the thrum of blood in his ears, and nothing else. No movement. It was as though Old Man had become a still in the never-ending movie of his life: no muscle twitched, not one straggly hair on his scalp waved; even his chest was motionless, devoid of evidence of heartbeat.

Is he dead? Scott thought.

'Big claim,' Old Man said. He turned towards

Nina, pointed at the book in her hands. 'Put that down. Tell more.'

'He can tell.'

Old Man turned to Scott and placed his hands flat on the desk. 'Human?'

'Papa – my grandfather – and his friend Lewis, they found some stone tablets in Africa during the Second World War. Brought them home, translated some of what was on them, and Papa became fearful of what they were discovering. And apparently of what Lewis would do with whatever they discovered. So fearful that he murdered Lewis and killed himself. Thirty years ago.' Scott lowered his head. Every time he mentioned Papa's crime he was filled with a mix of sadness and shame.

Old Man nodded. 'Lies.'

'No!' Scott said.

'This comes to light now?'

'He sent me a letter. I got it yesterday.'

'Yesterday.'

'We found the Lost Pages,' Nina said. 'In Cardiff. Found them and destroyed them, and the only way we could have found them was by following Papa's clues. The clues he sent to Scott in a letter, which took thirty years to arrive.'

'No human could translate the Chord,' Old Man said.

'Well, he did. Some of it, at least. And his friend was…not a good man. Papa realised that as they grew older, and as he approached death he knew what had to be done. They must have been so close to discovering where the Chord was kept. Papa completed the translation and killed Lewis before he could know.'

'Lewis is still here,' Scott said. 'He took my wife.'

'Took her alive?'

'Into the Wide.'

'Wide.' Old Man sighed, shaking his head. 'Nina, you tell too much.'

'He's like his grandfather, Old Man. He's able to know. All the things he's seen in the last two days, and he's nowhere near mad. Look at him. He could be the one who helps us...the one who finds the Chord of Souls. You know what that would mean? Peace, Old Man! Rest!'

'For some. For others, perhaps war.'

'War?' Scott asked.

'Not all immortals want the same thing,' Nina said.

'But war?'

'Who stands behind Lewis?' Old Man asked.

Scott shook his head. 'I don't understand.'

'We don't know,' Nina said.

Old Man nodded.

'Why is anyone behind him?'

'Human ghost, immortal power. Not on his own.'

Scott looked at Nina and she shrugged, but he realised that she had known this all along. She'd hinted at it, true, suggesting that someone was helping Lewis. But it felt like yet another way she was simply playing him for her own ends.

'My wife,' Scott said. 'I don't give a fuck about all of this. Keep your cure for cancer and your Linear A, whatever that is. All I want is to get my wife back. She's the whole world to me, not all this.' He waved his hand at the wall of journals to his right. 'She's been taken away and I want her, and I'll do anything necessary to get her back. Anything!'

Old Man pointed at Scott. 'You seek your wife.' He pointed over his shoulder at Nina. 'You seek the gift of death.' Then he pointed to himself. 'I seek all answers.'

'I know where it is,' Scott said.

'How?'

'Papa left a clue.'

'And how did he know?'

'We don't know,' Nina said.

'All a lie. Go. Search. Find the lie.'

'It isn't a lie!' Nina said. 'It can't be. The stone tablets were where he said they'd be, and they were real, Old Man. I couldn't touch them, felt sick around them, and Lewis appeared with the blights as soon as—'

'Lewis carried blights?'

'Directed them.'

Old Man nodded, but his face was grim. 'Proof. Not on his own. Guided by someone, just as you are guided by Nina, human.'

'We'll move on,' Scott said. 'We'll get out of your way and leave you in your hole, finding secrets and keeping them to yourself. I don't give a flying fuck. Do what you want. Sit here and jerk off for eternity if you must, but we came here because Nina said you may be able to help me. I know where that damn book of yours is, and if you don't help me I swear I'll carry that knowledge to my grave.'

Old Man leant forward again and smiled, displaying those gruesome teeth. 'There, you'll never be safe,' he said.

All three fell silent again. Old Man closed his eyes. Nina glanced across at Scott, then went back to browsing the journals, running her finger along the spines. None of them seemed to surprise her.

Scott felt a wave of queasiness sweeping through him, prickling cold sweat from the back of his neck and churning his guts. The pains in his arm and chest waved in again, a sick, rotten heat.

'I can cure,' Old Man said. 'For a price.'

'What price?' Nina asked.

'Chord of Souls comes to me.'

'What about Helen?'

'I can help with that. Give advice. Lend knowledge. But the Chord comes to me.'

'No,' Nina said.

'Yes,' Scott said.

'Scott, you have no idea—'

'Human knows I could torture,' Old Man said. 'Torture the truth.'

'You'd never do that,' Nina said. 'I've never known you to hurt a soul.'

'Been a long time, Nina. We've all changed.'

'The book comes to you,' Scott said. 'Now help us. Help me. Please!'

Old Man pointed to his messy cot in the corner of the room. 'Lie down.'

Scott did as he was told. There were a million questions buzzing around his head. *How do you survive? Where does the electricity come from? What do you eat? Do you go out? Where do all those holes lead to or come from?* But he was tired, and the thought of Old Man helping them was suddenly the most important thing he could think about.

He cures me, we go on, he gets the book, he thought. And on top of that, he realised that he knew absolutely nothing about what was going on here. Nina might well be playing him, but she was guiding him as well. Without her, this would end very quickly, and Helen would be gone for ever.

'Nina?' he said.

She offered her enigmatic smile. Nodded. 'Go on,' she said. 'It's a small price.'

'Small price for Helen, or for death?'

That same smile.

Scott lay down on the cot and closed his eyes.

Chapter Seven

real memory

Someone rustled around the cave. Muttered conversation. The sizzle of static, then the smell of something like cooking pork.

'Lesson in everything,' Old Man said, and Nina snorted.

Scott opened his eyes.

Old Man was sprawled on the ceiling above him, hands and feet hooked into cracks, head turned completely around so that his blind gaze met Scott's exactly.

'Best you sleep for this.'

Scott closed his eyes and found it easy to oblige.

He and Papa walk past the edge of their village and enter the woods. Instead of the familiar paths and streams and clearings, however, they find themselves in a blank landscape made of fog. There is no up or down, no left or right. Scott – barely into his teens – is startled, but Papa seems unconcerned. 'This way,' he says, and Scott follows.

They walk on nothing, and there is no way to gauge how far they have gone, neither distance nor time. Papa does not stop speaking, but Scott cannot understand what he is saying. He hopes it's not important.

Papa pauses, and as he turns around the forest appears around them again.

'This will do,' Papa says. 'It's a delicate operation. It involves all sorts of arcane methods and practices. I really don't think your mum and dad will be very pleased.' He smiles the cheeky boy's smile that sets him apart from so many other old people. It's a smile that communicates a sense of wonder that most lose when they hit puberty, accepting cynicism and self-obsession instead of the ability to dream and imagine beyond the confines of their own mind.

'When will it be over, Papa?' Scott asks.

Papa's smile drops. 'Oh, Scotty, it's only just begun.' He taps a fallen tree, clearing part of the trunk of moss and ants. 'Sit. Don't worry. Papa would never hurt you.'

Scott sits and looks around the forest, taking in all the familiar sights and sounds and enjoying the fact that, as always, they feel as new as the first time.

Papa is unbuttoning Scott's shirt.

'What's wrong, Papa?'

'Nothing yet.' But it looks as though Papa *can* see something wrong, even though where he touches Scott's skin Scott can feel nothing.

'Let's get to work,' Papa says. He kicks aside a pile of leaves and plucks some fungi from the underside of a rotten branch. He picks up a beetle and plucks off its wings. Ants, a grub from beneath the soil, the leaf from the third-lowest branch of a nearby oak sapling. He collects them all in his hand and stirs them, careful not to mix them so well that they lose their identities. Then he reaches out and takes something from the air that Scott does not understand.

'This isn't a real memory, is it, Papa?'

'No, Scott. Not really.'

Papa mixes the normal with the arcane, and he starts applying it to Scott's right arm and chest.

It hurts. Scott opens his mouth to scream, but the noise is far away. He looks around the woods, wondering where the scream is coming from, and the pain kicks in deeper and harsher. He screams again, pleading with Papa to stop, and tries to jump down from the fallen trunk. But Papa is still there, crying as he presses the strange mixture into Scott, pushing it through the skin so that it becomes a part of him.

The trees begin to sway, the woods to swim, and Scott cries out. Just before he closes his eyes and faints away, everything turns to grey once more.

Scott opened his eyes, and Nina was sitting beside him on the cot. Her expression did not change, but she put her hand on his arm. Behind her, Old Man scurried here and there, catching glowing things in his hands and mouth as they burst from holes in the wall.

Scott tried to speak but could not find the energy. He closed his eyes and let sleep take him again.

Next time he woke the light had weakened. There were only a few bulbs alight now, casting shadows across the cavern that he had not noticed before. Nina was sitting in the far corner of the room, one of Old Man's journals open across her knees. She did not even notice that Scott was awake.

Old Man hung from the centre of the ceiling like a bat. His arms were folded across his chest. He twitched slightly, muscles in his legs tensing and relaxing. His eyes were open, but Scott could not tell whether or not he was asleep.

He lay there for some time, looking around the subterranean room and trying to answer some of his own questions. But this place was as mysterious as ever.

Nina turned a page and carried on reading. She was frowning and stroking her chin gently with her forefinger as she read.

'What's that?' Scott whispered. His throat hurt as he spoke. He coughed, and Nina rose quickly to her feet. She placed the book delicately on Old Man's desk and brought Scott a cup of water.

'Drink,' she said. 'Try not to talk for a while.'

'What were you reading?' He sipped the water and sighed as it soothed his throat.

'Notes on the seventh and eighth senses.'

'Oh. Nothing too heavy, then.'

Nina smiled, and that pleased Scott. He felt so cut off from things, so alone, that her company – strange though it might seem at times – was important to him. It should have been Helen sitting by his sickbed when he woke up, loving him and telling him that everything would be all right.

'So am I better?' he asked.

She nodded. 'I knew he'd be able to help. It tired him out.'

'How long have I been sleeping?'

'A day. Maybe less.'

'A day.' He sipped more water, glad that the burning in his throat was lessening with every mouthful. Nina took the cup and he lifted the sheet, looking down at his chest. Where before there had been a spread of black skin and rotting flesh, now there was a sheen of pale scar tissue. It was almost as if Old Man had taken away the dead part of him and replaced it with something else.

'How did he do it?'

'I didn't understand,' Nina said. 'Just be grateful. I'm going out to get you some food. Stay here, rest, and as soon as you're strong again, we have to move on.'

Scott looked at Old Man. He was asleep for now, but if he woke up…?

'He won't harm you,' Nina said.

'How do you know?'

'That's not his way.'

'He threatened to torture me.'

Nina shook her head and laughed gently. 'That's not his way, Scott. Old Man is a man of peace. Always has been, always will be. That's why he shuts himself away down here.'

'Because not all immortals are as peaceful, right?'

'Not all, no.'

'And you?'

Nina stared at him for a while, then rolled her eyes. 'When you break all the laws of physics, do you seriously think there won't be a price?'

'Wait,' Scott said. 'Wait. Is that another—'

'*Event Horizon*. Cool movie, I thought. And Sam Neill is hot.'

Scott shook his head. 'I don't know you. First you're one Nina; then you change and—'

'I told you, there were many Ninas through the years. Now, I'm going to get food. Won't be long. Rest. Sleep. Soon we'll go for the book and get Helen back for you.'

Scott watched her leave. He looked at Old Man, asleep and hanging from the ceiling of his peaceful hidden retreat. And he thought of Helen.

I've been close to death and brought back for you, he thought. *Been to the edge of the route to the afterlife, and back again. I* will *find you.*

He remembered a holiday they'd had together to Cornwall a year before, and he fell asleep dreaming of walking across the causeway to St Michael's Mount.

* * *

A hand on his shoulder stirred him from his dreams. He was ravenous, and he wondered what food Nina had brought back.

Old Man sat beside him on the bed. 'Remember your promise,' he said. 'The book. To me.'

'I promise,' Scott said.

'I know so much,' Old Man said. 'So much information. So much knowledge. So many secrets. But there's so much more to know. Shame, if Chord of Souls left us for ever.'

'What else is in the book?' Scott asked. 'Apart from the immortality part. What else?'

'What did Nina tell you?'

'She said "stuff".'

Old Man nodded and turned away. 'Stuff. Good.' He went to his desk, sat down, and picked up his pen, and whatever Scott said to him – however much he pleaded for information or tried to enter into conversation – Old Man remained silent until Nina returned to the cave.

Scott's final few minutes in the cave seemed even stranger than everything that had gone before. He and the two immortals sat there and ate McDonald's. Old Man seemed especially appreciative of the meal, smacking his lips and nodding his head with each mouthful. 'Self-destruction can be fun,' he said as he tucked into his second Big Mac.

Scott walked the perimeter of the room a few

times to show Nina that he was strong enough to leave. In truth he felt better than he had for years, and after their brief pause he was keener than ever to get back on the trail. He had the skull key ring in his pocket and Helen in his soul.

As they prepared to leave, Old Man crawled across to the bed and pulled something out from underneath. It was an LCD television set. He arranged it on his desk, plugged it into a socket fixed loosely to the wall, and sat back in his chair.

'But you're blind,' Scott said.

'Am I?' Old Man looked at him with those milky eyes, and Scott began to doubt.

As they left, Old Man was illuminated by a rapid-fire splash of colour and light. The strains of Kerrang! TV accompanied them back out through the caves, and by the time they reached the outside, Scott had already begun to doubt that any of the past day had happened.

He felt better, yes. His arm and chest were almost back to their normal colour, he was rested, and he knew a little more about what they were doing. But the small opening in the hillside below Edinburgh Castle seemed to be an unlikely home for an immortal.

'That's why he lives there,' Nina said when he stated his doubts. 'He's in the heart of things, but so far away.'

'You collect dead hearts.'

'This one can't die.'

Scott went to ask more questions about Old Man
– electricity, oil, food? – but he thought better of it.
He liked the mystery. In that way if no other, he and
Papa were very much alike.

Chapter Eight

in memory of fleeting friendships

'I have some questions,' Scott said. 'I'm confused.'

'What questions?'

They were sitting in a cafe just off Princes Street. It was mid-afternoon, and the city was buzzing. People sat close around them, talking into mobile phones or having animated discussions with companions, eating, drinking hot coffee or cold juice, and catching snippets of their conversations made Scott want to know more.

He had never felt so distanced from civilisation. He wondered whether more knowledge would drive him even farther away.

'Well, aside from about six million questions about Old Man, there are these: Why are we looking for the book instead of for Helen? Who is behind Lewis? What was all that talk of war? Why are you so keen on destroying the book, while Old Man wants it handed back to him?' He took a sip of coffee and a bite of doughnut.

'That's it?'

'For starters.'

'If we look for Helen we won't find her. If we find the book, Lewis will bring her to us.'

'What makes you so sure?'

'He wants the book more than anything else. He wants an earthbound immortality. Papa stole that from him, and he sees it as his right.'

'OK. So who's behind him?'

'Another immortal. Not sure which one.'

'And they want the book because of this other "stuff" it has in it?'

'Yes. Same reason Old Man wants it. Same reason neither of them can have it.'

'These were the people you wrote the book with all those years ago.'

'Yes.'

'Can't any of you remember what's in it?'

'The basics, yes. Not the execution. Not the practice. At the time when we wrote it all down, we were only…'

'Human.'

Nina nodded. She took a drink of strong black coffee. It was her third cup.

Scott shook his head, looking down into his own brew. 'This is all madness. All I want is my wife. I don't want to get mixed up in—'

'It's inevitable. You know where the book is, and you're the only person. You get that, Scott? Now that Papa is dead and beyond reach, you're the *only one* who knows its location. That makes you special. That makes you R2-D2 in *Star Wars*. You have the information.'

'So why not torture it out of me, like Old Man said?'

'He was joking. But there are others…' She drifted off, looking down into her cup.

'Oh, great.'

They drank their coffee in silence, and it was a couple of minutes before Nina spoke again. 'I want the Chord of Souls destroyed because it should never have been written down in the first place. And Old Man wants it just because he's an information junkie.'

'What were those things coming out of the holes in his walls?'

'Information.'

Scott nodded as though he understood. Nina was driving him mad. She spoke to him, but said nothing.

'So what are we waiting for?' he said. 'Nothing like forging ahead blindly into something you don't understand that could lead to war.'

'The war comment—'

Scott held up his hand. 'Don't. Later, maybe. Not now. Unlike that weird Old Man under the hill, I can suffer information overload.'

He looked at the ghost that had been sitting in one of the window seats ever since they arrived. She stared from the window and drummed her fingers on the table, making a gentle tapping sound. A couple of people looked around now and then, or checked their mobile phones, or touched the radiator on the wall beside them to stop the water hammer. But none of them saw her. For them, she may as well never have existed at all.

They hired a car. Scott had half expected Nina to prepare them for another trip across the boundaries of the Wide, but she said that she could do that only if she knew exactly where they were going. Scott remained silent, offering up no information. She smiled and nodded, and he was glad. He had no real wish to visit that place again.

Scott drove them out of Edinburgh on the A70 and headed south. The sun was dipping towards the west, painting the sky a palette of oranges and yellows. His perception of day and night was totally confused. He felt jet-lagged. When all this was over and he had Helen back…

Tears threatened but he fought them off. Now was not the time. Crying felt like giving in.

'There's a trust issue here,' Nina said at last. She'd been totally silent for over half an hour, sitting back in her seat and watching the world go by.

'You sound like Oprah.'

'So you're admitting that you do watch TV sometimes, then?'

'Sometimes,' Scott said. 'Usually fantasy. Though none of it as far-out as this.'

'You should tell me what the skull key ring means.'

'You say you knew Papa. Don't you know?'

'No. I didn't know him that well.'

'Tell me about him. What you knew, and how. All I know of him is what he and I had, really. I'd like to hear someone else's stories.'

'If I tell you, will you tell me what the skull means?'

'Why not just wait until we get there?'

She was silent for a while, tapping her fingers on the dashboard. Trucks stormed by, and it started to rain. 'I'm afraid something may happen to you,' she said at last.

Right, thought Scott. *I buy the farm and the knowledge goes with me.*

'Lewis?'

'Yes. And whoever's aiding him.'

'Why would they kill me? Do that and they'd never…' Scott trailed off. *Have I learnt nothing?*

'You see?' she said.

'Yes. No need to explain. They kill me, stop me from setting off into the Wide. Interrogate me over there. But what can they do—'

'The dead can be hurt as well, if you know how.'

'Fucking marvellous.'

'So you see why I not only want to keep you alive, but also think you should share what you know with me.'

'I don't trust you.'

'Good. That's healthy. But believe me when I say, Scott, that we have to be here for each other in this. We *have* to.'

Scott watched water pushed up the windscreen by the air forced over the car. The faster he went, the quicker the water would be pushed. He was being driven in the same way: a splash of water in a rainstorm, forced onward by powers he could not possibly imagine or hope to understand. The only thing that offered him an advantage was the skull key ring and what it represented.

'Tell me a story from your past,' he said.

'Why?'

'Because I want to hear.' He flicked the headlights on and isolated their car more than ever. *Islands in the storm*, he thought.

'There are so many,' she said.

'The first one that comes to your mind,' Scott said. 'Keep me awake. I'm sleepy. You wouldn't want me to crash and die now, would you?'

'I've lost friends before,' Nina said. Then she fell silent for a couple of minutes as though regretting saying it. 'OK,' she continued. 'OK. There was Jack. He lived in Deadwood, and he was famous for shooting Wild Bill Hickok.'

'You're kidding me.'

'You want me to tell a story? Shut up and listen.'

Scott sighed and settled back into his seat.

'Not much of a story actually,' Nina said. 'Just about Jack. Wayward boy. He liked to brag about crimes he'd never committed, talk himself up. Carried a gun, like a lot of men did in those days. He travelled from town to town, robbing stores, rustling cattle, and he had this uncanny ability to dodge in and out of trouble like a slippery fish.

'I met him a year before Deadwood. He'd been prospecting for gold, but he'd grown bored quickly, and he'd taken to robbing the prospectors. I was one of them, but he'd left me alone. I was a woman and...well, I could look after myself. I'd already proved that several times.' She touched the mass of scar tissue on her neck, and Scott thought, *How bad must that have been to still be visible now?*

'I willed it to stay visible,' Nina said. 'In case you're wondering.'

Scott said nothing.

'So, one day there was a massive storm in the valley we'd been working. Landslides, new streams roaring down from the hillsides, and the river burst its banks and flooded hundreds of acres. Jack chose that night to rob the wrong man, who came after him. Jack burst into my tent. We stared at each other for a while – he was dripping with water and sweat, panting with fear – and then I ushered him under my bedclothes. Told him to shut up if he wanted to live.

'Bastard Bob – the guy he'd robbed – came into my tent, waving his gun and raging about how he'd seen the thieving little shit come this way, and he'd have his pound of flesh before the day was over.

I just looked at him, told him no one had entered my tent, and asked if he was really ready to search a lady's things.'

'So did he?'

'No. I stared him down, and he left.'

'Yes,' Scott said. 'I can imagine that working.'

'Jack stayed with me for four nights. Such a young lad, innocent, and doomed from the moment he was born. After that he left and I never saw him again. He was one of the few friends I've ever made.'

'You knew him for four days,' Scott said, aghast. 'He was a criminal and you saved him, and he was a *friend*?'

'Four days is a lifetime in the company of a friend, Scott.'

'That doesn't make any sense.'

Nina was silent for a few seconds, her breath hidden in the swish of the windscreen wipers. 'It does to me,' she said.

'So your friend went on to kill Hickok and—'

'Jack never killed anyone.'

'Then who?'

Nina was silent for so long that Scott thought she had fallen asleep. He glanced across at her, unable to see her eyes, and the third time he looked she had turned back to him. 'Something else,' she said. 'Jack just got the blame. So do you trust me now? You're Jack, Scott, and I've taken you in from the storm.'

'No,' he said. 'I don't. And we're not friends, Nina.' He expected her to start raging, and he had no idea what an immortal could really do when provoked.

'Fair enough,' she said. 'But you *will* trust me. You'll see that my cause in this is not totally selfish. I promise.'

'I hope so,' he said, and he really did. He liked Nina. She was so different from him that he could barely comprehend her, but there was still a humanity about her – something naive and primal, something almost innocent – that drew him. Old Man had lost his way ages ago, taking to a hole in the ground to survive. Nina was still out here. For Scott, that said a lot.

After an hour of contemplative silence, Scott said, 'I asked you to tell me a story, and now you've confused me more than ever.'

'Sorry,' Nina said.

'That's OK.' He drove on, wondering whether she was sorry at all.

They pulled off the motorway outside Preston and found a pub that had rooms to let. They'd come almost two hundred miles, and Scott was exhausted. Part of him wanted to carry on through the night, reach the place of the screaming skulls, and discover whether the rest of the book was there or not. After that, perhaps, would come Helen. But another part of him urged caution. Somehow it felt right to stop, rest, and take stock. Fatigue made the decision easier.

After checking into their adjoining rooms, they sat in the bar for a while, watching people come and go. The pub claimed to be one of the most haunted in Britain, but Scott had seen no sign of any ghosts. He was glad. He'd entered his room warily, knowing that he'd never be able to sleep where a wraith played moments from the past. He was briefly tempted to take the manager to task over the brash statement, but that seemed so crass. And besides, he had no way of backing his knowledge of the truth.

'There's never any real understanding, is there?' he said.

Nina was sipping at yet another cup of black coffee. 'What do you mean?'

'People. *These* people. They don't understand very much. Their knowledge is mostly constrained.'

'You feel you know more than them already. I suppose you do.'

'I do. The Wide, the Chord of Souls. You.'

Nina brushed her long hair back behind her ear, a surprisingly vulnerable gesture. 'After just a couple of days, too. Imagine how much I understand after much, much longer.'

'You haven't told me when you were born.'

'You'd never believe me.'

'I believe that you're immortal.'

'Do you?'

Scott nodded. He stared into her eyes. *Yes, I believe.*

'But deep down, you can't believe it. It's been only

two days, Scott. You've seen and heard a lot, but your conditioning—'

'I was conditioned by Papa.'

Nina looked away and smiled. 'Of course,' she said. 'I sometimes forget.' Scott was not sure whether there was a mocking tone there or not. She had a way of making him feel so inferior, an insect in the protection of a hawk.

'What about the others?' he asked. 'Tell me about them. Are they all like you? Or are most of them mad, like Old Man?'

'Madness is relative,' she said. 'You have to have something to compare it to. We're unique.'

'You're sure you're the only ones? Twelve immortals, and you're sure you're unique? Nature can't like that.'

'I'm sure it doesn't. And yes, I'm sure. We've had a long time to look for others.'

'Who told you what to write in that book?'

'I've already said, you can never know. No one can. It would change everything. A change that rapid and extreme would mean the end.'

'God?'

Her expression gave him nothing.

'If it was God, and the book is proof of His existence…I don't know, maybe proof would be a good thing. If everyone *knew* He was there, maybe the world would be a better place.'

Nina took another drink of coffee.

'Well…' Scott drained his drink and stood to get

another. He looked around the pub. A family sat in one corner, parents trying to keep their kids occupied while their dinner was prepared. A few couples were sitting here and there, a scattering of lonely men drinking lonesome pints, and a large family group sat around the other side of the bar, playing some sort of quiz and enjoying one another's company. It was an attractive place, but laced with the trappings of chaindom: stock menus, familiar wood and chrome fittings, and pointless beams newly cut to look old. 'I'll get us another drink,' he said. 'And then I'd like to hear about the others. If that's OK with you.' He walked across to the bar without waiting for Nina's reply.

I want to hear, because one of them has Helen.

'What can I get you?' The barman glanced across at Nina, then back at Scott.

'Abbott, and a black coffee, please.'

And I think she already knows which one it might be.

'Here on holiday?'

'No.'

'Right.' The barman looked at Nina again as he poured the pint, eyes twitching up and down as he sized her up.

Maybe she'll tell me if I tell her about the screaming skulls. But maybe not.

'Very haunted pub, this one.'

Scott handed over a fiver. 'No, it isn't.'

The barman gave him a weird look, scooped

change from the till, and dropped it on the bar.

'Thanks,' Scott said. He hadn't meant to be rude, but it was too late now. 'Cheers.'

The barman nodded and offered a brief smile before going to serve someone else.

He just doesn't understand, Scott thought. *He has no idea of what's out there. He doesn't even know his own pub.* For the first time since meeting Nina, he began to believe that a person could know too much.

Nina thanked him when he placed another coffee before her. She took a sip and sighed in appreciation. Scott did the same with his beer.

'So?' he asked.

'A dozen of us,' Nina said. She suddenly sounded keen to talk. 'Some, like me, have stayed in the world. We travel. Change names and identities when the time comes. Some learn things; others simply live to experience. Cleo – that's her name for now, last I heard – claims she's had sex with over six hundred thousand men and women. She never tires of it. Fucks her way through time, and there are legends about her everywhere she goes.'

'Quite a responsible way to treat immortality.'

'We weren't chosen for this, you know,' Nina said, a note of anger creeping in. 'We happened to be the ones to find it and write it all down. We're not some illustrious group handed a great purpose. There's no moral duty because we're immortal. Why should there be? Cleo enjoys herself, and what's wrong with that? Best thing to do with life.' She trailed off, stroking her finger around the rim of her cup.

'You haven't told me what you do,' Scott said.

'You wanted to hear about the others.' She glared up at him, forbidding any response, and carried on. 'Three of us disappeared soon after we wrote the Chord of Souls. No one has seen them since. Perhaps like Old Man they went underground, and who knows what's become of them? There's no telling. Maybe they're lying mad at the bottom of potholes, or perhaps they slink through life below the radar of civilisation, doing their own thing and feeling no need to be a part of anyone else's immortality.'

'What do you mean?'

'Some of us meet up. Every hundred years or so, six of us gather together to discuss what we've been doing. A couple like to...play games. Sometimes dangerous games.'

'Dangerous for who?'

'For the pawns they use.'

'The people, you mean.'

Nina nodded. 'The people. The two who play like to pitch people against one another, either singly, in small groups or – once or twice – in armies. They play.'

'What does the winner get?'

'A point.'

'That's it?'

'Yep.' She finished her coffee before it had a chance to cool down. 'Last I heard it was level at seven hundred and fifty-three points each.'

Scott shook his head in disbelief. 'You're immortals, and you play games or travel the world fucking everything in sight. Why don't you...? What about...?'

'What? Are we talking morals again here? There're no great tasks for us, Scott. There's just a curse that we brought on ourselves, and some of us handle it better than others. And in different ways.' She snorted. 'You haven't heard the best yet. Tigre. You'll *love* him.'

'Not sure I want to know.' He swigged his beer and considered walking away. He could put down his glass and leave, go out to the car and drive to the place of screaming skulls on his own. Leave this woman behind. This madwoman, who had broken into his house searching for Papa's note, and who ever since had been dragging him along like a pawn in whatever game it was *she* chose to play.

'Well, you asked, damn you! And you *will* know!'

A man at a neighbouring table glanced across, then away again when Nina looked at him.

'One of us went mad right at the beginning,' she said, lowering her voice. 'Midnight that first day Tigre tried killing himself. Slit his throat, stabbed himself in the heart...and he just got better. So through the night he moved on us, singly at first, and then attacking us when we came in couples or threes to see what was happening. Blood everywhere. Pain, so much pain. And the agony of not dying.

'So he fled out into the desert. We didn't follow.

We were confused, shocked, and for us it was the first and only proof we needed that what we'd done the day before had been for real. So we left him, thinking we'd never see him again. We had no concept of time back then. A few days could be a long time, but it took us a while to recognise decades and centuries and…They say time is unforgiving, and I'll attest to that.

'First time he appeared again was thirty years after that first night. One of us had been wandering northern Africa and she came across a massacre. The sand was red for a hundred steps in every direction, and at the centre of the blood stood Tigre. He was cut and slashed and gored with spears, but he was still alive. There were a hundred corpses piled around him. Bits of bodies. He was the only living thing in sight. He ran.'

'And since then?' Scott asked. 'He continued, didn't he? This Tigre. Carried on killing.'

Nina nodded. 'Became very good at it. We never went looking, but sometimes the signs were obvious, and word often reached us. He's been executed for his crimes at least a dozen times that I know of. Spent a lot of time locked away in places where they don't favour execution. But he always returns to his ways. Where there's a war, Tigre will appear. He takes sides only if it will make the killing easier. Sometimes he doesn't take sides at all, and then he'll become the stuff of legend and myth. Demon of the battlefield, and for some, an angel. And when there's not a war, he finds other ways to satisfy his killing rage.'

'Why does he do it?'

'I told you, he's mad. I think he's still trying to kill himself. Destroy his wretched soul with slaughter in the hope that his body will eventually wither away with the shame of it all. The uselessness.'

'You think he's the one behind Lewis?'

Nina's face dropped. 'I hope not,' she said. 'Scott, I sincerely hope not. I think that if it was him we'd know by now. He'd have come against us himself instead of sending Lewis and the blights. He'd have…'

'I'd be dead.'

'It's all he knows. Yes, you'd be dead.'

'And so would Helen.' Scott drank some more beer, but suddenly it tasted bitter and stale.

Nina touched his arm and squeezed, and Scott felt the pressure. If she'd done that a day before, it would have been a dead part of him. He owed her that, at least.

'Helen is alive,' she said.

Scott nodded. Although neither of them could know that for sure, he took comfort in Nina's certainty.

They ate a small dinner – Scott found that his appetite had all but vanished – and then went up to their rooms. They did not say very much. Nina waited outside her door while Scott unlocked his, and when he glanced up there was a strange look on her face. *I'm married*, he thought. And as if reading his mind once again she smiled, went into her room, and closed the door behind her.

Exhausted though he was, he lay awake for a long time, staring at the ceiling and trying to discern truths in the shadows of trees speckling the plaster. He thought of Papa and where he was now, way beyond the Wide. He thought of Tigre, the murderous immortal trying to kill himself through slaughter. And all the while Helen was there, innocent in all of this, stolen away by Lewis and kept in a place she did not know and could not understand. His own brief sojourn into the Wide had been bad enough; what would she be feeling?

He closed his eyes at last, but tears of guilt prevented him from going to sleep.

Chapter Nine

whole new world

In the morning the sun rose on a whole new world. Plants had grown infinitesimally overnight, air had moved away and been drawn in from elsewhere, dew hung on blades of grass like brief diamonds, a new blue stained the sky, and all living things were closer to death. Scott sat on the wide window sill of his room and stared out over the pub garden and the countryside beyond, trying to see import in the way sunbeams textured the ground and mist gave contour and depth to the morning scene. He had slept for only a few hours, waking just before sunrise and sitting here, staring out at the dark. He'd watched for shadows moving where they should not, but it was a time when even the dead were silent and still.

Next door he could hear Nina snoring. It was an incredibly human sound, unconscious and unbidden. It altered his perception of her. He wondered how long it would take before he began to take her strangeness for granted.

Papa had taught him that being different was no bad thing. He'd spoken at length about the way some people were wired differently, built by nature to make them wonder and quest, rather than think and live themselves into a rut that held false comfort and little hope. He told Scott that these people often found life difficult, because society forbore existences that went against the norm. *There was a man who liked to speak to bees*, Papa once said. *He practised it over the years, asking them how they could fly with such small wings, how they could steer a hive to pollen-rich areas just by performing a dance, and after thirty years of speaking to them, he said they were starting to talk back. He claimed they told him secrets, though he never revealed what those secrets were. People asked him, of course. Secrets are intriguing, even for those who aren't wired that way. But the man said he could never betray the bees. He was considered mad by then, and when he died, he lay amongst his hives for six weeks before anyone found him. He'd decomposed, but they found the bodies of sixteen rats, a dozen birds, and a fox nearby, all stung to death. His bees had granted him natural rest, not consumption by carrion creatures. And even in death he's still thought of as mad.*

Over the years, Scott had met many people who wanted to know his secret. They'd talk about Papa and what he had done, and the majority were there simply because they were prying, craved scandal, or held some grim fascination of murder. Only a small minority asked because they perceived a story behind the story. They saw strangeness and were drawn to it, because beyond strangeness lay knowledge. These were the few he even bothered speaking to.

Wait till they ask me about this, he thought, sitting there in that wide window seat. *Wait until they ask where Helen went and how I got her back.* He watched a cat slink across the pub's back garden, dew speckling its fur. And he knew that whoever asked, he would never tell.

Nina's snoring had ceased. He heard no movement next door, and he was about to stand when there was a soft knock at his door.

Nina stood in the hallway, dressed and washed and looking as though she had never been tired before. 'Shall we?' she said.

'Can you give me a few minutes?' Scott rubbed his eyes and realised how tired he still was. 'Didn't sleep too well. You?'

'The sleep of the innocent,' she said.

'Right.'

'Can I come in while you get ready?'

Scott held the door wide and Nina breezed past him. He'd never seen her carrying a bag or purse, yet she smelt of freshly washed skin and exotic perfume. Perhaps that was her natural smell.

She went straight to the window seat and sat down, looking out the window. 'Nice view,' she said. 'Beautiful sunrise. See anything worth seeing?'

'The view. The sunrise.'

Nina looked around the garden and beyond and, seemingly satisfied, turned back to Scott. 'We've got a few minutes,' she said.

'Until what?'

'Until we need to go.'

'Why?'

'Nothing.' She shook her head but would not meet his gaze.

'Nina?'

'Get ready, Scott. We'll grab breakfast on the hoof.' She nodded at the bathroom door, then turned back to the garden.

'What are you watching for?'

'Nothing.' Her voice echoed from the cool glass and sounded strangely flat.

Scott wanted to say more; he felt a tension in the room now, something sharp that could hurt if he struck it the wrong way. But he went into the bathroom, ran a sink of hot water, and started to wash.

When he stood up and wiped his face, there was writing in the condensation on the mirror: *She will slay you.* It was written in large, spidery letters. Water ran from the letters' lowest points, dribbling down and pooling on the mirror's rim. They had just been written.

Scott dropped the towel and spun around. He scanned the bathroom. It was small, but he looked into all its corners, high and low. There was nothing behind the shower curtain, no shape cowering in the bath, no slip of something that should not be there, hiding beside the closed door.

He picked up the towel and wiped the mirror, then ran more scalding water.

'Almost done?' Nina called from beyond the door.

'Two minutes.' Scott glanced at the door handle, half expecting to see it moving as Nina tried to enter. It remained still. He put his head to the door, closed his eyes and concentrated, but he could not hear her moving about. When he looked at the mirror again there were more words drawn there: *Lose her.*

Nina tapped on the door. 'Scott, we need to go.'

'Just a minute!' he called.

'Scott…' She knocked again.

He flushed the chain and looked around; there was one window, painted shut and too small for him. No other way out than through the door.

Who's talking to me? he thought; then he whispered the same question, so low that his words were hidden by the sound of water filling the tank. He watched the mirror, waiting for the response – a name, perhaps, an explanation. But there was nothing new. Only those words, *Lose her,* fading.

How was he supposed to trust them?

'Papa?' he whispered, but nothing proved him right.

Why would Nina slay him? He did not know. He knew virtually nothing other than what she chose to tell him, and that could have been skewed for her own reasons. But there was Old Man. He existed, and fantastic though the other things Nina spoke of sounded – immortals playing games with the world's armies and fighting lovers, another who tried to kill himself through murder – there was no reason to suspect that she lied.

'Scott!' Nina said. 'I'm coming in.'

'Hang on, I'm—'

The door burst open. Nina came in and looked everywhere before seeing Scott.

'You ready?' She glanced at his bare chest; what did she think of the grey hairs there? How did the evidence of ageing really sit with her?

Scott nodded as he slipped on his shirt. If he was going to tell her about the writing, now was the time. And he should. Perhaps she would understand. But something held him back. Not a suspicion that the writer was right – not yet, at least – but doubt.

As they left the building and got in the hired car, Scott was more aware than ever of the rubbings in his back pocket.

'Why are we leaving so quickly?' he asked. Nina was sitting in the passenger seat, tense and twitchy. She had adjusted the wing mirror on her side so that she could watch behind them as they drove. 'What are you looking for?'

'Just a feeling.'

'What sort?'

'That we're being followed.'

Oh, yes, not far wrong there, he thought.

'Who'd be following us?'

'If I knew I might not be so worried. Just drive. I'll watch.'

Scott drove. He was heading south, and quite soon he would have to get the map out and start planning the end of their journey. That would be when their destination became clearer to Nina, and whoever else might be following them. The farther they went – the more time that passed – the closer they drew to the Chord of Souls.

She will slay you, the words had said. Why? Nina could not touch the book herself – none of them could, so she said – so surely she needed him?

'When this is over,' he said, 'and you've got what you want from the book and seen it destroyed… what about me?'

'You'll be back with your wife.'

'If we can get her from Lewis.'

'We will. I'll help you.'

'Yes, but…I'll know. I'll have seen the book. Read some of its pages. I know about you, and I know about Old Man in his hole in Edinburgh.'

'What are you hinting at?'

'What happens to me?'

'I've told you, you go home. Your wife goes with you, and you do your best to carry on. Forget this happened. Consign it to your dreams.'

'That's too much of a happy ending. Things like that don't happen. There's always pain to carry forward, and trouble tends to tag along too. I can never see Helen and me sitting in our living room, watching a movie on DVD and sharing a takeaway. There'll always be something else beyond our window. I'll *always* remember those faces at the glass. And I see them now.' They had just passed a cluster of ghosts beside the road, victims of some long-ago accident. Two parents, two children, just standing there as though waiting for a bus to the afterlife they had always been promised.

'I'll make sure that fades with time,' Nina said. 'I know words that will shield that part of things for you.'

'Consign me back to normality?'

'But that's what you want, isn't it?'

Lose her, the words had said. And much as that made no real sense right now, still the adventure of it excited him. 'I'm not sure, Nina. I'm not sure I'll be able to do that. It's not the way Papa made me.'

'I know.' Nina suddenly sounded terribly sad. 'But I'm doing my best to make sure things turn out well for all of us.'

Scott nodded and drove on, his mind in turmoil.

Nina sat back and seemed to relax. She raised her knees against the dashboard and crossed her hands over them, still glancing at the mirror every few seconds. He didn't trust her, but he did like her. Though they had been together for only three days, she had told him much more than a few words scrawled in steam.

But the doubt was there. Planted, it would

require little to urge it to sprout and grow. *She will slay you. Lose her.* Those words, simple and chilling, replayed themselves over and over in his mind as he drove. As time went on, the voice whispering them sounded more and more earnest.

'I'm so tired,' Nina said. Neither of them had spoken for a while, and the sound of the road was becoming soporific.

Scott glanced across and saw that she was crying. He had never seen that before – had not thought it possible – and it shocked him. He'd come to believe that she was immune to such displays.

'We could be close to the end,' Scott said.

Nina nodded. 'We could be. Or maybe not.'

'Which number am I?'

'What?' Nina sat up straighter, but she did not look across at him.

'How many other people have you used to help you? Mortals, helping an immortal seeking death. How many?'

'Three,' she said.

'In all that time?'

'Yes. Three whom I got to know, and who claimed to know where the Chord of Souls was kept.'

'What happened to them?'

'They died.'

Silence for a while, and then Nina sniffed. Wiped her eyes. Sobbed.

Scott slowed and drifted over towards the hard shoulder.

'Don't stop,' Nina said. 'Keep going. I'm fine.' She wiped her eyes again and sat up straighter, and when he looked over Scott could see that her tears had already ceased.

'What are you sad about?' he asked.

'I'm beyond sad. Like I said, I'm so tired. I'm craving death more and more, and the closer we get to the book, the more I'm eager to end things. I had to learn patience quickly, to begin with. Took on tasks that would take a long time, just to *pass* the time. I once walked from Constantinople to Paris, and at every town I stopped to collect a wound. Sometimes I did it myself in whatever room or hovel I slept in for the night. Other times I invited someone to give me a scar, entertaining them with my willingness to take the knife or sword, the whip or spike. And on occasion I picked a fight. Lost on purpose. Welcomed the agony of what should have been death. It was my journey of scars.'

'So where are they?'

'Faded, with time. I used to renew them to begin with, but then I left them to disappear.'

'Is it because this is your last journey?' he said softly. He was remembering the morning's beautiful sunrise, and wondering what Nina must have thought of it.

'*Fuck*, no. I don't give a shit. If you did tell me where this place was, I'd try to get us there through the Wide. I've no desire to say goodbye to the world, Scott. I've been in it far too long to miss it.' She laughed bitterly, then rested her head back and closed her eyes.

'If I told you…' he said, but he could not finish.

The ghosts saw to that.

'Scott, drive on.'

'No!'

'They're ghosts.'

'But *look* at them!'

Tyres screeched, the car slewed to the right, horns sounded behind and around them as startled drivers braked and fought to maintain control of their own vehicles. As far as everyone else was concerned, Scott had slammed on his brakes for no reason. The drivers would be cursing him, hating him already, and perhaps some were even now imagining how they would make it from their crashed cars, find him, and punch him down. *You risked my family, you lunatic… You fucking idiot!…What the hell do you think you're playing at!…*

'Look at them,' he said again, because he could not tear his eyes from the forest of ghosts spanning the motorway. There were hundreds of them, all staring directly at him, and as some of their mouths fell open, the cry of burning brakes gave them voice.

'Scott!' Nina shouted, but it was already far too late.

* * *

'As long as you're in control of your own destiny, you're responsible,' Papa says.

Scott is climbing a tree. It's the sort of thing his father would frown upon – he'd tell him to come down before he hurt himself – but Papa allows him to carry on. There's little that Papa won't let Scott try, and once or twice the thirteen-year-old has been slightly perturbed by this. They once sat in the woods drinking cider, and when Papa carried Scott home later that afternoon, Scott remembered only flashes of the argument that erupted between his parents and grandparent. Mostly he recalled only shouting, but somewhere in there was Papa's soft, enthralling voice, trying to explain, trying to give reasons.

'Can I go higher?'

'Don't know; can you?'

Scott looks up. The branches grow closer together up here, and they're thinner, and he's sure he can feel the actual trunk of the tree bending slightly as he moves. But there's one route he can see, and at its end is an old bird's nest. No treasure is worth anything without trials to reach it. 'Think so,' he says.

'Just remember,' Papa says, 'I'm only watching. It's you who has control. If I weren't here right now, everything would be the same. If I vanished from the world and left you alone for ever, the moments between my vanishing and you coming down from there wouldn't change. You're climbing, you're holding on, and you're the one in control.'

'I'm going a bit higher,' Scott says. He doesn't like Papa talking about not being here. He knows that one day that will be the case – Papa is growing older, after all, though in Scott's memory he has always looked the same – but the thought of a world without Papa is unbearable.

Scott grabs a branch and angrily hauls himself higher.

The branch breaks. He falls.

'Scott!' Papa's voice is concerned, but there's also something else there: excitement.

Scott slips down and bangs from branch to branch, then manages to gain a handhold again. There was no risk of his falling all the way to the ground, not really. But his heart is thumping and adrenaline flows, and there's a part of him that is thrilled at what just happened. *I had control* he thinks, *and I lost it and found it again. I was responsible.*

'I'm OK!' he shouts. He turns to look down at Papa, and the old man is shading his eyes from the sun as he looks up, grinning from ear to ear. 'I'm going back up.'

Scott climbs higher than he had intended. He goes right to the top. By the time he reaches the ground again he's slipped twice more, and his trousers are torn, and there's a cut on his calf that needs stitching, though he hides it from his parents and it eventually heals into an ugly scar.

Usually the memory stops here, but on the way home now Papa says to Scott, 'I've only ever lost control once. I slipped and stumbled, but I quickly started putting things right, and now if you'll help me we can finish this thing together.' In the memory he turns around and Papa is not talking, but his voice is stronger – and closer – than it has ever been before.

'You can't die!' Nina screamed, and Scott thought, *How nice of her to be so concerned.*

He struggled to keep the car straight, just as he tried to take his foot from the brake. But he could do neither. Instinct said, *You can't just run those people down,* while good sense screamed at him, *They're ghosts! They're dead already!* By the time he tried to separate those disparate voices the car started to spin, the tyres shredded, the wheels threw up a gush of sparks and pained squeals, and the car flipped over onto its roof.

Something struck them and set them spinning. Scott's senses were attacked and, because everything was so overpowering, they felt almost dulled by the onslaught. The noise, the heat, the taste of burnt rubber, the feeling of his body being buffeted, the sense of metal crunching as something else hit them, arrested the spin and started the car rolling...

Something grabbed Scott. Hands clawed into his shoulders and neck, holding on tightly, and even through the chaotic movement of the crash he felt them pulling. He opened his eyes and saw Nina before him, kneeling astride his braced legs with arms outstretched, eyes slitted almost closed, mouth working as she muttered something he could not hear. She appeared immune to the crazy forces the car was subjected to, and though her hair rose and swayed manically, her body remained still and in control.

She's in control, Scott thought. *She's responsible.*

His surroundings changed quickly. The movement calmed, the noise and smell withdrew, and somewhere in the distance there was an explosion of fire, heat, and noise that should have been much louder.

When all movement and noise and terror ceased, Scott opened his eyes. There was a man standing in front of him. One side of his face was bruised black, and his shoulder drooped at an odd angle, and for a second Scott thought he was a victim of the crash. Then he opened his mouth and only silence came out, and Scott knew he was a ghost.

He sat up and looked around. He'd obviously been thrown from the car. He was sitting on a steep bank, and the car was farther down in the ditch, steam gushing from its ruptured front end. It curled above road level, and a breeze dispersed it to the atmosphere.

There was a small fire below the car, flaring now and then when petrol dripped from somewhere and gave it more fuel.

Nina, Scott wanted to say, but nothing came from his mouth. He realised that he could not hear anything.

More wraiths appeared around him, joining the man in his blank-eyed stare. There was a woman with a burnt face wearing charred yellow dungarees, a teenage girl holding a little boy's hand, a man carrying something red on his back, an old woman using two sticks to stand upright on the stumps where her feet should have been...they all came to him, talking silently and ignoring the chaos of the accident. These were the people he had braked to avoid, these and hundreds more. These were the ghosts.

He tried to ask what they wanted, but he could not speak. He could not even hear the blood in his ears, the click of his throat, the hiss of breath forcing in and out of his bloodied nose.

He watched their faces and tried to read what they were trying to say in the movements of their mouths, the hopelessness in their eyes. *Help me,* the young boy seemed to mutter. *Only you can help,* the old woman mimed. *Save me,* the woman with the burnt face said, and Scott looked away because all of these were wrong. He was seeing words that would not be spoken, and reading into them impossible ideas. He closed his eyes and leant forward, but something touched his eyelids and forced them open again.

The young boy was kneeling before him. The teenage girl – his sister? – stood behind the boy, hands on his shoulders. He'd used his thumbs to lift Scott's eyelids.

The boy spoke, and somewhere in the distance Scott heard the faint breeze of his voice. *Don't just leave us here*, it said. The boy started to cry, and when he leant back into his sister's embrace, Scott's eyes stayed open.

He held out his hands, shook his head, and tried to ask them what he could do. His voice was still absent, yet his actions seemed to make sense. The ghosts – and there were more joining them every minute – all raised their arms and pointed to the southwest. They said two words, and in their unity their voices became audible: *Screaming skulls*.

There was a disturbance farther back in the crowd. The ghosts swayed and scattered and the disturbance rushed closer, barging through them as though they were little more than forgotten last breaths.

Scott cringed back, trying to claw his way up the bank, pushing with his feet, and remembering the image of Lewis hovering above him while the blights formed in the impossible distance. 'Get away from me!' he shouted, and his voice was shockingly loud as it burst through the bubble of silence.

More ghosts faded, merging with the air like steam from the crashed car.

Nina came up the hillside, looking around at the ghosts, up at the sky, and then straight ahead at Scott. She was covered in blood. A slab of her scalp had been torn off, one eye socket had shattered and was leaking down across her face, but even as she climbed closer Scott could see that strange reversal already beginning in her wounds.

She reached Scott and held out her hand. 'Quickly!' she said.

'What's happening?'

'Lewis.' She grabbed Scott's hand and started hauling him up the bank, but his hand slipped from hers. There was so much blood.

'Nina…'

'I'm *fine*.' She glanced back at him and her eye socket was already scabbing over, the deformed bone re-forming. 'Now come on!' She pulled again, he crawled behind her, and even though she had strength he had not even guessed at, still he froze when he saw what he had done.

After the brief silence following the crash – induced by shock, perhaps, or maybe the ghosts had lured him closer to the Wide for a time – the noise was tremendous. Most of it was caused by the fire. A truck transporting live chickens had ploughed into a builder's truck, and some sort of gas canister must have exploded. The truck was an inferno, and the fire had leapt to the truck as well. Chickens darted here and there, flaming across the road before the fire made them still, flapping uselessly at the air, screeching as they died and cooked. The smell was sickeningly mouth-watering, and Scott closed his eyes. *Could be more than chicken flesh cooking here*, he thought.

People were shouting. Someone screamed. Drivers from the other lanes had stopped and were leaping the central barrier, dashing to the several crashed cars to help. One of the vehicles was dangerously close to the burning truck, paint blistering and windscreen shattering from the heat as Scott watched. Its twisted door had already been kicked open, and a man stood on the hard shoulder with his wife and two children, watching their car begin to burn.

'I did this,' Scott said.

'You OK?' A man ran across the road to them, glancing at Nina's wounds and cringing as he saw what was left of her eye.

'Fine,' she said. 'Scott…?' She tugged at his hand, but he would not move. *How can I leave all this?* he thought.

'You don't look OK,' the man said, face growing pale. 'Come over here, sit down, the services will be here—'

'I'm fine!' Nina said again. She put her hand to her scalp, her face, and looked at the blood. 'It's slowing already.'

'You're in shock, love,' the man said. He looked terrified, but he was a good man trying to help. 'I saw this type of thing on TV once; the shock's protecting you, but you really need to sit down and—'

'You'll be in shock soon,' Nina said quietly. Scott could not see how she was looking at the man, but he saw the sudden doubt in his eyes. *Doesn't really know what he's seeing here*, Scott thought. *He'll remember this for ever.*

The man turned and left, glancing back once.

'He only wanted to help,' Scott said.

'We need to go.'

'Where? How?'

'Anywhere away from here. Can't you feel it? Don't you sense things changing?' She spit her impatience.

Scott felt nothing. Only the shock of the crash, the shame at seeing the pain in those ghosts' eyes.

And then he saw the body lying a few steps from the burning truck, its charred yellow dungarees, and he would have screamed if Nina had not tugged him hard.

I caused this! he wanted to shout. *I killed her.*

He followed Nina, terrified now of looking back. Afraid that he'd see more bodies lying in the road or crushed in their overturned cars. A girl and her brother. An old woman. Others.

'It's closer, much closer,' Nina said. 'There's someone strong with him. Someone who can lift the veil and keep it lifted. It's building. Can't you feel it?'

And now he could. The air seemed to be vibrating, thrumming against his eardrums and urging his hair to stand on end. His balls shivered and crawled.

They ran on ahead of the accident, passing

stopped cars and seeing the surprised expressions of those inside and mingling on the road.

They see Nina, and perhaps some of them know she should be dead.

'We need a car,' Nina said.

'Can you just *drive* from this?'

She glanced back and shrugged. Blood still dribbled down her face, but the wounds were closing now, the rent in her scalp already covered with fresh skin and sprouting a fine fuzz of new hair.

'You don't know?' he asked.

'I don't know everything.' She stopped beside a silver Mondeo. Its door was open, engine running, driver's seat empty. 'Get in.'

'We can't just—'

'It's only a car.'

'I'm not on about stealing. I'm on about *leaving*. I caused all that.' He glanced back at the accident, his eyes drawn straight to the yellow-dressed corpse. *I caused that.*

'No, you didn't,' Nina said. 'The ghosts did. And whoever drove them. Not you.' She opened the passenger door and nudged Scott, urging him to get inside.

A man standing beside another car turned around. 'Hey!'

'Fuck off,' Nina said.

'But that's my—'

'Fuck...off.' She spoke quietly, but somehow managed to project all her years into those two words. The man looked down at the ground and backed away like a cowed dog. He did not say anything else. The woman he had been speaking to closed her car door, wound up the window, and looked the other way.

Scott sat in the car and slammed the door. Nina climbed in beside him. She was looking in the rear-view mirror, glancing around like a bird with a broken wing awaiting the arrival of a cat.

'I don't see anything,' Scott said. 'But I can feel it.' The air seemed to dance with potential, as if every atom were preparing to move somewhere else. Maybe it was like this before a hurricane or a tornado.

Nina pulled off, steering slowly between other cars that had stopped to see the accident behind them. When she reached open road she floored the accelerator.

Now that detail had been stolen by distance, Scott could look back. He turned in the seat, wincing as he started to discover injuries he had sustained in the impact: a sore shoulder, bruised ribs, bloody nose. But he was glad of them. In some small way, minor though they seemed, they marked him for what he had done.

Smoke rose thick and heavy above the motorway. He could still see the flames at its base. They glinted from the windows of parked cars – those involved in the accident, and those that stopped to help – and the farther away they moved, the more the fire seemed to flicker.

It disappeared long before it should have.

'There's something wrong with the air,' he said.

Nina nodded. 'It'll follow.'

'What is it?'

'A rent into the Wide.'

'So who—'

Nina took her foot from the accelerator. The car began to drift, then slowed. She stared from the windscreen, mouth hanging open and head shaking ever so slightly. 'Him,' she said at last, and Scott turned to see what she had seen.

Chapter Ten

the testimony of scars

The man was made of scars. He was naked but for a blood-red cape, clothed otherwise in a testimony of wounds that gnarled his flesh, darkened his skin, twisted his limbs, and slashed him from left to right, up and down. Shadows hid in the depths of old cuts. Some bled darkness that turned red only when it touched sunlight. His head was almost devoid of hair, and the only features that made sense were his eyes and mouth. In his left hand he carried a sword, in his right, a pistol. Strapped across his back were a bow and a quiver of arrows, and there were knives tied to his legs. The only real adornment was a silver chain around his neck. The pendant was a hand grenade.

'Tigre,' Nina said.

'You only told me about him yesterday.'

'I haven't seen him for ever.'

He was standing beside the road, surrounded by a haze in reality. Ghosts walked by him, emerging from the haze and wisping away in the bright sunlight. He stood like a stone in a river of the damned, and though the ghosts mouthed silent pleas for peace, he had eyes only for Nina.

She stopped the car and opened the door.

'Nina!'

'It's OK.'

'How do you know? Nina, I'm scared. If he's behind Lewis, why is he here?'

'It's OK,' Nina said, but Scott was certain she had not heard a word he said.

Here was the immortal attempting to die through slaughter.

Scott watched, helpless, as she left the car and walked towards the man of scars. She passed through a haze of ghosts without noticing, and their cries were as silent as ever.

He could get in the driver's seat and go. Run them down, leave them spread across the road so that they would be out of action for a while, head into Wales and find the place of the screaming skulls. He could do that, but he was still not sure how he felt about travelling on his own. *Lose her*, the writing on the mirror had said, but he had no idea who or what had written those words.

Somewhere ahead of him – both in distance and time – Helen waited. If he did everything right, maybe he would have her back. He thought of her easy smile and the way she sighed against his neck when she came, the sound of her laughter and the birthmark on the top of her arm, shaped so much like the boot of Italy that they had once taken a holiday there, just in case fate was trying to guide them. They had returned, and she had not been pregnant, but they had never laid the blame at fate's door.

'I'm coming for you, Helen,' he said.

Nina had almost reached Tigre. The two stood a dozen paces apart, and the haze around Tigre settled down, fading away to the view that should be there. Behind him Scott saw fields, a farm, some hills, all normal things, always meant to be.

The ghosts were gone again. *Some I see in the Wide; some are visible here. What's the difference? What am I seeing, and why?*

So many questions. So much more to know. And if he drove away now, he would be on his own.

Scott turned sideways and exhaled onto the window. He watched as the condensation slowly faded away, but nothing was written there. 'Help me,' he whispered. He breathed out again. No message. '*Help* me, please.' One more time with the same result.

Nina was tall and beautiful. Watching her from a distance as she talked with someone else, he truly realised this for the first time. But her beauty was a result of her presence, such a powerful sense derived from all the history she had seen, everything and everyone she had been.

Scott opened the door and stood from the car.

'Is that him?' Tigre said. Even from this far away, with cars still passing by in the opposite lanes, Scott heard those words. The man's voice sounded as ragged and torn as the rest of his body, and Scott wondered how many times he'd had his throat slashed.

Nina glanced back at Scott and smiled. He wasn't sure whether the smile was for him or Tigre.

Nobody seemed to be noticing this strange exchange. No cars came from the direction of the accident, but the traffic on the other side was still moving, slowly now so that the rubberneckers could get a good look at the carnage a mile behind them. Scott saw people looking from car and coach windows, but there was only a vague interest in their eyes. Most of them were straining to see ahead, find the fire, see sights that they would have nightmares about later and probably never forget.

How many of them will be able to close their eyes? he thought. It would not be many. People just weren't made to look away.

'Your wife?' Tigre growled.

Scott walked to Nina and faced the man. Up close his wounds were even more grotesque, but Scott tried to maintain eye contact. It was impossible. Tigre's eyes had seen so much, and though dead as stone, they held such power that it almost hurt to look there.

'Helen,' Scott said. 'A man called Lewis took her, and I want her back.'

Tigre laughed. It was so unexpected that Scott found himself letting out a giggle as well, and Nina was also smiling.

'Good for you,' Tigre said. He nodded, staring at Scott, and Scott realised that it was impossible to tell what he was thinking. No smile was possible in this mangled flesh. No delicate expression, no intricacies of appearance. His face was a mask of scar tissue, destined always to look cold and hard.

'Where is she?' Scott asked.

'I don't know.'

Scott looked at Nina. She seemed bewitched. There was half a smile on her face and a dreamy look in her eyes. It did not suit her at all, and Scott nudged her arm. 'What's happening?' he said.

'What's happening is, Tigre has come to visit.'

Scott remembered her tales of his slaughter, a mad immortal using his own gift or curse in an attempt to cultivate the death of his soul. Looking at this thing before him, he wondered whether he had succeeded long ago.

'Can you help us?' Scott asked.

'Help?'

Scott waited for Nina to speak, but she said nothing. She was simply staring. They stood that way for a time, listening to traffic passing them by, the wails of distant sirens, and out over the fields the lone cry of a buzzard.

'Then I'll go on—'

'Is it really you beneath all this hurt?' Nina said.

It was as if she had not even heard Scott speak. She went on, slipping into a language he did not know, but the subtleties of her voice were evident. There was something here that he had yet to really hear from her: compassion.

Tigre answered in the same language, and they were both silent again.

Scott turned and walked back to the car. Every step of the way he expected a hand to fall on his shoulder, or a bullet to sever his spine. He climbed into the driver's seat and slammed the door, and Nina and Tigre still stood facing each other. Nina's hip was tilted to one side in eternal provocation.

Even when he started the engine, neither of them looked his way.

She will slay you, those words had said. A secret message from a secret benefactor? Scott slipped the car into first gear, and a bullet shattered the headrest beside his ear.

He shouted, fell forward, took his foot from the clutch, and stalled the car. He touched his ear and felt hot blood seeping from a dozen tiny wounds. When he sat up again and looked through the windscreen, Nina and Tigre were no longer there. A neat bullet hole sat directly in his line of sight.

Scott turned and saw Nina beside the car. She'd just opened the driver's door, standing back as if to allow Tigre to view him. Tigre was standing by the concrete divider. Tensed. Ready for flight or fight, and Scott knew which.

'Does he really need to see the lengths I'll go to?' Tigre asked Nina.

'I don't—' Scott began.

'Scott!' Nina hissed.

Tigre stepped over the divider and held up the pistol, aiming it at an oncoming bus. His red cloak fluttered in the breeze from passing traffic.

'*Does* he?'

'No,' Scott said. 'I don't need to see.'

Tigre hesitated for a few seconds, tracking the bus as it passed him by. Then he lowered the gun and came back across the road.

More sirens wailed, but Scott knew there would be no help there.

'I'll be there,' the scarred man said. 'At the end, I'll be there.'

'I want what you want,' Nina said, and Tigre laughed so long and loud that even Nina seemed uncomfortable.

And then the scarred man walked away. Scott watched him go, trailing ahead of them and then turning down the embankment. He disappeared for a while, then came into view again in a field, walking slowly, his direction wavering, as though he wasn't exactly certain where he needed to go.

Nina watched him as well. Scott stole a glance at her, and her expression had slipped. Where before there had been nostalgia, now there was a quiet sadness.

'What was that?' Scott asked.

Nina turned, and for the briefest moment she looked at him with such contempt that he thought she was going to lash out. Crush him beneath her boot, perhaps, as one would crush a slug. He was a nobody, a nothing, a simple necessity, and though she might be immortal, she already seemed bored with his company.

She looked down at her feet and shook her head, sighed. 'He wanted to talk,' she said.

'He brought all those ghosts. He made me do that…because he wanted to talk?'

'Maybe he thought I was driving.'

'He thought…?' Scott looked in the mirror, seeing fire still glinting behind them and smoke billowing skyward. Somewhere in that smoke, perhaps, the ashen remains of dead people. There were flashing blue lights there now as well, and he wondered how long it would be before a man told the police about the injured woman stealing his car.

'He wanted to make sure we were doing the right thing,' Nina said. 'If we weren't, he'd have shown you what he can do.'

'Is he just walking away?'

She shook her head. 'He'll be watching. He needs us to find the book for the same reason I do…except that he's wanted to die from the moment we were made immortal. Imagine.' She spoke the final word to herself, whispering it again and staring after Tigre.

'He laughed when I mentioned Helen.'

'Just one woman. This is so much larger.'

'Not to me.'

'No, not to you. Good. Keep it that way. There may be those who try to persuade you otherwise.'

She will slay you. 'I've already been warned,' he said without thinking. It seemed the right thing to say at that moment, a comment to draw her out or pull her closer to him.

'And?' She didn't even ask what he had been told, or how, or even by whom. Perhaps she already knew.

'And I have to trust you.'

Nina nodded, walked around the car, and sat in the passenger's seat. 'Good,' she said. 'But there's still a lie in there. Trust me enough to tell me where we're going? We can be there much faster.'

'No,' Scott said. 'This is about Helen, that's all, and the skull key ring is my map to her.' He started the car and pulled away. The bullet hole in the windscreen whistled as they picked up speed.

'Tigre wanted to take you into the Wide – properly kill you – and get it out of you there.'

Scott shivered. *Those eyes, sizing me up.* 'Why didn't he?'

'We need you. None of us can touch the Chord of Souls.'

'Nice.'

Nina sighed. Scott sensed a blizzard of memories around her, and her silence seemed to confirm that. So he drove on, and with every mile that passed beneath the wheels, trust became something farther removed than ever.

Scott turned on the radio to see if there was any news about the accident. His memory kept returning to that woman in the yellow dungarees, her head burnt and mouth hanging open, and how she was somebody's mother or wife, daughter or sister.

I caused that. However much he tried to persuade himself otherwise, he could not alter the truth.

He was instantly grateful for the chatter. Nina seemed to be asleep, though he sensed her attention focused directly on him, and the Mondeo purred efficiently along the motorway. The local radio deejay tried valiantly to be amusing, and it wasn't until the hourly news came on that there was the first mention of the crash.

Scott slowed as he listened to the report, trying to put himself there. But through all that he heard, he could not find a connection. They described the accident and its aftermath – vehicles involved, the fires, the traffic queues and disruption – and it could have been anywhere.

All but the numbers. These he used. He whipped himself with the rough edges of five dead to inflict wounds on his soul, scored shameful trails across his mind with the sharp realities of a dozen wounded.

'Hear that?' he said. 'Five dead. My fault.'

'Tigre's fault. I doubt he'll even add them to his tally.'

'And what is his tally? How many has he killed?'

'I have no idea.'

'Does he?'

'Oh, I'm sure.'

'I have a tally: five dead.' Scott pressed the accelerator down, edging over a hundred miles per hour and imagining plunging the car into every bridge they passed.

Chapter Eleven

the loyalties of flesh and blood

It was late afternoon. They had crossed the border into Wales, and Scott was very conscious that he would soon have to consult the road atlas. And soon after that, when they approached the place where the skull was leading him, Nina would know.

If she wanted to slay him then, there was nothing he could do about it.

Over the past hour he had considered trusting her, telling her about the writing on the mirror. There was so much more going on here than he could even begin to understand, but he was also comfortable with the slight power he seemed to have right now. The more he told her – the more she took control – the less leverage he maintained. And this was all about Helen. Nothing else mattered but her.

You're in control; you have responsibility, Papa had said, and the same seemed to translate the other way as well.

He pulled off the motorway and stopped. Nina looked over at him, eyebrows raised.

'I need to piss.' He stood from the car and climbed a gate into a field, standing behind the hedge to urinate. He was constantly looking over his shoulder. He had seen three ghosts since leaving the scene of the accident, all of them wandering sadly across the road where they had presumably met their ends. One of them he had driven straight through. He did not want to see another one now.

Back in the car, Nina was waiting for him with the map on her lap. 'How close are we?' she asked.

'A couple of hours. Maybe more. Maybe less.'

She nodded. 'It'll be dark when we get there.'

'I don't think I want to go there in the dark.'

'I can protect—'

'It's not that. Not really. It's the place. If we spend a long time looking, I'm afraid of what will happen to Helen. We need to go straight there, do what needs to be done. And I don't think it's going to be easy to find.'

'Why not?'

'Well…it doesn't really exist.'

Nina nodded slowly, looking away from Scott. 'Right.'

'But neither does the Wide.'

Nina looked down at the map in her lap, her fingers steepled against her nose.

'How old are you, Nina?'

'Old.'

'Surely you can wait another night to die?'

She looked up quickly, and he saw something he did not understand in her eyes. Was that anger? Excitement? Jealousy?

'I can wait,' she said. 'But we have to be careful. This close…anything could happen.'

'But nobody knows—'

'This close, Lewis might take a guess.'

Could he know? Scott wondered. The House of Screaming Skulls was a place he and Papa had read about together, but could he have mentioned it to Lewis as well? Surely not. Surely if that was the case, then Papa would have never guided Scott there.

But at the end, after so long trying and such fear over what he had accomplished, perhaps Papa really had lost his mind.

'He won't guess right,' Scott said.

'He may. I already have a pretty good idea of where you're taking us.'

Scott started the car, eased back into the traffic, and said no more. Things were coming together. This had started only three days ago, but already there was a definite sense that the end was in sight.

And if Nina thought she knew where they were going…

She will slay you. Lose her.

Something would happen tonight.

They found another roadside pub. Neither of them was hungry, and they received strange glances when they booked two single rooms.

'Drink?' Scott asked. Nina looked very tired, and he knew she did not mean it when she nodded.

Coffee for Nina, as usual, and a pint for Scott. Its taste and smell brought back a sudden rush of memory, so rich and powerful that he closed his eyes to hold on to it, willing it to continue like the best instance of déjà vu.

The woman walks across the river bridge in Caermaen, a little village in South Wales, emerging from the heat haze above the river like an angel forming from light. Scott is sitting on the riverbank drinking, watching the water and the world go by. He has just been for a job interview and, pleased with how it went and glad that it finished early, he decides to have a few drinks before catching the train home. He is on his third pint. He's just entered that phase where the tastes and smells and colours of the beer combine to form an overall experience, soothing his senses and yet helping him to see clearer than ever. So she walks on, short pleated skirt and loose blouse reflecting sunlight and camouflaging her in its glare. Long hair, he can see that. Slim, fit, pert breasts, long legs – way out of his league, but it's always fine to look, and today of all days he feels more confident, more in control. Perhaps it's the fact that the interview went so well, or maybe it's just the beer talking, but he can't help trying his luck. *And an angel appeared before me,* he says as the woman draws level with him, and she steps below a tree and out of the sun as if to offer him his first real look. She is gorgeous, as he first assumed, but there's something else about her that weakens him to the point of collapse. It's her eyes; they're stunning. Like globes of fire, twinkling with intelligence and humour and strength. She smiles, and the colour of their flames changes. *I'm no angel* Helen says, one hand on her hip, the other stroking the hem of her blouse. And ever since then he's called her Angel because, in his heart and mind, she always will be.

'Are there angels?' he asked. 'Are there demons?'

Nina took a sip of coffee, and Scott wondered what memories she could be feeling right now. 'There are things,' she said. 'I've seen some and heard of others. I don't know what you'd call them.'

'Heaven? Hell?'

Nina shrugged. 'I'm just immortal. I don't know everything.'

'But don't you want to?'

She looked at him, her eyes sad. 'The more I know, the more I wish I didn't.'

'How comforting.'

'So don't ask me any more.'

He sipped more beer, she drank her coffee, and partly because he sensed she wanted to go to bed, he ordered two fresh drinks.

There was so much to ask and say, but they sat quietly in the bar. Scott remembered Helen, struggling to think of her in the present tense. He came close to tears several times. *The beer,* he thought. *The tiredness.*

But it was the fear of grief that brought those tears from him. That, and the growing idea that there was absolutely nothing he could do to help.

They went upstairs, stood outside their respective doors, and Nina gave him that look again. *She could have anyone she wanted,* he thought, *but not me.* He opened his door, offered her an apologetic smile, and went into his room.

He locked the door behind him. He hated empty bedrooms. In over twenty years together, he and Helen had slept apart only a handful of times, and never very well. He felt incomplete without his wife. Half a person.

In the bathroom he ran a sinkful of scalding water, and returned several times to see whether there were more messages on the steamed mirror. But it remained untouched. He wrote, *Help me,* and when he returned a few minutes later, it was still there, alone, almost steamed over again but mirroring evidence of his hopelessness back at him.

He sat by the window for a long time, because he did not feel at all tired. He had turned off the light so that it did not throw his shadow outside, and he watched the darkness grow more complete as dusk settled into night.

It has to be tonight, he thought. He would creep out and go to find the House of Screaming Skulls, and then whoever had left that message for him would help him get Helen back.

What if it was Lewis?

Then he would deal with that when the time came. Lewis wanted the book; that was all. Not revenge.

What if it was someone else? Someone even Nina doesn't suspect?

What would be, would be.

'I have no idea whether I'm doing the right thing,' he whispered, breath steaming on the window glass. It faded away to reveal a ghost standing in the pub garden.

It was a woman, dressed in dark colours that helped hide her away, but Scott could see her face. Even from this distance her sunken eyes revealed her true nature. She waved to him, beckoning him down from the room, and for a second he reached out and unclasped the window catch. She seemed excited, agitated, and she waved more quickly. Every few seconds she glanced to her left – checking Nina's window, Scott guessed – and she began to nod as Scott stood and shrugged on his jacket.

All he knew was from Nina. Even what Old Man and Tigre had said had been explained to him by her, not them. She had stepped into his life straight after Helen was taken away, steered him, and even driving towards the Screaming Skulls he felt that she had been guiding their path. She treated him like a child. Sometimes he felt safe with her, but other times when she looked at him he felt like a rabbit in a python's glare. And what she wanted from these hidden pages of the Chord of Souls...he did not know. To die?

Was it that simple? For Tigre perhaps, because he seemed like a simple being: made immortal and craving mortality, he had spent centuries seeking death.

But Nina was far more complex. There were depths to her, places he had not even glimpsed that could contain all manner of desires, hopes, cravings. *What else is in the book?* he had asked, and she had replied, *Stuff.*

Before he went on, he needed to know more of what this *stuff* entailed.

He would not discover that from Nina.

He opened the door carefully, crept out onto the wide landing, glanced back at Nina's door to make sure it remained closed. And he froze in his tracks.

There were a dozen ghosts standing outside her room. They had their hands pressed firmly against the door and frame, but they had all turned their heads to stare at him. Their eyes were wide and expectant. One of them nodded, his long hair flowing as though he were underwater. Another opened her mouth to speak and Scott turned away, not wanting to read her silent words.

He walked down the curving staircase, and every step of the way he felt dead people staring at his back.

He reached the lobby of the pub's accommodation wing. The building was still silent. At the front door he slid aside a couple of bolts, turned a key, and then Nina started to shout.

'Scott! Don't go out there!'

He turned and looked up at the landing. The ghosts were still gathered at her door, and now they were leaning back, fingers and hands curled into the wood, using whatever impossible purchase they had to keep the door closed as Nina tried to haul it open from the inside. Her voice was muffled by more than the door. There was a distance there that had nothing to do with space.

'Don't go!' she said, her voice even farther away. Several of the ghosts faded and moved through the door and wall, and when she next shouted he could not even make out her words.

Exercising his own will by leaving Nina, Scott suddenly felt directed more than ever before. There was nothing he could do to help her; go back now and he would be lost. All he could do was go through with this. Fate had him in its grasp, and nothing as negligible as his own fears would distort it from its path.

He closed the front door behind him, and Nina's shouts became nothing.

It was cool outside. A breeze had risen to flap his trouser legs and pluck at his jacket. There were few cars left in the pub car park, and the road beyond was silent. A small shadow dashed across the tarmac, several more moved around one of the cars – night creatures foraging, perhaps killing. A bat flew overhead. In silence nature expressed its true, irrefutable ownership.

Scott headed towards the back garden, and as he turned the corner he came face-to-face with the ghost.

The woman looked quite normal, yet there was no doubt that she was dead. There was something about her, a sense of nonbelonging that even the darkness did nothing to lessen. And a silence. No breathing, no sighing, no sound of cloth moving against itself, no crunch of gravel or whisper of grass beneath her feet. The ghost's ties to this world were severed. It was a visitor here now, a lost soul doing its best to find its way somewhere better.

Help us, she mouthed. The words were unmistakable. She looked at Scott as she turned and started walking, never taking her eyes from his face.

Scott followed. He watched the ghost's feet where they passed across the ground. He did not wish to see her eyes…those deep, desperate eyes.

Something cracked behind and above him, and when he looked up at the facade of the building, he saw something stretching out of one of the windows. At first he thought it was a gush of flame and smoke, but then it took form and he saw that it was an arm, twisting and flexing as it tried to reach farther. A voice came with it. 'Scott.' It was Nina's voice, but distorted, as if filtered through a thousand other mouths. The hand opened and closed, fingers dropping sparkles of light that faded into darkness as they fell towards the ground.

'I'm sorry,' he said, but the admission made him feel worse.

The hand was drawn back inside the shattered window. It did not want to go, but something tugged at its flesh and bone, fingers clawing, nails screeching against the glass that remained.

'Will they hurt her?' Scott asked the ghost before him. Her expression did not change and she carried on walking. *Help us,* she mouthed again.

They could hurt her, but they can't kill her, he thought. If they could, perhaps she'd let them.

There were more strange sounds from behind, but Scott no longer looked. It sounded like a struggle, and below that – almost subaudible – a moan of desperation that he hoped never to hear again.

'My wife,' he said, filling his head with his own voice. 'Helen…it's all for Helen, and everyone else is involved because of themselves. Sorry, Nina, but it'll work out. It'll resolve itself.'

The ghost still looked at him over her shoulder as they walked. He only glanced at her face before looking away again. She was lost, and there were no answers there.

They reached the end of the pub's long garden, passed through a rotten wooden gate that was jammed permanently open, and entered an area of undergrowth gone wild. A stream gurgled somewhere to Scott's left and the ground turned marshy. His shoes sank with every step, sucking and popping as he lifted his feet to walk on. He watched the ghost's feet barely touching the world.

He blinked and the ghost was gone. He blinked again, thinking his vision was teasing, but he was alone, standing in a small clearing carpeted with rotten newspapers and a pile of soggy porn magazines.

There was a mattress shoved under one low, wide bush, with a few tattered sheets of polyethythene drawn across the bush's branches and pricked onto its thorny limbs. A few empty cans, a smashed whiskey bottle, and an underlying stink of waste. Scott wrinkled his nose and took a backward step, but then a shadow moved.

He squinted and peered across the clearing. Something had shifted beneath the tree over there, a shadow that had seemed merged with the thick trunk but which now stood and detached itself, walking out into the sparse moonlight.

I can hear its footsteps, Scott thought.

'You one of them?' The voice was gruff, yet tinged with fear. Bravado went only so far.

'Are you?'

'What you think, fuckhead?' The shadow stamped on the ground, flapped its arms, slapped its own face. 'Flesh and fuckin' blood, man.'

'Me too.'

'Yeah?'

'You ever heard one talking?'

The man's silence was heavy with thought. 'Don't know,' he said finally. 'Maybe.'

'I'm sorry I'm here,' Scott said. He started backing away, keeping the stream to his left in the hope that it would guide him back to the pub garden. Once there, maybe he could take their stolen car and head for his final destination.

'You Scott?' the voice said.

Scott froze. 'You are one of them?' he asked again.

'No, man. Flesh and fuckin' blood, like I said. Look!' The man walked forward and stood outside the tree's shadow, letting starlight touch him. He was much younger than he sounded, barely out of his teens. Jeans, sweatshirt, black jacket, the beginnings of a beard, long dark hair forming a chaotic shadow-halo around his head. His face was drawn and pained, and even in this poor light Scott could make out the skin and eyes of a lost man. The smell of stale alcohol was strong. A bottle swung from his left hand, almost empty and seemingly forgotten.

'How do you know my name?'

The man shrugged and put on a mock-posh voice. 'Seems I have you at a disadvantage.'

'So, how?' Scott looked around for the woman's ghost, thinking that maybe she was watching to see what would happen. But all other shadows acted as they should.

'Old dude told me. Spooky fucker. Dropped me a bottle of good stuff and twenty straights, said there'd be same again if I passed on the message.'

'What message?'

The man smiled, showing off teeth that belonged to someone three times his age. 'What'll you give me for it?'

Scott shook his head and turned his back, ready to walk away.

The man was on him in a second. The bottle clunked him on the side of the head, a leg twisted in front of him, and there was a sharp push between his shoulder blades. Scott went sprawling, hands slipping in the slime of rotting magazines, and the man dropped down onto his back. Hands reached around and clawed at Scott's face, and he almost gagged at their stink.

The man leant down and whispered into Scott's ear, 'Be a good boy for Daz, now, and you'll get your message. But it's like…power. I got something to pass on, you got something you have to hear, so there's a trade there, see? A fair trade. Fuckhead.'

'I don't have anything,' Scott said.

'Nothing to give?'

He shook his head, trying not to breathe in Daz's foul stench.

'Well, we can sort something out.' Daz sat up again, and Scott heard the sound of a zipper opening. 'Get a load of this, mouthful and a faceful, and I'll tell you what the old dude said.'

Scott closed his eyes and thought of Helen. He could conjure no memories – could not even picture her face – but the idea of her was there with him, strong and comforting and warm with love. He smiled into the mud and sent his own love back to her.

Daz shuffled forward, one hand reaching down to turn Scott's head to the side, the other beating rhythmically between his legs.

Scott lay loose and weak, letting Daz turn his head. He opened his eyes.

'Here you go, fuckhead. Get some of this; here you go. Old dude said I should give the message so you remember it, so here you go. Fuckhead.'

Scott tensed his shoulders and arms and lifted up, twisting his body at the same time, throwing Daz off his back and standing in one movement.

Daz shouted and went sprawling across the mound of mouldy newspapers.

Scott kicked something, bent down, and picked up the whiskey bottle. He went after Daz before he had a chance to stand, swinging the bottle high and hard and wincing as it connected with the man's forehead. It rebounded with a dull thunk, somehow remaining whole, but Daz's struggles slowed.

Scott threw the bottle into the dark and dropped down astride the man, pinning his arms to his side. He punched him in the face. He hadn't punched anyone like that since he was eleven years old and got into a fight with the school bully. Back then the sensation of his fist connecting with someone else's nose had frightened him with its primal violence, but now it felt good. He did it again.

'Fucking pervert!' he said, striking out again and again, face and neck and chest. Daz tried to mutter something, and Scott punched him once more, though some of the anger had gone out of him now, leached away and already turning into a crimson shade of guilt.

'Enough?' he asked. Daz was not struggling; nor did he make a sound. He simply stared up at Scott, the stained whites of his eyes catching starlight. He nodded.

Scott stood and backed away, letting the man come to his knees. He was struggling to tuck his flaccid cock back into his trousers, a pathetic, pitiful action that made Scott look away.

'The old dude,' Scott said. 'Tell me what he said. I've got a twenty here for you if you tell me. Buy yourself a few bottles. Better still, some deodorant. But tell me now, or I'll get fucking angry again.'

'Man, I'm just flesh and blood, you know?'

'And what does that *mean*?' Scott felt his anger rising again, unfamiliar and disconcerting.

'Guy has his needs, man.'

'His needs? So you try to stick it in my face to satisfy your needs?'

'Old dude said—'

'Just what *did* he say?' Scott stepped forward, and Daz flinched away, falling onto his back and holding up both hands. Scott's shoulders sagged and he shook his head. 'Damn it, Daz, just tell me. I need to get out of here. You have no idea, no inkling.'

'I do,' he said. 'I seen them. Thought I had before, for years, but I seen them tonight, plenty of them. Walking around as if they're lost. None of 'em talk to me. Finished the bottle and they still didn't go away. And they only came after the old dude went.'

'What did he look like?'

Daz shrugged. 'Old.'

'And he said…?'

'OK, gimme a sec.' Daz sat up and rubbed at his mouth. There was a dark trail leaking from it, blood blackened in the starlight. He coughed, spit, touched his forehead, and winced.

'Waiting for me to apologise?' Scott asked.

'No, man.' Daz looked up at Scott, sad and wretched. 'So, the old dude said: "There's a guy called Scott who you'll meet. Give him a message from me. Tell him to lose Nina, go on his own, find the book."' He looked away and shook his head.

'That's it?'

'No, trying to remember… Yeah, find the book. And stay with it. It has more things in it, dude said. Then he said, "Everything will come together. Things will work out. Be explained."' He nodded, frowned. 'Yeah, that's it.'

'Sure?'

'Yeah.'

'More things?'

'That's what he said.'

Scott dug out a rolled-up twenty-pound note

from his pocket and dropped it onto the mass of torn, wet newspaper.

'Oh, hey, man…'

'Give you something to do,' Scott said. 'Sort yourself out, Daz.'

'Will they leave me alone now?' the man asked. He sounded desperate for the right answer.

Scott thought about lying. Giving this wretched excuse a scrap of hope. But right then, he couldn't find such benevolence within. It had been driven too deep, and he left with a comment that chilled him even as he spoke. 'No,' he said. 'They're always here. Always have been. Always will be.'

As he walked back through the bushes he heard Daz somewhere behind him, moaning and crying as he nursed his bloody wounds and bruises. Just someone else whom Lewis had used, abused, and left shattered. A lost soul in waiting.

'Hey, Scott!' Daz called as Scott reached the gate back into the pub garden. The voice was muffled and confused by the vegetation, but Scott still heard. 'One more thing the old dude said. Me, I hope it's true. I hope it fuckin' happens to you, man. Said she'll gut you soon as she's finished with you. Yeah. Sounds good to me, fuckhead.'

Scott worked his way around the perimeter of the pub garden until he reached the car park. He kept his ears open in case Daz had decided to follow and his eyes on the pub. There was no movement and no sounds of pursuit. *Where will Nina be now?* he thought. *Still trapped in her room? Still hemmed in by ghosts?* He was running blind, and the more he heard and saw, the more confused he became.

She'll gut you as soon as she's finished with you.

Surely Lewis had not written those words on his mirror? He was more direct than that, more intrusive, like introducing Scott to Daz to pass on a message. But if it had not been him, then who else was warning him away from Nina?

'Need to do my own thing,' he whispered to the night. It did not reply.

Climbing into the car, he saw a ghost standing against the wall of the pub, so still that it might have been painted there. It watched him leave. He felt its eyes on him, and as he accelerated quickly towards whatever fate had in store, he wondered to whom the ghost would report.

More things, Daz had said. *It has more things in it.* Scott remembered the quote from Hamlet, and he wondered just what *more things* could entail.

Chapter Twelve

in the gaze of the real world

As he drove, Scott began to feel incredibly exposed. Though darkness accompanied him all the way into Wales, held back only by the twin spears of the car headlights, he felt as though a thousand eyes were watching. He was the centre of attention for many people he could not understand. He sensed the minds of things focusing upon him, and he kept glancing left and right, as though expecting to see something monstrous lunging out of the night. *More things*, he kept thinking, and he wondered what more things in heaven and Earth could be. *Stuff*, Nina had called the rest of the book. But she had refused to state who or what had told her and the others to transcribe the Chord of Souls in the first place. Perhaps they had received it in their minds, projected there by forces or presences way beyond humanity's comprehension. Or maybe something or someone had dictated to them, sitting there day after day as Nina and the other eleven immortals hacked and chiselled the book into solid stone slabs, bringing it into being for the first time. The travel writings of some vast, ancient spirit, or the musings of the last of a long-lost civilisation. Nina had said that to reveal where the Chord of Souls came from would change everything.

'God?' Scott muttered. The car headlights dimmed and brightened slightly, as though the darkness had pulsed inward for an instant. 'Maybe it really was God, and the book is proof of His existence.'

Scott was a casual believer. He never prayed or went to church, but he had always been content in his belief that there was more to life than living: there was dying as well, and what came after. What he had seen since Helen had been taken confused him, though he had not even begun trying to make sense of what it all meant. It confirmed that there was some sort of existence beyond death – at least, he thought it did – but it also seemed to hint at a truth he found almost too painful to bear: that after death, there could be pain. Fearing God was all about looking for your own salvation, wasn't it? Looking forward to an eternity of heaven?

If so, then what was the Wide? If there *were* different routes to heaven, and many who never made it there, Scott really did not wish to know. He did not want to face the prospect of being lost in the Wide, skimming its outer fringes or wandering its endless depths for ever. He saw lost souls and the echoes of those long gone, but there had been nothing yet to show him what these wraiths really were.

He and Helen enjoyed talking religion, and approaching it from diverse angles. *What would happen*, she had once suggested, *if God revealed himself to everyone? If the world was given incontrovertible, undeniable proof of His existence, would it make it a better place?* Scott had argued that it was impossible; that proof was unworkable if richness of faith were to be maintained. But Helen had shaken her head and run with the idea, and Scott now remembered the long, heated discussion it had initiated.

God as an object or process, not a belief. A definite fact, like gravity, the sun, or electricity. Scott's take was that life was ruled by faith, and that gravity and evolution were still only theories that many believed in. He had faith that when he turned a corner in the car, there would not be a wall of glass built across the road. He had faith that when he blinked his eyes, they would open again onto the same scene he had been seeing when he closed them. He had faith in many things, and perhaps the strength of that faith was exactly what made them so. If he *truly* believed that, when he next blinked, he would open his eyes onto a blood-red landscape with towers of carbon issuing clouds of flying demons, then maybe that would be so.

If that's the case, Helen had said, *then God exists in six billion different forms.*

'I don't care,' he told the darkness. The car rumbled on, and around the next corner there was only road. 'All I want is Helen back.' He blinked, and the view remained the same. 'Leave me alone.' He sighed, then shouted it again: 'Leave me alone!'

He drove on, still feeling watched, still believing that he was at the centre of some vast web of beliefs and impossibilities. If he drove fast enough, perhaps he could escape.

In his right front pocket, the skull key ring pressed into his leg. Papa had touched that. He'd bought it for Scott after they'd talked about the Screaming Skulls, a conversation that his parents would have hated but which Papa revelled in. There had been mention of the Skulls on a TV program, and Scott had wanted to find out more. Back then there was no Internet, so Papa took him into town one Saturday and they sat in the library for the afternoon, digging out old volumes about myths and legends, unsolved mysteries and the unexplained. Even here there was only passing mention, because the Skulls were so ambiguous. Some books seemed to suggest that they had never been seen, while others printed eyewitness accounts. Some said that the last time anyone heard them scream was a thousand years ago, while one book suggested that they could still be heard today, echoing around the Welsh valley where their home had once been. A folded valley, the book said, wrapped up by magic and neglect, twisted in upon itself so that it was no longer there. But ghosts didn't need the physical to exist…and on the darkest, coldest nights of the year, the Screaming Skulls cried out from their hidden home, seeking a peace that would never come.

There was no clearly defined cause for their screaming.

Scott and Papa had fun making up some reasons.

Now, Scott did not find quite so much pleasure in those memories. He could not recall any detail of the conversation he and Papa had in that library, and though he remembered taking notes, he had no idea where they were now. He could not even remember reading the notes again after writing them that first time. It was as if the Screaming Skulls were trying to remain misty in his memory, steering him away from where they were supposed to be.

But he did remember one image from one of those obscure books: a map.

'Not far from here,' he said. He stopped at the side of the road and dug around behind his seat for a road atlas. Flipping on the inside light solidified the darkness outside, and he tried not to look up at the windows as he examined the map. He traced the route of one river to where it met another, found where the two valleys intersected, and that was where the hidden valley was alleged to be. Folded away in time and perception, perhaps it would reveal itself to Scott.

Or perhaps not.

Either way he was out here on his own, for good or bad. Nina would be pursuing him. Lewis seemed to be guiding him. Tigre wanted to see the book when it was found, and Old Man had made him promise to take the Chord of Souls to Edinburgh.

The folded papers in his back pocket suddenly felt much thicker than they were. 'I could burn them,' he whispered. 'Give their energy to the night.' But now that he had made them exist, destroying the papers seemed grotesque.

He had shattered those first few slabs on Nina's say-so. Now, it was time for him to take control.

He parked and waited for sunrise.

Scott had found the place where he had always believed the valley to be. He could remember looking at the old map with Papa, and Papa saying, *Here it is.* There had been little fanfare and no real sense of import. But now, over thirty years later, Scott realised that had been the single most important moment of communication between the two of them. The old man must have understood that; it was not long before he killed Lewis and himself. Sitting in the stolen car, watching night sucked from the sky as the sun made its proud return, Scott could remember nothing more about that moment. Perhaps Papa had meant it that way. Hidden knowledge, locked away in the young boy's mind to be retrieved again later, when it was most needed.

'But we only guessed,' Scott said. Outside, the emerging countryside did not argue.

Ancient civilisations used to believe that the sun was a god, for ever fighting off the scourge of night-time to return triumphant each morning, sometimes stained with its enemy's blood. And through sacrifice, they had offered it the blood it needed to keep itself strong. As Scott watched the sun appear above a hill to the east, he wondered what sacrifice Papa had made when he killed himself. Maybe it *was* simply madness, but he thought not. This was much more complex and far-reaching than that.

For the first time since making them, Scott took the folded sheets of paper from his back pocket. Papa's letter was mixed in with them, and he read that again first, seeking any new clues: a key to new memories, perhaps, or more detailed instructions of what he had to do. But there was no more. It must have served its purpose, because the letter did not strike him nearly as hard as it had the first few times he read it.

He unfolded the sheets of paper, smoothed them out, and used dawn's early light to examine the rubbings. They were all strange. The shapes could have been images of creatures of the time, though Scott barely recognised any of them. A limb here, a wing there, but they were all unknown. Other shapes merged into one another, forming a strange symmetry that steered its way across the paper. Perhaps the language was in this symmetry instead of the shapes themselves? Few characters repeated themselves, and when two did, the repeated shape was always slightly different, as if already changed by the appearance of the first. They made no sense to Scott. He ran his fingers across the rubbings, trying to remember what touching the actual carvings felt like.

Nothing. But he did not have any understanding of such things, and immersed as he was in this strange world, there was no reason he should be able to read the Chord.

Others would, he knew. The immortals. Old Man or Tigre or Nina, or one of the others. Perhaps they would even recognise their own hand, the shapes of their own lettering from so long ago.

He had yet to decide what to do with these pages. The consensus seemed to be that the Chord of Souls should be destroyed, but this came from Papa – who undoubtedly had been badly affected by whatever he had translated – and Nina, who was immortal. Surely there were things in the book that would benefit humankind? Old Man claimed to understand a cure for cancer, and if he could acquire that knowledge through time, what greater knowledge could there be in the Chord of Souls? The idea of destroying such potential seemed ludicrous.

Scott rooted around in the car's glove compartment. There was the usual car service guide and instruction books, but he also found a reporter's notepad and a short green pencil. The first few pages of the pad were taken up with a kid's scribbles, but the rest was blank.

'Here's potential,' he said. He folded the rubbings and put them into his back pocket, while the folded notebook and pencil went into his front pocket.

He felt armed.

When dawn had burnt away much of the darkness and pulled a soft mist from the ground, Scott stepped from the car and started walking.

It was cold, quiet, the air filled with the chill potential of a unique new day. Papa would have loved this. They had often gone walking together in the early morning, when the only vehicles around were milk wagons and farmhands driving to work. The silences between these intermittent vehicles had been what Papa called—

'It's the real world.' Birds chatter all around them, the volume of their song seeming to increase every time Papa and Scott pause. 'Stop. Our footsteps aren't real.' They stop and lean against a gate. The field beyond is a sea of mist, marred here and there by ghostly cows. The mist moves slowly, like a blanket covering the waking ground. There is not a breeze in the air. The gate is cold and beaded with moisture, and Papa touches the water and puts his fingers to his mouth. 'Taste the morning,' he whispers. Scott does so, and it is forbidden and mysterious.

They wait there for a few minutes, seeing and hearing the world waking around them. 'Why do you call it the real world?' Scott asks at last. He thinks he has an idea, but he wants to hear it from Papa's mouth. The old man has a way with words.

'Well, it's not really,' he says. 'Not as real as it could be. We're here, for a start, and though we're still we're tainting the scene. Our hearts are heard by something; something else smells us. And their fear of humans changes their behaviour, which changes the scene. But it's as close to real as we can get, and that's good enough for now.'

'But we're part of the world.' Scott watches Papa watching the cows. The old man doesn't reply for several minutes, and Scott becomes a large part of the silence. He opens his mouth and tries to breathe lightly, remaining as still as possible so that his clothes don't rub together. Eventually a motorbike roars in from the distance and passes them, startling the cows and causing a slight ripple in the air that upsets the mist.

'We weren't a part of it long ago, and one day we won't be again,' Papa says. 'One day, all people will be gone. It's inevitable. While some of us are doing our best to make sure we live on, there are others striving to end it all. And it takes only one of them to succeed. There's that old saying: we have to be lucky all the time, and they have to be lucky only once. So we'll end, and the world will go on, and that will be the real world once more.'

The cows calm down and the mist starts to settle, but the disturbance has been set, and it slowly floats and billows away. 'I don't understand.'

'We're just visitors here, Scott,' Papa says.

'I don't—'

'Let's get home, son.'

'Papa?'

Papa looks down at him, reaches out, and touches his forehead. His hand is warm. He smiles. 'Let's get home.'

In that remote Welsh valley, there were no human-made sounds to break the reality. Scott paused every few seconds to give the solitude of the place its freedom. Even footsteps broke the magic. To the south lay a large mountain, ridges rising up on either side like wide shoulders. Its summit was hidden in a heavy mist, and wisps of mist also wandered its lower slopes. To the north – Scott's right – lay a range of hills, and in between was a wide, gently sloped valley, evidence of the last great ice age. The road curved its way down into the valley and along its base, and here and there he saw the white blocks of farms. He was willing to bet that they were deserted. He saw no signs of cattle, and the fields themselves seemed to be given over to natural growth. The hedgerows marking their limits had burst out of orderliness, haemorrhaging into the fields in wild abandon. *Of course they wouldn't stay here,* he thought. *They're close to another world, and that's enough to scare anyone.*

A hundred steps farther on he saw the first ghost. It was a man dressed in clothes Scott did not recognise from any history book. He was standing out in a field, looking up at the mountainside as though awaiting the arrival of someone or something. The wraith was weak and forlorn. He glanced back at Scott but looked away again.

Scott paused and watched the ghost. It waited for a while longer, then drew its sword, knelt, placed the point against its sternum, and fell forward. Scott gasped and stepped back. The ghost fell to the ground and quickly melted away, as though Scott were viewing months of decay in the space of seconds. Then it manifested again, standing and watching the mountain for someone or something that had never – and would never – come.

'There's another valley,' Scott shouted. He felt vaguely ridiculous talking to this ghost – an echo – and he did not like the sound of his own voice spoiling the peace.

The ghost turned and started walking towards him.

Scott backed away, suddenly wishing he had simply carried on along the road. The apparition approached, legs passing through the long grass without disturbing it at all. The man was short and wiry, heavily bearded, and sporting a leather tunic studded with strange metal sigils. His cheeks and forehead were scored with harsh tattoos, the skin raised and scarred where the designs had been clumsily carved.

Scott recognised some of them. *What the hell is this?* he thought.

The ghost came closer, and it had no eyes. They had been torn out, leaving sickly strands hanging over its cheeks. Blood ran over the designs there, giving them the promise of colour.

When the man was a dozen steps away he stopped and opened his mouth. *Screaming Skulls,* he said, and his voice, though a whisper, hurt like a sudden cold breeze.

Scott grimaced and went to put his hands to his ears, but the man's empty eyes grew wider.

You seek them? he asked.

'Yes,' Scott said. The marks on the ghost's face were reminiscent of the language of the Chord of Souls and some of the signs Papa had used in his letter. He could not tell whether any of them matched exactly, but they were too similar for it to be coincidence. 'Who are you?'

Long dead. The ghost sighed. *Long, long gone.*

'The Skulls?'

Me. The eyeless ghost turned and looked up at the mountainside.

'Can you guide me?' Scott asked. 'Tell me? The hidden valley is here. I need to know the way.'

I see you, the ghost said. *I hear you. You know the words that will show you the way.*

'I'm not sure. Will you tell me?'

And be more damned? The man turned and faced the mountain, drew his sword, and fell on it again.

Scott backed away as the wraith turned black and melted into the ground. His flesh disappeared, bones weathered until they sank down, and even the metal sigils on his tunic rusted away to nothing. For a moment the scene was part of the real world, but then the ghost came into being again and started walking back towards the mountain. He did not turn around. Perhaps he had already forgotten that Scott was there, or maybe he had yet to find out.

Scott walked on, thinking about what the ghost had said, and Papa's strange sing-song words came back to him once again. He muttered them as he walked. They had never sounded right coming from a human mouth, and here in the silent valley they were like stains on time itself.

As he walked, he felt the very real sensation of moving from one place to the next.

To the north, between two of the low hills, a valley appeared.

Scott paused and sank to his knees. Behind him the old ghost was killing himself again, and before him was the valley containing the House of Screaming Skulls. Scott could not help but connect the two.

He had those signs tattooed into his skin, he thought. *Part of the ancient language used to write the Chord of Souls. Perhaps it spread. Maybe there always was more than just the book.* He touched the papers in his pocket, stood and started walking again.

The real world watched him leave.

When he came to a point where things changed, he paused. The new valley lay before him. A few steps ahead a road began. It was as though it had heaved itself from the soil, pushing up out of the ground, birthed from rock and mud and roots to provide a raised, level surface into the valley. There were drainage ditches on both sides. No road markings, no cats' eyes, no signs that it had ever been used. In places weeds had grown through, forcing open the compact surfacing and sprouting like hairy boils on an old woman's face. It curled its way into the valley, seeking the lowest points like a river, and disappeared into a hazy distance. The valley sides were streaked purple, green, and brown with heather and bracken. Rocky outcrops on the western hillsides hid shadows from the morning sun, while the eastern slopes were still in darkness. Trees grew here and there, and at a couple of places Scott thought he saw the glitter of waterfalls. Perhaps the road bridged the streams, but he could not tell from here. A few birds fluttered about, and not far away he saw the throats of rabbit holes. There were no cattle; indeed, no signs at all of this place ever having been touched by man, apart from the curving, relatively smooth road.

Things looked normal. But they felt all wrong.

This valley had not been here moments before. Or

rather, it had been here, but Scott had not muttered the words that would open up his perception and allow him access. This was a ghost road leading into a haunted valley, and he wondered why he could not yet see the dead.

He stepped forward a few paces until he stood on the road. Turning around, he suddenly expected to see that the true valley behind him had vanished, leaving only the blank paleness of the Wide. But he could still see the road perpendicular to this one, his car, and out in the field the sad shape of the wraith forever waiting. He was almost tempted to go back, climb into the car, and leave. For a moment even Helen felt distant, an old memory from three days before that he would eventually forget, like thirty-year-old dreams that occasionally came back to bite. But he could not go back; he knew that. Perhaps he never would. He had come so far and seen so much, and though he had yet to understand, he knew that he had changed for ever.

He started walking. And it was as if taking his steps into this valley made it aware of his presence.

The first ghost appeared in a field to his left. It was far away, but it immediately started walking towards him. He quickened his pace but soon realised that he could not avoid a meeting; the ghost flowed, shifting position wherever necessary to make sure their paths would eventually cross.

A second ghost materialised on the road far ahead, and then a third. The farther he walked, the more shapes emerged from nothing, taking form and converging on him.

I could turn and run! But he had a feeling that once out of this valley, he would be unlikely ever to find it again.

His heart beat faster as he slowed his pace. Even though the morning sun warmed the side of his face and neck, a cold chill clasped his spine. The ghost nearest to him was already close enough for him to see the tattoos on its face.

He stopped in the middle of the road. At his feet a spread of poppies had broken through the road surface, their delicate stems and brittle flowers using time to triumph over the compacted layers. He moved forward, careful not to tread on any of the blooms, concentrating so hard that he noticed the ghost only when he stepped into its embrace.

Scott cried out. For an instant before he stumbled back he felt all the pain, the loss, the anguish of this wandering soul. His arms pinwheeled as he struggled to maintain balance. He looked down and saw that he'd stepped on some poppies, and when he looked up again more ghosts were joining the first.

There were men and women, a couple of children, and they all bore those strange tattoos on much of their exposed skin. Face, necks, bald heads, arms, hands, legs…images and sigils he recognised as the language of the Chord of Souls. Their appearance here gave him no more clues as to what they meant.

They're like a living book, he thought, but of

course that was wrong. All these people were dead. Their bodies were probably long since rotted away, gone to dust and bone, all their experiences, loves, and losses faded with time. These sad echoes were all that was left, and Scott wondered how far each of them had made it across the Wide before becoming lost.

'Who are you?' he asked. The ghost near the car had spoken. A horrible sound, chilling, a voice from beyond the grave and between heaven and hell. But if they could tell him something that would take him one step closer to Helen, then he would suffer the fear. He would hear their words. 'Tell me,' he said.

The ghosts spoke in unison. *Go no farther.* It was a hundred times worse than the first ghost's voice, tearing into Scott's core, crawling through veins and bones until it reached the heart of him and punched him there. His heart fluttered like a trapped bird. He gasped, coughed, and went to his knees, looking down at a crushed poppy bloom.

'The Chord of Souls,' Scott said.

Go no farther. The whispers combined to make a voice like a hurricane.

'I have to find it,' Scott said, his own whisper directed at the ground. He stared at the crushed poppy because he did not want to look upon the ghosts. They reminded him of what he might be, and perhaps what Helen already was. 'I *need* it.'

The Chord is not for the living.

'Then who is it for?'

Not the dead.

'Not the living or the dead?' He wondered whether the poppy had a spirit of sorts, and if so, where he had sent it by stepping on the flower. Its crushed stem stained the road. The blooms were creased and ruined. If it was not already dead, then its potential for life had been wiped out.

No one…nothing…

'Who are you?' he asked, and then he looked up because he suddenly needed to know. The ghosts stood in a semicircle before him, several deep, blocking the road. There must have been forty of them. They wore a variety of clothes, from rough leather wraps to more modern garments. They were staring at him intently, never blinking. Some displayed wounds, others none. All of them had tattoos.

No one, they said.

'You have words from the book on your skin.'

They said nothing.

'Are you part of the book? A living part? Dead part?'

*No part. We tried to steal, to translate, but…*Their mouths hung open and moved, but the movements did not match the words. Each utterance seemed to freeze the air before them. Scott looked down and saw a fine frost on the road, dappling the crushed poppies white.

'I need to find the living book. I need to see it and know it. My wife is in the Wide and I must have her back.' A couple of the ghosts had seemed to flinch at the mention of the Wide, but they said nothing. They just stared. Perhaps they meant to be threatening. He stood. 'Are you going to stop me?' He walked forward.

The wraiths closest to him raised their hands, palms out, as if to ward him off. Scott kept walking, looking down as a hand and arm passed into his chest. *This is when I feel it clasp my heart*, he thought, but there was no sensation at all. He pressed on, squinting as if to lessen the amount of pain and distress he saw on those lost souls' faces. They did not move out of his way. If anything they bunched together, forming a barrier through which he would have to pass in order to continue. He paused, but only for a moment. *They're wisps of air*, he thought, *or even less. They're not here. They don't touch the world, don't affect it. They're just paintings on my imagination.*

He walked on, coming close to one woman's image, pressing face-to-face, pausing before passing right through.

Those ghosts back at the pub, holding Nina's door closed, keeping her in...

He saw nothing unusual inside the ghost's head, nothing but blankness. When he emerged he was faced with the head of another, and this time he did not pause.

They were holding the door closed, pushing through walls, and from the shouts it sounded as though they were restraining her. Holding her. Touching the world.

He passed through two more, and none of them moved aside. They started screaming. Each scream was timed with the next, so that it sounded like one massive cry emerging from a single source, misting the air with ice-cold condensation and forcing Scott to press his hands over his ears.

Someone must have been controlling them, just as Lewis controlled those ghosts outside my house. These… they're not controlled by anyone. The only thing that controls these is death.

He passed the final ghost and hurried along the road. The scream stopped immediately, echoing away to nothing against the valley slopes. Scott glanced back, afraid that he would be pursued, but the ghosts were motionless. They had turned their heads to look at him, every single one. In their eyes sat an accusation that they could not voice.

'I'm sorry,' he said. 'I don't know what you lost, or when, but I can't afford to lose any more. I have to find my wife.'

A little girl emerged from the group of phantoms. She walked quickly towards Scott and paused a few steps away. In life she must have been very pretty, but death gave her only coldness and a strange, unsettling hunger. *If she's in the Wide, she's lost.*

'No. She's being held there. He knows where she is, the person holding her. And he'll give her back to me.'

The Wide is the universe.

'Why have you got those tattoos on your skin?'

The girl looked sad. *We thought they were part of the word.*

'What word?'

The girl blinked and ghost tears fell.

'The word of God?'

She blinked again. Then she turned and walked back to the ghosts, disappearing between their legs and bodies, merging with them until she was nowhere to be seen.

'Why are you all trapped here?' Scott still did not understand. Why could one dead soul find its way across the Wide, and so many others become lost? Was it all to do with faith, or physics?

'Fuck this.' He turned his back on the ghosts and walked on.

Be warned, they said, a final stormy outburst that raised the hairs on his neck and set his balls crawling. He turned to ask them why, but he was just in time to see the spirits spreading out from the road, crossing the fields, and disappearing into sunlight or shadow.

Chapter Thirteen

sigh in a hurricane

The ghost road was empty of ghosts, yet it was still haunted. Scott stayed to the centre of the road, and with every step he sensed more and more that this entire place was redolent with the past. Trees looked real, but could also have been the image of every tree that had ever grown. The hills appeared timeless, yet there was something about the way the air smelt, the sunlight hit the ground, the breeze played with his hair, that set Scott thinking. If he had seen this place only after first muttering words from the Chord of Souls, then surely the two were irrevocably tied together? This was more than just a hiding place for that book.

This was its home.

The road curved around a rocky deposit in the centre of the valley – a small hill topped with a sprouting of trees – and as he skirted the hill he saw the body beside the road.

He paused, waiting for it to stand and perform

some sad, repetitive act of suicide. It did not move. He walked closer, picking his steps carefully through another spread of wild poppies growing across the road like spattered blood. When he reached the corpse, Scott stood still for a long time, staring down at its face and wondering what he was supposed to do.

The woman had been dead for some time, yet the dry, cold air here had held back the rot. Her clothes – modern leathers, belts, and clasps – had sunk around her as her flesh dried and shrank. Her face was drawn, eyes little more than pips in their sockets. *Why hasn't anything eaten her?* Scott thought. He had seen birds and insects, and had heard larger things moving out in the fields. But nothing had planted eggs, taken bites out of her flesh, nibbled at her fingers, or pecked out her eyes.

'Go,' Scott said. 'Fade away.' He reached out to touch her, drew back. She looked like no ghost he had ever seen. They usually seemed to represent the owner's soul at the time of death, either directly before or straight after their time on earth had ended. Sometimes they repeated the final seconds of their life, as if trying to rectify a flawed performance. Other times they just wandered around being wretched.

He looked into her eyes, but there was nothing to see in those dried-up things.

He reached out again and touched her jacket. It was real. The leather was hard and dried by the wind, but it was solid beneath his fingers. He shoved, increasing the pressure until the body shifted with a crack and crackle. It had been here for a long time.

Scott looked around, wondering whether this woman's soul was another lost one. 'I hope you made it across the Wide,' he said. 'I hope you found it and crossed over to whatever's on the other side.' He touched the skin of her face, tracing one of the tattoos as though reading in Braille.

The ghost rose from its corpse, screaming.

Scott backed away, a small moan escaping him.

The wraith stood – feet still planted in its corpse's boots – turned around, and looked down at its dead self. It screamed again. Its hands went to its face and held it, covering its eyes and trying to shut out the light.

The scream was more real than anything Scott had yet heard from a ghost.

'Are you him?' she said, turning to look directly at Scott.

'No, no, I'm just…' He trailed off, and the ghost glared at him.

'You *must* be him. You're here. Alive. You *have* to be.'

'I'm sorry,' Scott said.

'Then why are you here?'

'Why do you seem alive?' Scott asked. 'I've seen a hundred ghosts over the past couple of days, but you're talking, asking questions. Reasoning.'

'Reasoning,' the ghost said, glancing back and

down at the body it had once inhabited. 'How reasonable is that?'

Scott shook his head, not knowing what to say.

'So, why are you here? This is a ghost road in a ghost valley. We're locked away in here. We have to be. We can't let just anyone—'

'I'm here looking for the House of Screaming Skulls,' Scott said.

'Why?'

'There's something there I want.'

'Why do you want the Chord?'

'Then it *is* there!'

'Why?'

'To free my wife. And destroy it.'

The ghost lowered its head sadly, looking down at where its feet touched those slowly mummifying in their shoes. 'A selfish act, as ever.'

'No, no. I want to destroy it. I'm told it has to be destroyed. I've already crushed part of it to dust.'

The ghost whirled on Scott, eschewing contact with its body to move across and stand face-to-face. 'You found the Lost Pages?'

'I did.'

'And…?'

'They're gone.'

The ghostly woman stared at him, reached out, and placed her hand on his forehead. He almost felt her fingers touching him…almost. Perhaps it was subconscious.

She smiled. It was grotesque, a smile belonging

to no human, dead or otherwise. Then she cackled. 'You might really be the one,' she said.

'The one?'

'The one to touch the book. Come with me.'

'But—'

The woman grabbed him. Her right hand sank into the flesh of his arm; she grunted as she exerted great will, and then she turned and started running along the road. He ran with her because he had to; her hand had formed itself around his bicep, crushing the skin and clasping hard enough to cause instant bruising.

'We'll travel soon,' she said.

'Travel?'

'Not long now. Oh, dear sweet fucking heaven and hell, not long now!'

She had left her body behind without a backward glance, and it was only then – stupidly, crazily – that Scott realised that this ghost wore no tattoos.

'What are you?' he said.

The woman did not turn. She ran on, hand clasped around his arm, her feet making a greater impact noise every time they hit the road. She seemed to be forming with every step they took, becoming more solid, and he wondered how something dead could suddenly seem so alive.

'Not dead,' she said. 'That's what I am: not dead. Old. Very, very old. But soon that age will be nothing.'

'But—'

'Shut up. Follow.' She squeezed his arm harder, eliciting a scream of agony that almost made him pass out. But she dragged him upright and slapped him across the face with her free hand. It felt very real indeed.

Scott realised with a jolt that she must be one of the missing immortals. Perhaps she had been waiting here for ever.

'A hop, skip, and jump,' she said, skidding to a halt close to an ancient ruin. It was the first sign of habitation that Scott had seen, apart from the road. One wall was all that remained, an arched doorway at its centre, and all around its base were the tumbled stones of the rest of the building.

'A church?' he asked, and that seemed to cause much amusement to the woman. She laughed so hard that she had to bend down, holding her stomach, yet never letting go of Scott for an instant.

'A church!' She gasped through tears of mirth. 'That's a good one. Good one!' She calmed herself and started mumbling. Scott knew the sound of those words.

He also knew the nature of the light appearing in the ruin's doorway.

A pale, even light, sickly grey. The way to somewhere else.

'Hop, skip, and jump,' she said again. 'Come on.'

She dragged Scott towards the doorway. There was nothing he could do but follow.

* * *

They went into the Wide, but it was not like the first time with Nina. She had carried him in, easing him through the veils that separated this world from the next – thin veils in places, but defying time and reason nonetheless – and guided him across the boundary of that endless place. She had protected him, trying to make the trip as comfortable and as easy as possible. It had been awful.

Now, they burst through the doorway the woman had created and emerged deep in the Wide. There was no preamble, no prelude to their arrival, no warning: one second she was dragging him across that strange ghost road towards the ruined archway; the next he had left the world entirely.

Scott's heart stopped. He gasped: there was no pain, but the sudden absence of something barely acknowledged was a shock.

The woman dragged him across a wide expanse of nothingness, and the sense of space around them was heavy, intimidating, threatening. When he was a child, Scott had dreamt a particular dream whenever he was ill. He had found it very difficult to explain when he woke up, but it terrified him, and chased him from sleep with the mockery of something knowing it could never be changed or understood. There was something about space in there, a great, crushing expanse of potential pain that crowded in at him where he stood on top of an impossible hill. The hill was split in two by a giant wound, stitched here and there, but still gaping to show its horrible insides. The threat that this stitching would break at any second was every bit as frightening as the weight of space around him. Pressure from below, pressure from above, and he was dwarfed by it, compressed to nothing resembling a living thing. He was a grain of sand, a spit in an ocean, a sigh in a hurricane, and every single instant of that dream threatened him with becoming utterly lost.

Upon screaming himself awake he had usually found his parents with him, cooing and soothing and not understanding anything he had to say about the hill, and the sky, and the held breath of that place waiting to blow him away.

Papa had understood. He'd been there twice when Scott awoke, and both times he had seemed more relieved than Scott to see the boy rising from sleep with only tears to dab away. *That's no good place to be,* Papa had said, and Scott had buried his face in Papa's familiar-smelling shirt.

This is no good place to be, Scott tried to say now, but his breath had left him. No heartbeat, no breath, and he opened his eyes to fight against whatever was happening.

He could not move. The woman dragged him through the space, and for as far as Scott could see there were spirits standing motionless, too lost even to drift around anymore. They wailed, and their cries formed in the air around them like smoke above a battlefield. He could smell their torment.

I'm not going to be like that, he thought. He

fought. He raged against the darkness and strove towards the light. He kept Helen in his mind, because she was in here, somewhere, a prisoner of Lewis, and when the idea was spawned that she was already one of these lost souls, he shoved it aside, refusing even to accept the possibility.

No! he shouted, voice silent, but the notion all there. His heart thumped and he smiled in delight.

The woman looked back and grinned. There was only pure madness there, an age-old insanity that recognised a change closing in.

And then her grin began to fade.

Scott struggled to free himself. It felt as though her hand had merged with his flesh. There was no blood, but surely his skin must be pierced, the meat of him crushed and parted?

The woman began to scowl. They moved onward and she looked back, and anger flooded her eyes.

Scott averted his gaze, but there was nowhere else to look. If he looked beyond this strange woman into the Wide he felt sick; his insides churned and tumbled, and he fell a thousand feet in a second. So he stared back, and it was then that he realised she was no longer looking at him. She was looking past him, back the way they had come. And she was furious.

Scott tried to turn, but all the forces acting on him felt wrong. When he went to turn his head, his hand flexed. If he tried to move his toes, his shoulders tensed. He blinked his eyes and sniffed, and he smelt time rotting away to nothing.

He thought that if this ride continued for much longer, the woman may as well leave him here. He would be dead, lost, doomed to wander the Wide for ever, and for ever wondering whether Helen was still alive.

The Wide began to darken. Scott closed his eyes and his senses screeched as input hit him once again. He struck a hard surface, smelt age and mould, heard the impact of his body against stone, tasted blood as he bit down on his tongue, and then there was a long, high scream from somewhere above him, and the next taste in his mouth was someone else's blood.

Before now, Scott had only ever tasted his own blood. This new blood was stale, sickly, rancid. It smelt bad. Perhaps the blood of all immortals was like this.

He rolled onto his side, sat up, and looked around. He was sitting on a large paved area in front of a tall, wide house. The house had three stories, and each story held eight windows across its length. The facade was otherwise bland and unremarkable: bare stone, no ostentatious features or aesthetic flourishes. There was an arched doorway, and some of the windows on the top floor were fronted by small cast-iron balconies. Several of the windows were open, curtains billowing. He could not tell whether or not anyone watched from inside.

The woman who had dragged him here through

the Wide was sprawled on the patio a dozen steps from him. Tigre stood over her, legs planted wide, brandishing a short sword in each hand. The side of his head glittered with blood, but it was not his own.

The woman was gashed in a dozen places. Blood spewed from her wounds, finding the natural low points of the patio. The stone was sun-bleached, and the blood formed strange, squared patterns on the ground.

'I thought I'd lost you for sure,' a voice said.

Scott turned and saw Nina standing a few steps behind him. She was shaking. Sweating. Her eyes looked watery, those eyes usually so dark and unreadable. 'Someone told me you'd kill me,' he said.

'Who?'

'I'm not really sure. Not anymore. I thought maybe it was Lewis, but then I met her...' He nodded across at the slumped shape. The woman started moving, pulling an almost-severed arm back against her chest, raising her head so that blood-soaked hair drooped heavily to the ground.

Tigre lashed out with his swords. They made meaty impacts as they penetrated flesh and struck bone. He stood on her back and forced her down as he withdrew the swords. More blood flowed, and she was still once more.

Scott flinched away, turned to look at Nina. 'Why is he doing that?'

'It's what he does.'

'But who is she?'

'We think she's Yaima. One of us. One of the originals.'

'An immortal,' Scott said, stupidly pleased that he had been right.

'I haven't seen her for six thousand years,' Tigre muttered. He knelt beside the tattered body and thrust his sword deep into her chest. 'Her heart's still strong, Nina. Want to collect?'

'Are you OK?' Nina ignored Tigre, seeming genuinely concerned as she knelt beside Scott and touched his face.

'I'm really not sure.' He glanced up at the house. Was that a face he saw at one of the windows, stepping back into shadow as he looked? 'I don't think so.'

'She was brutal with you,' Nina said. 'She didn't care. Straight into the Wide, and that's just not right. That's no place for you to be.'

'You took me there.'

'I was careful.'

He remembered the time Nina had taken him through, and compared it with the trip he had just survived. And he nodded, because she was right. Before he had come out feeling disconcerted and upset; now…he was utterly unnerved.

'Why did you run?' she asked.

'I thought you wanted to kill me.' He looked at her carefully, trying to read her reaction. She'd had a long time to practice hiding her feelings.

'Why would I possibly want to kill you?' Nina said.

'Why wouldn't you?'

Nina shook her head, confused. 'I don't understand the question.'

'I don't understand any of this, but I have to because of Helen. So when I start getting messages that warn me away from you, what am I supposed to do?'

'Talk to me about it.'

'I don't know you!'

'So therefore you don't trust me?'

'You're just the immortal who happened to visit me, and who happens to have taken me with you. It could just as easily have been her.' He pointed at the woman squirming on the ground. 'Or him.'

Tigre glared at Scott, his expression hard with scar tissue.

'Just because I'm immortal, that doesn't mean I'm inhuman,' Nina said.

Scott snorted and turned away, but there'd been something in her voice that struck a chord. After all, out of the immortals he had met so far, she was the most like him. She smiled and laughed, felt pain, and suffered the sting of loneliness.

Scott stared up at the house, wondering which windows hid faces and which hid something else. It was a haunted house; that much was clear. It stood in a valley hidden away behind the veil dividing the world from everything else. Perhaps it had been here for ever. And inside could lie his salvation.

Save us, he had seen the silent ghosts mouthing at him. *Help us.*

'So whom do I trust?' he asked, still looking at the house. He heard movement behind him, felt Nina's hand on his shoulder.

'I promise you I'm on your side,' she said.

'Why me? What am I? I know it's not just Papa, not just because of him. I'm something more, aren't I?'

'You're mortal, unchanged by the book's contents. You can *touch* it. To the likes of us, it's as ghostlike as the truly dead. We can't touch it, can barely see it, and being around it...'

'What?'

'It was horrible,' Nina said, and Scott knew that she was telling the truth.

Tears burnt behind his eyes, and he was not sad that his vision blurred. Nina came in close until all he could see was her face. 'So what happens now?' he asked. 'What do I have to do?'

Nina looked over his shoulder at the house. 'Let's knock on the door and see what answers.'

Chapter Fourteen

fabled screams

This was the House of Screaming Skulls. Papa and Scott had read about it and seen obscure mentions on late-night TV, but Scott had never believed he would ever find himself here. It was fabled, like Oz or Atlantis. A place of the world, but not within it. A story.

He rapped his knuckles against the door. There was no echo, as he had expected. There was barely any sound at all. He knocked again.

Nina stood beside him, while Tigre hung back. He had sliced the woman in two across her chest and kicked her halves apart, smearing viscera and blood across the concrete area. Since then, Scott had tried not to look at her. But he could hear wet, sticky movement behind him as she tried to rejoin herself, and her gargled threats, which were sounding more malevolent with every heartbeat.

He knocked again. Nina shifted impatiently beside him. Glancing at her, he noticed her extreme discomfort for the first time. She was sweating, blinking quickly, and her breath came in short, fast gasps. He looked around at Tigre, but the mutilated man's face remained a feature of fights and violence.

'Maybe no one's home,' Scott said. 'Who'd want to live here? Local pub must be miles away. And imagine having to clean all these windows.' He looked at the facade rising above and around him, jumped when a light curtain billowed from one of the windows. There was no breeze outside to cause that; maybe the air inside was being disrupted. 'What's in here?'

'Nobody knows,' Nina said. 'As far as I know, no one has ever been inside.'

'No one?'

She shrugged.

'Great,' Scott said. 'Great.'

'Move aside,' Tigre said. 'Let me open the door.' He hefted his bloody swords and stepped forward.

The front door clicked and opened a hand's width.

Scott stepped back. Nina remained where she was, but her shoulders tensed, hands fisted.

The air shifted slightly, as if the house were exhaling past them. It smelt stale and musty, and it carried the taint of an abandoned abattoir: no fresh blood, but plenty of deathly echoes.

'I don't like this place,' Scott said.

'The book,' Nina said, and there was wonder in her voice.

'It really is here.' Tigre stepped forward and put a hand on Nina's shoulder, squeezing slightly. 'It really is here!' Then he turned to Scott. 'Ready to help, human?'

Every nerve in Scott's body, every part of his mind, told him to turn and run. *It's a brain*, he thought, and though the idea repulsed him, he could not shake it. *A brain, a mind, a consciousness without a soul. And it's barren.*

'I'm not sure I can,' he said.

'Helen,' Nina breathed. 'She's out there, where you've just been. So lost. And the only way I can help you get her back—'

'I'll go,' Scott said. 'Of course I'll go. But it's not a house.'

Nina shook her head. 'Never thought it was.'

Tigre laughed. It was a gruesome sound, yet so unexpected that it lifted Scott's spirits. 'If it'll make you feel any better, I'll go first.' He sheathed the swords and pulled a dull black object from a holster on his hip. 'People used to call me Death,' he said. 'It's all I've ever wanted.' He stepped to the door and kicked it open all the way.

Inside the house, out of the sun, they could have been anywhere. The entrance hallway was large and grand, but possessed a depressing taint of age. It was like a great country house that had fallen into disrepair, a mansion whose better times were decades or centuries in the past. It was a place way past its prime. Perhaps it had always looked this way.

The floor was laid with massive marble slabs, six feet square. The centres of these slabs retained their beauty, but the edges were dulled and darkened with moisture penetration. There were rugs here and there, most of them threadbare, and their colours bled pale, a couple bearing black-edged holes as if they had been burnt. The walls were lined with dark timber all around, pocked here and there with doorways. Every door seemed to be closed. A staircase began in the centre of the hallway fifteen steps in, rising straight up, then splitting and curving to the left and right. The balustrade was ornately carved, the treads inlaid with individual carpet squares, the risers painted with elaborate representations of what appeared to be hunting scenes. The walls were also decorated with paintings, though much of what they depicted was hidden by a heavy sheen of dust and dirt that had accumulated over the centuries.

Some areas seemed to have been cleaned, and others had been left to gather time.

One strange affectation was a stag's head, mounted at the first stair landing where the separate stairways curved left and right. It was huge, the antlers long and convoluted, though their ends had turned dark and crumbled to dust. Its eyes glittered with reflected light. Scott stared at it, fully expecting it to blink.

Living up to his promise, Tigre went first. He moved forward across the marble floor, pausing when he stood on the first rug. He held the machine pistol down beside his leg, its short barrel resembling an extended finger. Scott hoped he was ready to point at the first hint of danger. *I can die; they can't,* he kept thinking. But he was trying to convince himself that he was in a position of power. If he died, they would not find the book, nor be able to read the words they had written so long ago and now forgotten. It was in their interests to protect him.

'Strange,' Tigre said. He moved a few more steps, then stopped again, standing on the next rug. He lifted one foot, then the other, looking around as he did so. 'Illusion,' he said.

'All of it?' Nina asked.

'Some.' He walked on.

'What does he mean?' Scott asked.

'The house isn't really here.'

Scott moved sideways and placed his hand against the wood panelling. It was cool and rough, spiky with hardened varnish spots. When he rubbed his hand across its surface it scratched his skin, tickled his fingertips. 'It feels real to me,' he said.

Nina glanced back and shrugged. 'Come on.' She followed Tigre, and Scott hurried to keep up.

They headed for the foot of the staircase. As they came closer, Scott could make out details on the painted risers. Starting from the first one, the pictures seemed to tell a story: a chase, a hunt, a kill, and farther upstairs there looked like revelry and celebration.

There were very few humans in the pictures.

'My God, what are those?' he whispered. The main figures in the paintings were tall, cloaked creatures with muscled arms and chests, and bare skulls atop their shoulders. Some of the skulls still carried shreds of bright red meat, and one or two still had shrivelled eyes in their sockets. But most were skeletal from the neck up, the sliced surface of their necks blackened with hardened blood.

'Screaming Skulls,' Nina said.

'But they're not real, right? Not like that?'

Again, she only shrugged.

'Around here,' Tigre said.

'Yes, I think so too,' Nina said. There was a quaver to her voice, and for a moment Scott thought someone else had spoken. He reached out and clasped Nina's shoulder, and she turned to look at him. Her eyes were wide and frightened. Her face was pale and spotted with beads of sweat. The house was cool.

'What is it?'

'The Chord of Souls is very close,' she said. 'It's a ghost to us, but it's like poison also. We're breathing its air. Invading its space.'

'And Tigre?'

'He just can't show the pain.'

'Do you think—'

'We need to move on, Scott. We're so close. Helen, remember? All for Helen.'

Helen, he thought. He remembered her face, and for that he was glad. He remembered her voice and her smell, the touch of her lips against his neck and her hand on his thigh. He could remember all of that, and the memory had the power and immediacy of one that would be lived again. 'We'll do this,' he said. 'We will.'

A voice shouted out behind them. It was pained and distorted, but loud enough to make Scott jump.

'They're here for the book!' it said. 'They're going to destroy the book! Smash it, crush it, make it into dust!'

Scott and the others spun around, Tigre dropping to one knee and raising the gun.

The door stood open, and bleeding in through the entrance was Yaima. She had dragged her upper body across the forecourt and up the steps to the door, and now her bodily fluids added to the moisture permeating the old marble slabs. She was raised on one hand, face held high, and there was a frightening clarity to her expression as she stared at Scott. 'And they have a human!' she bellowed.

The air exploded around Scott and he curled up on the floor. Tigre stood and fired another burst from the machine pistol, and when Scott looked again the woman was lying against the open door, her head shattered. Blood settled around her in a fine mist. Sunlight glimmered on the spread of brain matter spattered against the door, nestling in fresh bullet holes and slowly running down to the ground. All parts of her seemed to be drawing together, obeying some incredible attraction that would seek to rebuild her tattered form.

'So much for the element of surprise,' Scott said, and then the screams came down around them.

He had never heard a sound like it. They started as normal cries, then rose in volume and tone until they were something more, something almost solid that sliced through the air and penetrated his skull, twisting inside his ears like poisonous insects seeking escape. He clapped his hands to his ears but it had no effect; the screams were already inside. They echoed in his skull. They pierced his flesh and resonated through his bones, vibrating each joint until it felt as if his whole skeleton were readying to burst apart.

He screamed himself, but the sound was lost. He fell to his knees, bruising them on the marble floor – it was still there, though Tigre had claimed the house to be illusory. Something tumbled into him and he saw Nina, her body twisting and face contorted with the same pain.

Tigre stood before them, legs shaking, scarred flesh vibrating, either from the noise or the fear it instilled. His arm rose. He was fighting, struggling to maintain control, railing against the onslaught of sound that came at them again and again in solid waves.

The screams went on. Scott was beginning to lose hold of his senses. Hearing was still there, torturing him with its honesty, but his sight was wavering, and though he opened his mouth to shout he could not utter a word.

Tigre clasped his right wrist in his left hand and raised it, pointing the machine pistol past the staircase at the shadows beyond.

And in those shadows…

The pictures on the stair risers had come to life. A dozen shapes emerged and manifested as the Screaming Skulls, flowing slowly, long robes tied open around their shoulders and falling down to pool on the floor around their feet. Their arms were bare, muscled, pale, and mottled with flowery blood-red spots. Their chests and stomachs were exposed; similarly muscled, they flexed and squirmed as though containing a thousand lizards and snakes trying to escape.

Their heads were skulls. They wore wide necklaces of dried, caked blood, extending down from the limit of their flesh and flowing across their chests and shoulders. Above the necks, bones had been stripped clear of all flesh. The skulls were yellow, like bones left out in the sun for too long. None of them had any scraps of flesh remaining, eyes in the sockets, or mummified scalps. They were all hairless. Most still had teeth, though there were also many gaps.

Their mouths hung open as they screamed.

Tigre's machine pistol spit fire for a couple of seconds before falling empty. Three of the Screaming Skulls staggered back, clasping big hands to the wounds in their chests and arms. Then they stood upright again, and their mouths opened once more to add to the cacophony.

Tigre shook his head and stepped back, blood flowing from his mouth. His hands moved expertly as he swapped magazines and fired again. Bullets slammed home in one Skull's stomach and sent it folding to the floor. Tigre raised the gun and fired at exposed bone, but the bullets ricocheted, splintering the staircase banister and exploding plaster dust from the ceiling.

Nina stepped forward and kicked out at one of the Skulls. It fell over and its scream ceased for a few seconds, but it was soon on its feet again, helped by the figure Tigre had shot. Their screams recommenced.

Scott had taken his hands away from his ears. The pain was still intense and shocking, but if he wasn't to curl up and die here, he had to move.

He had no idea what he could do. He stared at the grinning faces of these monstrous things, watched Tigre shoot them down to the ground, saw them haul themselves or one another back to their feet and advance some more.

They were slow, but what did speed matter when they could not be stopped?

Nina came to him and cupped her hands around his left ear. Even shouting, she could barely be heard above their shrieks.

'Go farther. Go *deeper*. Find the book! And when you do, stay with it. I'll come.'

'How can you…?' he started to say, but she pulled back and shook her head. She looked weak and uneasy, and he knew it was not all from the effects of the Screaming Skull's cries. She jerked her head behind her, urging him to go.

He looked. He would have to pass these things… unless he went upstairs. Tigre and Nina had been certain that the book was beyond the staircase, but in a place this size there had to be another way down.

Tigre's gun spit lead for another few seconds, and several of the Skulls staggered back and fell. Most of them rolled and twisted back to their feet, but one stayed down, hands clutching its stomach. It was still moving. It turned its head, and its empty eye sockets fixed on him.

Scott dashed to the right and headed for the foot of the stairs.

A Skull appeared before him, sliding into view across the marble floor. It faced him and screamed, and the proximity seemed to amplify its effect. Scott went to his knees and fell forward, reaching out and touching the first of the stair risers. The Skull bent down and moved its face closer to his, mouth agape, blackened teeth promising unknown pain were they to connect with his very real, very human flesh.

A foot connected with the side of the Skull's head and it spun, striking the floor on its side and flailing its limbs as it tried to stand again. Nina grimaced at him, jerked her head towards the shadows behind the staircase. *Go,* she was saying, but Scott already had his plan, and in a spur-of-the-moment decision he decided to stick with it.

He stood, leapt over the sprawled Skull, and sprinted up the staircase.

The tone of the screams changed. He thought the volume had increased, but glancing back he realised that it was because every Screaming Skull was now looking up at him.

They started rushing for the stairs.

Tigre opened up again, cutting several of them down, standing astride one of the fallen and emptying the magazine into its chest. When he turned, reaching into the small bag over his shoulder for another magazine, the thing below him reached out and tripped him. Then it sat up, pale orange dust spewing from the holes across its body.

Scott ran. He did not think about direction or purpose. Where the staircase split he headed left on a whim, glancing up at the huge stag head guarding the way. It gave him no clues. He knew that the Skulls were following him; their screams cut in like heated knives, their footsteps transmitting through the stairs to meet his own. Tigre's gun fired again, there was the sound of metal on metal, Nina shouted, and then he found himself faced with the entrance to two corridors. One led left, the other at a right angle led deeper into the house. He chose that one.

There was a set of doors into the corridor, blocked open by objects that had lost their shape with webs and dust. He kicked them aside – dust clouded, piled books scattered across the floor – and turned to slam the doors.

The Screaming Skulls bore down on him. They moved unnaturally, flowing rather than running, as though they were not quite a true part of the scene. *Not ghosts*, he thought, and they confirmed that by slamming against the closed doors. He turned a big, ornate key, and something gave a satisfying click.

The doors would not hold for long. He ran.

Not ghosts, but not here either. Bullets punch holes in them and dust comes out. No brains, no minds...

More gunfire, more clanging of metal. He heard heavy footsteps on the stairs, and hoped that Tigre and Nina were coming this way as well.

The book is here, he thought. *Below me, deeper down, so Nina said. And that immortal, dragging half of herself to the door like that:* And they have a human! *she shouted.*

He ducked left into a side corridor, then right into an open space with a large table piled with books, faded tapestries on the walls, and two doors in each wall to choose from.

Only I can touch the book.

He wondered what the books on the table might contain, and whether any of them may be useful. Tigre had called the house an illusion, but Scott was not so sure. Perhaps it was convenient that a book such as the Chord of Souls would be hidden in a place like this, but if it was an illusion, why not have it perfect? Wallpaper hung from the walls, lath-and-plaster ceilings dipped heavy with damp and rot, and all the riches this place had once contained were now faded and holed.

It didn't matter.

He looked at one of the tapestries. It depicted a fight, and the two things fighting were like nothing he had ever seen before. They had arms and legs, muscles and skin and hair, but beyond that he could not identify them. They were difficult to look at. *Angels and demons,* he thought, and the idea did not sit well.

He heard the Skulls running through the house, screeching louder each time they turned a corner and found only more shadows.

Scott had to choose a door. He did not think too hard, just stepped forward and reached out for a handle. He thought this route would take him deeper into the house. Beyond the door was a short corridor, ending at the head of a tightly curving staircase. 'Down,' he said. That seemed right.

He shut the door behind him, frustrated when he found there was no lock.

There were no longer any windows. He looked around but could perceive no obvious light source. It was much like the Wide, evenly lit from nowhere. That gave him no comfort at all.

The staircase was steep, its treads cast from stone, worn into shallow dips by centuries of feet. The walls were rough-cast plaster, any paint long since flaked away to reveal the paleness beneath. Scott started to descend, counting the steps as he went. He held on to the central pillar, running his other hand along the curving wall, wishing that there were a handrail. The stairs were narrow and tight, and he could see only a few steps ahead.

He paused after eighteen steps. *Should be on the ground floor again by now*, he thought. He opened his mouth and breathed lightly, listening for any sounds of pursuit. He could still hear the Screaming Skulls' piercing shrieks, but they were in the distance, muffled by floors, walls, and the spaces in between.

There were no other sounds. The door at the end of the corridor above remained closed, while whatever lay at the base of the staircase offered no clues.

Scott continued down. *So close to the book. So where is Lewis? And what really happens when I find it?*

There were so many unknowns. Nina and Tigre claimed they wanted to read the book only to discover how to die. Lewis wanted it in exchange for Helen. Old Man wanted it for knowledge. How to achieve any of these aims, Scott had no idea.

He moved on, descending slowly and pausing every few steps to listen.

When he had counted thirty steps he stopped again, looking back the way he had come. He must surely be below ground level now, yet still the staircase went on. Perhaps he had gotten lucky and the book was down here. But if that were the case, surely it would be guarded?

The staircase ended without warning. There was a room, and Scott recognised it. There were two people here, and he recognised them as well. They were sitting at a table, sharing a weekend broadsheet paper and all the extras that invariably accompanied it. They looked quite happy and content. They did not look very old.

'Mum?' he said. 'Dad?'

They looked up, and they were not pleased to see him.

'Scott,' his father said. 'You been out with that crazy old fuck again?'

'That's my father you're talking about!' his mother said, but she spoke with half a smile.

'Well, he's still crazy,' his father said. 'Remember that time with the dominoes?'

Scott's mother laughed. 'Yeah, there is that. You're right. Crazy fuck. And speaking of which…' She stood quickly, sending her chair tumbling, and pulled off her blouse. Her heavy breasts swung free.

'Mum,' Scott said, blinking. 'Dad?'

'Stay away from that old prick,' his father said. 'He'll bring you nothing but trouble. Just look at you now!' He also stood, unzipping his trousers and releasing his erect penis. He stroked its end and smiled at Scott's mother.

She turned to Scott, rucking her skirt up around her hips. 'Yes, just look at you. Trouble all around.

And it's all his fault.' She glanced over her shoulder, bending and offering herself. 'Dad's fault.' Scott's father positioned himself behind her, looking down. He thrust forward, and she screeched. She looked at Scott again, her eyes half-closed and hair swinging with each thrust. 'Crazy, crazy fuck,' she said, but now she seemed to be talking to herself.

'You're not real!' Scott said. 'You're not even ghosts!'

'You don't believe in ghosts, do you, son?' his father said. His voice was distorted by grunts.

Scott closed his eyes and walked forward. 'Not real,' he said. 'It's this house playing with me. It can't have me, so it's playing with me.' His legs hit a table, and he heard a cry between pleasure and pain fade away into some unimaginable distance. 'I love you, Mum and Dad.'

When he opened his eyes the room was empty. No table, no chairs, no decor, just bare walls and a rough concrete floor. Scott sighed. It had seemed so real, and he knew he had to shed it as a memory.

'What the hell was that?' he whispered. The words echoed back at him, making him more confused than ever.

There was a sound behind him. It had come from the mouth of the spiral staircase. A crafty footstep falling too hard, followed by the panicked shuffling of someone trying to fall silent.

He moved across the room to the door. It was heavy and functional, an unpainted timber-framed and braced door with iron hinges and a chunky lock and handle. *It'll be locked; it'll be locked, and I'll have to go back up those stairs.* He touched the handle. It was warm. *It'll be locked and—*

The sound came again, a secretive rustling. It seemed closer. Sound would carry well down the funnel of the staircase, but it could also mean that whatever pursued him was nearing the bottom.

He heard its breathing: quick, panicked. Or fast and hungry.

Scott turned the handle and the door opened. The hinges were surprisingly silent. He emerged into another long corridor, bathed in the same even light as the rest of the house. *I'm below the building now,* he thought. *Way below. Deeper. Perhaps in an older version of the house.*

Papa stood halfway along the corridor.

'Papa?' Scott said. He closed the door behind him. The old man smiled just the way Scott had always remembered.

'Little cunt,' Papa said.

Scott shook his head and closed his eyes. 'Not there,' he said. When he looked again his grandfather was walking towards him.

'Little *cunt*! You think I really loved you? You think I'd send you a message from the grave, when you were so useless you could barely mutter your own name?'

'I know you're not there,' Scott said. 'And if you are, then you're not really Papa.' The vision grinned.

'You're one of *them*' Scott pointed behind him. 'So show me your skull, and scream if you think it can hurt me more.'

'I gave you everything I knew, and you never even realised it,' Papa said quietly, and his voice grew sad. 'All that potential I planted in you. All the power I offered. And look at you. What do you do? What's the point in you? You take up space; that's all. You're a waste of air. Remove you, and there's no effect on anyone, because you're *nothing*.'

'I love you, Papa,' Scott said, and he smiled at what the image represented. His smile saw past the false face and twisted words.

'Love? Little shit. Don't you fucking dare try…' Papa faded away, carrying the bitter voice with him. The corridor was empty once more.

'Try if you have to,' Scott said. 'I know who I am. And I know the people I love.' He walked on, finding fresh confidence in his defiance of these hallucinations. The house was playing with him. But why? Did it – or the Screaming Skulls – really think a few nasty visions would make him turn back?

The corridor's concrete floor turned to dirt, and the rendered walls became naked rock. The light remained level; its source was still mysterious, but its effect negated shadows. That was good. Anything could hide in shadows, and Scott was coming to believe that everything did.

He could make out tool marks in the stone walls. That meant that the tunnel had been carved out of the ground. There were drifts of stone shards and dust piled where the floor met the wall, and he shifted one pile, wondering what he would find. It hid nothing. Perhaps it had been there for thousands of years.

He walked a dozen more steps, then turned around. He was now in a cave, looking back along a tunnel that turned a corridor. This felt like a barrier that had to be passed, a changing point in his quest, and he had crossed it willingly.

The heavy door handle at the end of the corridor began to dip.

Scott turned and ran. The tunnel split and he took the left fork. (*Always go left,* Papa had said; *in a maze, always turn left.*)

'Scott!' To begin with he thought it was Nina. The turn in the tunnel hid his line of sight, so he went back the way he had come.

Should be running away, not toward. But something about that voice…

'Scott?'

That's not Nina.

'Scott.' There was defeat there, and wretchedness, and he had never heard Helen sound like that in all their time together.

'Helen?' He rounded the split in the tunnel and looked back towards the door, and there she stood, Helen, his wife and love. She looked totally defeated, even when she looked up at him. She smiled – she *grinned* – but seemed somehow reduced. 'That's not you,' he said. And he turned to walk away.

'*Scott?*' She screamed his name, and she was already running at him when he turned back.

'You're not…' he said, but then he frowned. *My wife? Is that my wife? I'd know her anywhere…but this is nowhere.*

'Oh, babe,' she said, voice jarring with the impact of her feet against the dirt floor. She was out of the corridor now and into the tunnel, her arms stretched out for him, and as he realised for certain that he would *always* know his wife – and this was her – the door opened again, and Lewis stepped through.

Helen ran into Scott so hard that they both toppled to the ground. Relief and delight faded quickly when he shifted her aside, looking past her splayed legs at Papa's dead friend. He was running at them.

A Screaming Skull sounded from somewhere close by.

Lewis paused, looked around, then came on again. His old man's face was lined, but no longer ugly. There was a purpose there that gave it something of a glow.

'Helen,' Scott said, and she smothered his face with kisses. 'Angel, we have to…We've got to…'

'We're together, we're home, we're together, we're home…' She could say nothing else, and she punctuated each word with a kiss.

She felt good against him. She felt right. And

while he knew that this was no vision, Scott had never before felt so threatened.

'Scott,' Lewis said, 'we need to talk.' Helen raised herself up above him, looking down. Tears dripped from her face onto his, and they made him cry. 'We really do,' Helen said. 'We really need to talk.'

'We have to keep moving.' The ghost of Lewis seemed pained with every word he uttered. His face was drained with effort, paled by death. Scott could not trust him for a second.

'I'd rather wait for Nina,' Scott said. 'So are you bringing blights to try to kill me again?'

'I didn't try,' Lewis said.

'Then why?'

'There are reasons.' He kept glancing back at the door, and ahead at where the corridor split. Impatient to move, afraid to stay.

'You OK, Angel?' Scott said. He buried his face in Helen's hair, smelling her, feeling her, pressing his hand against her face where she cuddled into his neck. She was shivering, her teeth clacking together. Her skin was cool and clammy. It was not a Helen he had ever known, and his hatred for Lewis was growing by the second.

'Listen to him,' Helen whispered.

'What?'

She nodded at Lewis. He shimmered against the wall, as though cast there by an old movie projector.

'He's a liar, and mad,' Scott said. 'He took you and tried to kill me.'

'Why would I try to kill you if I want the book?'

Scott shrugged. 'Because you're mad.'

'I have answers,' Lewis said. He held his hands out, palms up. 'I swear I have answers. But you need to move. I can go from here at any time, but you...' He looked back at the door. 'They're coming down,' he whispered.

'The Skulls?'

'All of them.'

'What about Nina and Tigre?'

'Tigre is here?' If it was possible for a ghost's visage to pale even more, Lewis's did so.

'He was fighting the Skulls while I...'

'The book is much deeper,' Lewis said.

'I can't trust you.'

Lewis came forward, stepping across the tunnel without touching the ground. He placed one hand against Scott's cheek; Scott felt it materialise until it was real, and he saw the effort in the ghost's eyes.

'I'm doing this for Papa,' Lewis said, and with great effort he slapped Scott around the face. 'I'm doing it for *Papa*! If you want to help him, do as I say. Listen to me. Helen knows...she knows it all. She can tell you while we go. But we have...to...*go*!' He turned and moved away along the tunnel.

'We have to go,' Helen echoed, and at last she sounded like herself. She pulled away from Scott's side, then looked back and grasped his hand. 'He's telling the truth, babe. If you still love Papa, we have to follow Lewis.'

Scott allowed himself to be led by his wife. *She's so beautiful*, he thought. 'You're so beautiful.'

She smiled meekly. 'Not like this.' Then her face fell. 'I saw so much, Scott.'

'*Him.*'

'He protected me. I'll tell you. Follow me – follow him – and I'll tell you what I know.'

'How do you know?'

'He told me.' She nodded at Lewis's back. He took the left fork in the tunnel, moving quickly.

Scott shook his head. *They're coming down,* Lewis had whispered. *All of them.*

And as if conjured by thought alone, a scream erupted back along the tunnel.

'Run!' Lewis said. They ran.

'Lewis and Papa were good friends right until the end,' Helen said. 'And they still are.'

'Papa's gone. Beyond the Wide. Heaven, or whatever's there.'

'No, babe.' They were running, and sadness jarred her voice. 'He's not gone. Papa and Lewis were researching the pages of the Chord of Souls they found in Africa. Sifting through the clues. And it was Papa who discovered where the rest of the book was being kept. He'd already known for a long time how dangerous the book would be, not only in the wrong hands, but in good hands as well. Such power, and such potential for corruption. So as soon as he discovered the location of the book he killed Lewis, then himself. There was no way he could let that knowledge out. Nor could he live with it. Maybe he *was* mad, slightly. But Lewis doesn't think so.'

'Why is Lewis still here? Why didn't he cross over?'

'He would have. But before Papa could reach the Wide, the Screaming Skulls took him! His knowledge of where the Chord was must have woken them, and they couldn't risk any of the immortals intercepting him while he crossed the Wide.'

'So where is he? If he's not alive and not dead, where is he?'

'He's here somewhere. Deep down, close to the book. They have him trapped across the Wide. This place, and another. A terrible limbo. There's nowhere for him to go, and he's suffering, Scott. Suffering badly.'

'The note…?'

'It was only recently that Lewis managed to communicate with him, via the blights. Papa wrote the note through him, but he knew only an immortal could read its language, and that they would be drawn to you. He put you in danger, but he had to. He wants you to find the book and destroy it.'

'And set him free?'

'No,' Lewis said from ahead of them. 'I'll have to look at it first. Find out the words to say, the spells to break.'

'You talk as though it's a book of magic.'

Lewis did not answer. The ghost chose which turnings to take; they jogged behind him, and minute by minute the recurring screams seemed to be fading. *Lost them*, Scott thought. But it could not be that easy.

'Who are the Screaming Skulls?'

'I don't know,' Helen said.

Lewis stopped. Scott and Helen leant forward, hands on knees, catching their breath.

'Who are they?' Scott asked.

'Guardians of the Chord of Souls.'

'But who put them here?'

'I don't think even the immortals know what they are or where they're from. My guess is they were put here by the book's true author.'

'Nina told me that she could never reveal who or what that was. She said it would change everything.'

'Perhaps it would,' Lewis said.

'You don't know?'

'I'm just a ghost. But I think Papa does.'

Scott shook his head, hugged Helen close to him again. She gave him comfort, but peace seemed so far away. 'All so confusing,' he said. 'What about the blights?'

'Sorry,' Lewis said, though there was little apology in his expression. 'I needed you to see Old Man, and I knew Nina would take you to him after that.'

'Why?'

'Because if anyone should have the book, it's him.'

'After you've freed Papa, I'm going to destroy the book.' Scott saw something dark pass behind Lewis's eyes, as though there were a ghost within the ghost.

'Good,' Lewis said. 'That will set many free. The route to the Wide has been confused by Papa's imprisonment.'

'So that's why ghosts have been asking me to help them.'

Helen swayed and slumped to the ground, pressing her hands to the stone to prevent herself from falling over. 'I don't feel too good.'

'*You* did this!' Scott spit at the ghost.

'I had to make sure you'd come! You wouldn't have believed me otherwise.'

'I don't believe you now.'

Lewis shook his head, turned, and started walking again.

'Where are you going?'

'To Papa. To the Chord of Souls. Then you can make up your own mind. What have you got to lose?'

'I'm getting out of here with Helen.'

Lewis said nothing, but simply turned and continued on his way. A distant Skull scream seemed to vibrate down Scott's spine.

Scott watched the ghost go, feeling torn a dozen ways. 'What about Nina?'

Lewis paused and turned back. 'Bastards want the book for the knowledge they lost. They don't want to *die*! They want to live on, with everything else the book can give them. Can you imagine Tigre with the power of a god?'

Scott shook his head. *I believed her. Maybe I still do.* 'Have you been leaving messages for me?' he asked.

'She will slay you. Lose her.'

'I don't believe she would.'

'We have to go deeper.'

They went deeper. Lewis led the way, silent most of the time. He moved with the ease of every ghost Scott had seen, but he was graceless. Perhaps he was pained, as well. If he really had purposely remained on this side of the Wide to help his old friend, perhaps pain was all he knew.

The tunnels curved down, passing through larger areas where carvings and paintings covered the walls. Most of them were senseless. They told stories with no endings and presented images without beginning. They exuded age, misplaced knowledge, and things that should never be known, and Scott found them more frightening than anything he had yet seen in or below the House of Screaming Skulls.

There were screams pursuing them. The Skulls knew where they were heading, so it was just a matter of time. A race. It was all down to speed.

Scott had Helen back, so it should have been over. His love, his angel was with him, running by his side even though she looked exhausted. She was a different woman; he could sense that very clearly.

She had been in the Wide with Lewis, and though he had apparently protected her there, she had seen things that no living person should ever see. Whether she had come back stronger or edging towards destruction had yet to be discovered.

It should have been over. But it was not.

Lewis seemed to be failing. His image faded in and out of focus, and though he moved just as easily as before, he seemed more pained than ever. He shimmered and flickered, and more than once Scott held out his hand and looked at it to test his own vision.

'Lewis,' Scott said, but the old ghost kept moving. They passed through tunnels and caves, and here and there were whole rooms, carved perfectly square into the rock of the earth and decorated with old paintings, swathes of faded cloth, or mosaic images buried into the wall. These mosaics used many mediums to communicate their image: pebbles, shells, coloured glass, and once what looked like a vast array of stained teeth. They did not pause long enough to examine any in great detail, and for that Scott was pleased. Everywhere down here felt wrong. He could not translate the mosaics, but even looking at them left a filthy taste in his mouth. He could not make out anything recognizable in the paintings, but somehow they communicated the presence of greater, less understandable things.

'What made these places?' he said, and when he

looked at Helen he saw that they were having the same effect on her.

'Don't want to know,' she said.

'What is this place?' Scott asked.

'Same answer.'

Lewis paused and seemed to gather his strength. Though he was a ghost, he seemed grateful for the rest. 'One of a thousand ancient places,' he said.

'How ancient?'

'Old.' The image of Papa's friend looked around the tunnel they were in, tracing one ambiguous finger along a ridge in the wall. 'So old.'

'And the Chord of Souls has been here ever since it was written?'

'That, I don't know. But I've heard whispers. I think much of what you see on the walls down here are images of old wars, and they all pivot about that book.'

'I want this over with,' Scott said. 'This isn't for me. I don't like this. Papa was the one; he was the one always searching further, looking deeper.'

'Of course,' Lewis said. 'But he needs you to save him.'

'You're here.'

'Only a mortal can touch the book.'

Scott nodded. 'Nina told the truth about that, at least.'

Another scream from behind them. It seemed to be answered by many more, or perhaps they were echoes.

'We should go,' Lewis said. 'Not far, I think. I'm feeling…I don't think it's far.'

'Will I know Papa?' Scott said, suddenly terrified at what he was going to face. The book was one thing, but the tortured soul of his grandfather, dead for thirty years yet still held here by the Skulls…that was so personal.

'You will,' Lewis said, smiling. 'He's not far away at all.'

They moved on, passing through more long tunnels and occasional rooms. The screams harried them, echoing from deep pits, erupting behind or in front of them, and which were screams and which were only echoes was impossible to determine. At any moment Scott expected the way to be blocked by one of the Skulls, its fleshless head gleaming in the strange light of this place older than history.

He also wondered about Nina and Tigre, and the immortal woman sliced in half outside the house. *This is far from over,* he thought. He squeezed Helen's hand again to make sure she was real, and she smiled at him. *I have Helen, but it's far from over.*

'Here,' Lewis whispered. 'He's here.'

They emerged from a narrow tunnel into a wide room. Its air shimmered with strange light and shadows with nowhere to hide. One side of the room did not exist; it disappeared into the sickly haze of the Wide, vast and endless. It was Scott's nightmare of crushing space and suffocating distance come to life.

Sitting at the centre of the room, on an old timber chair pitted with woodworm, an old man. Papa. His image was indistinct, and it blurred away into the Wide, as though grasped by something deep in that endless place and stretched for ever. He moved, his head shifting slowly and setting the stretched image vibrating across the room.

Scotty, a voice said, and Scott fell to his knees, crying, pressing his hands to his ears and then cupping them there to catch anything else that was said.

'Papa,' Scott said.

Hurts.

'I'll help you, Papa.'

Hurts, Scotty.

Scott did not know what to say. How could he comfort someone whose soul was subject to such pain? What could he really say that would not come across as an empty platitude? *I love you*, he could say, but the old man knew that well enough. *I'll help you*, he could say again, but what if that turned into an empty promise? He had no idea what had happened here and what would continue to happen. These were laws he could never understand, and he was an ignorant among these beings: ghosts, immortals, Screaming Skulls. He was mortal. He had lived half a life, and his vision found it difficult to look any farther.

'Lewis stayed with you,' he said, and Papa seemed to sigh in response. 'And so will I.' Papa's image lowered its head, bending across the room.

Scott refused to let go of Helen's hand. She had closed her eyes and covered them with her free arm, rejecting the sight. The Wide hung before them, a continuous extension to the room they were in, and Scott felt dwarfed by all around him, a mind without intellect.

Stronger than you know, Papa said, and for the first time it sounded like the voice of the old man he knew and loved. *Chord of Souls has to go, Scott. I span the Wide. I know what wrote it. Don't let Nina...don't let any of them...* Scott felt the effort there – the pain Papa suffered in projecting his voice in that way – but Papa had done it for him.

'I'll do it, Papa. I'm not afraid. Nettles don't sting on Saturdays.'

He felt an overwhelming flow of love then, as though the whole world were smiling at him.

'Come on,' he said to Helen. 'You're staying with me whatever happens.'

'They're here,' Lewis said. 'They're *here*!'

Something forged along the tunnel behind them, pushing air before it and projecting screams that crushed Scott and Helen down to the ground.

Shapes emerged from the Wide, coalescing into two humanoid figures that disturbed Papa's endless image, sending ripples that caused him to add his own silent scream to the room.

Lewis cowered back against a wall, and he and Scott locked eyes.

Now, Lewis's gaze said. *Your only chance.*

Scott saw Nina and Tigre form fully from the Wide. Nina's eyes flickered around until they settled on Scott. They were unreadable.

The Screaming Skulls burst from the tunnel, an eruption of bone and fury.

Shadowy blights flickered into existence around Lewis like negative fireworks.

Scott stood, lifted Helen to her feet, and ran for the only exit available from the crowded room.

Papa's voice followed him. *Don't wait for me, Scotty, or anyone else. Understand? Go safe.*

'How do you know it's this way?' Helen asked.

'I don't. Nowhere else to go.'

'But what if we're—'

'Look.' Scott pointed ahead at swathes of spider-webs hanging across the tunnel. They were heavy with dust, and dried things hung here and there, wrapped in silken threads. 'No one's been this way for a long time.'

'I don't like it here,' Helen said. 'I really need to go home.' She was struggling to hold in her tears, strong as ever, but a single drop escaped her right eye.

Scott watched it run down her cheek and drip from her chin. 'I can't do anything for us,' he said. 'Not right now. I'm as lost as you are, but I need you strong. Are you strong?'

Helen sniffed, nodded. 'You know I am.'

'I know you are.' Scott smiled. 'You ready for this?'

'Spiders? No. Hate the little fuckers.'

Little? Scott thought, looking at the webs. But he did not want to make matters worse.

He went first, and when he touched them the webs were surprisingly light. He felt the subtle rip as he ran his hand through them, but no spiders scurried from out of sight to bite his hand, and there were no thumps on his shoulders or cries from behind.

Helen still held his other hand. Her grip hurt. Scott squeezed, and she held tighter. It felt good.

Web was collecting around his hand and across his sleeved arm. It was all but weightless, and even the hanging dead things were light to the touch. Sucked dry, perhaps. But he tried to cast that thought aside.

The light still came from somewhere, exuded from the walls or born of the air itself. Perhaps this close to the rip into the Wide – the rent through which Papa's tortured soul was stretched – the air lit with what was beyond.

Past the webs they found a room. It was still, silent, and there was nothing there that should have felt threatening. Yet upon entering, Scott and Helen moved sideways and pressed themselves back against the cool walls. *So old!* he thought.

Age itself seemed to have a personality. He could tell that no one had been in this room for…ages. Literally ages. He could feel the slick, dank air that had not been breathed, see the layers of dust that consisted of no human skin, sense the impossible age of the things in this room almost exuded as aromas, such was their power. The level light remained, though it seemed darker than anywhere else in the tunnels. *Did this room exist before we set eyes on it?* he thought. *Was it here before I pushed through the last web and we emerged from the tunnel? If so, what was it like?* As a child he had often imagined the words of his favourite stories pressed together in closed books, unreadable in the darkness between pages, and unread. He had wondered whether the stories were still there. He'd asked Papa once, and Papa had said that stories are made, created, and understood by the reader. The book is just a collection of words. It had confused him then, and it still did now.

Spread across the floor and leaning casually against the wall were the stone tablets of the Chord of Souls.

'This is it,' Helen whispered, and Scott thought, What *is it?* It was not a comforting thought. It personalised the impersonal, and he did not like that idea. Had these tablets contained anything before he and Helen appeared? Had they meant anything? He could not know.

'Lewis needs to see something of this to free Papa,' Helen said.

'No,' Scott said. 'Papa told me not to wait.'

'But—'

'They have to be broken. Destroyed.'

'It's amazing,' Helen said. She stepped forward into the miasma of age and history, knelt before one slab and traced a carving with her forefinger. 'It's *incredible*'

Scott tried to pick up a slab. He pried his fingers beneath its edge, pushing through a small drift of dust that may have taken thousands of years to build up. The stone lifted with a dry exhalation. 'Helen, I need to trust you,' he said.

'Scott…'

'Please, Angel. I mean it. I need to *trust* you.' He took the folded exercise book from his front pocket. The pencil fell out and clattered onto the stone he was trying to lift, rolling into a carved channel.

'What are you doing?'

'Something secret. Will you help?' He plucked the pencil from the stone and leant the slab against another, bent forward, closed his eyes, and blew. Dust and grit pricked at his face, and he wiped it from his eyes before looking again. The stone was bare, begging to be read. He tore a sheet of paper from the book and pressed it to the stone surface. When he inclined the pencil and rubbed, impressions emerged from the tablet.

'I'll help you,' Helen whispered. She reached out and he gave her the exercise book. Their fingers touched briefly. She started tearing out its blank pages.

'I don't know if I'm doing the right thing,' he said.

Helen shook her head. 'Maybe with this there is no right and wrong.'

They started taking rubbings of the stones. Scott was crying, and at first he attributed it to the dust. But then he scolded his dishonesty and thought back to that image of Papa, trapped from here and across the Wide by the Screaming Skulls. It had seemed like a faded representation of him, lacking the vitality and intellect of the man and yet still so certainly Papa.

'How dare they?' he said.

Helen did not answer. She was being methodical, clearing dust from slabs, handing paper to Scott, then stacking the traced tablets against the far wall.

There were over forty tablets, but they worked quickly together.

'Nearly done, Papa,' he whispered. He hoped that he was doing the right thing. Even unable to read or translate what was before him, Scott could feel the potential radiating from these pages. *Maybe I'm affected by them even as I see them,* he thought. *Perhaps Helen and I will be changed by this for ever.*

Helen glanced over, a twinkle in her eye. And he knew that he was right. Every second that passed changed both of them. He only hoped that when this was over, they could still recognise each other. And themselves.

They worked on. Scott traced; Helen pocketed the finished pages. And time started to fade. In a place this old, perhaps it had little meaning. Scott had a crazy vision of time sprinting onward way above them; cities rising and falling, empires fading to dust and new ones rebuilding themselves from the rubble of the old, people being born, living and dying in endless cycles that sometimes seemed so futile, but actually meant so much.

For a moment he circled a position of such complete understanding that he gasped and fell onto his back. He stared at the ceiling and knew that the truth was there, just beyond his sight. He reached out, almost able to touch it. 'Have you ever felt as if you know almost everything?' he said, and Nina was above him, glaring down into his eyes and reaching out to hold his shoulders.

She pressed him down into the stone and leant in close. 'Not yet,' she said. 'But soon.'

Helen screamed. Scott turned his head and saw her held back against the wall by Tigre, the man of scars. He looked back up at Nina, her face upside down above his.

'I trusted you,' Scott said. 'For a while, at least.'

'I never meant to harm you,' Nina said.

'What do you mean?'

She looked around then, and he saw an animation in her eyes that had been so lacking. It was as if coming into this room of frozen time and painful history had brought her to life. 'Things have changed,' she said.

'Let Helen go.'

'Not yet. The book. I need the book, need to read it, and then you and Helen can go free.'

'And what then?'

'Sit up,' Nina said.

She moved her weight from his shoulders and Scott sat up, slipping the pencil beneath his leg, glancing across at Helen. *It'll be OK,* he tried to communicate, but she had her eyes closed against the man holding her.

'What?' Scott asked again. 'You read the book, remember what you were told, and then eternity becomes a much more attractive place. Is that it? More power, more knowledge?'

'It's probable that once you leave here, you'll never see us again,' Nina said. 'There's such power in these pages, but it's above the knowledge of mere humans.'

'You're weak,' Scott said, and he could see it. Her eyes were hazy once again, her skin pale and mottled, and even Tigre's legs were shaking. 'You shouldn't be here.'

'Tigre.' Nina uttered his name so casually that at first Scott was not aware of what she had done. But then he heard the sickening snap of breaking bone, and Helen screamed, and Tigre looked at him with something in his eyes that could have been a smile.

'Helen!'

'Just her arm,' Nina said. 'Lots more bones left. Or perhaps her eyes next. This isn't me, Scott; you should know that. It's not my way. But I'm learning.'

'Just leave her the fuck alone.' He rose to his knees and turned to the next stone tablet. He picked it up, blew dust from it, and then heaved it as hard as he could at the wall.

The effect was staggering. He was hoping for a break, perhaps several cracks, but the tablet shattered into a hundred pieces, dust and grit exploding from it and scraping against his skin, shards ricocheting around the chamber, and even before they had all settled on the ground, Nina was shouting.

'One for one!' Scott said. 'Just one page, but there are lots left!' He held his breath. Helen was still whimpering, but there had been no fresh breaks. *They won't really harm her*, he thought. *Not badly. They kill her, and I have nothing left to live for.* But the thought of them torturing her to get to him…

'You're not in control, Scott!' Nina shouted.

'Neither are you. We have a trade to make.'

Nina pursed her lips, looked at the shattered pieces of stone, then nodded. *She must be wondering what is lost for ever*, Scott thought. And then, looking down at the dust and stone shards, so was he.

'Clean them and stack them up,' Nina said. She moved to the slabs Helen had already stacked against the wall, swaying as she stood before them.

They're weak, Scott thought. *They hurt Helen because they're weak. It's a pretence. I am the one in control here. Papa? Is that right? Am I in control? Am I responsible?*

Scott searched for Papa's voice, but heard nothing.

The tattered soul of the old man was so close, but it was also way beyond him now. Scott could save him from further suffering, but they would never again have one of their talks. *I'll miss you,* Scott thought.

He bent and lifted another slab. He sensed Nina tensing behind him as he did so.

'You can't touch these,' he said. 'I know that wasn't a lie, at least.' He hefted the slab – it was heavy, but still light enough for him to manipulate – and showed it to her. 'See anything good?'

'Don't fuck with me, Scott.' But Nina was leaning forward, looking as if she were going to be sick but still fascinated, unable to help herself, staring at the stone – the page from the Chord of Souls – and grimacing at the pain it caused her.

Her mouth suddenly dropped open in wonder. 'I carved that one,' she said.

'Have it back.' Scott threw the stone with all his might. He fell backward, scrabbling on the ground for a heavy chunk of the tablet he had smashed, and as his fingers closed around one the slab struck Nina.

'Helen, down!' he shouted.

Nina screamed.

Helen slumped to the floor with a groan, legs folding beneath her, and Tigre's grip slipped on her broken arm.

Scott threw the chunk of stone tablet at the scarred man's back. It sailed high and struck him at the base of the skull.

As Nina's first scream began to fade, Tigre's cut in.

Scott had no idea what to expect. *It's a ghost to us, but it's like poison also,* Nina had said about the Chord of Souls. As her second, heavier scream sliced around the enclosed space, Scott realised just how true that was.

The stone page had ghosted right through her. The movement had shoved her back against the wall, and the tablet lay shattered behind her. It had been a lucky throw; the initial impact had hurt Nina, but the stone shattering behind her, peppering her back with rebounded shards, had driven her to her knees. 'No!' she wailed again and again, and she seemed to dance as she reached for the places she had been touched.

Tigre's cry ended abruptly.

This is when he cuts me to pieces, Scott thought. But he was wrong. Tigre was suffering in silence. Where the stone shard had struck him and passed through, an open wound grew. Blood spilt, bone shone grimly through the rent in his scarred flesh, and he hissed as he grabbed Nina's arms and dragged her from the room.

'I'm not seeing any of this,' Helen said. Her head was turned to the side, broken arm cradled in her lap.

'We have enough,' Scott said. He shoved the crumpled pages into his pockets and lifted another slab. *This could be the map to Atlantis,* he thought, and he threw it into a corner of the room. It shattered. Perhaps even these stone pages were so old that time had made them brittle. Or maybe it was the forbidden knowledge that had done that. Maybe this unexpected release was giving the Chord of Souls power to aid in its own destruction.

He kicked another slab and it cracked in two. Stomped on one half, and that piece turned to shards. Again, and there was only dust beneath his heel. He picked them up, threw them, smashed them to pieces and stomped on the pieces until they were gravel. The dust of the Chord of Souls filled the room, and he wondered what arcane knowledge he and Helen were breathing in. Given forever, perhaps the dust could be re-formed, a jigsaw that would take eternity to complete. But Scott felt such a sense of rightness in what he was doing that he thought the Chord would never allow itself to be discovered again.

Who wrote you? he thought. *Who knew you? What gave you away?* He was sure he would never know.

There was one slab left. It sat against the wall beside Helen, and she had placed a sheet of paper against it and traced it. She was crying. 'There's so much here,' she said.

'Maybe, but we're only human.' He picked up the slab and threw it into the far corner of the room.

And then there was a voice in his mind, so rich and vibrant that he fell to his knees with the shock of recollection. *They've stopped screaming, and they're letting me go.*

'Papa!' Scott shouted.

You're a good boy, Scotty.

'Papa, won't they come for me? Aren't they the guardians?'

Once. But time can change so much. Now they feel it; they want only release. And Scotty, release feels so good. I'm going. Slipping away. Lewis is with me… Lewis, my old friend.

'But he only wanted the book for himself.'

Of course, I know that. He's only human.

'Papa, don't go. Not yet. There's still so much to say!'

Always…to say…talk to me…

'Papa?'

…in your dreams…

And that was all.

'He's gone?' Helen said.

Scott nodded. 'And Lewis.' He felt suddenly deflated, as though something momentous had refused to happen. 'What did I do here?'

'You set Papa free,' Helen said. 'He's proud.'

'Not that. This.' He pointed at the mess of stones and dust around them. 'Helen, what have I done?'

'I really don't know.'

They sat side by side, breathing in the dust as it slowly settled. A spider scuttled in from the tunnel, perhaps upset at finding its web broken. It scurried across the stones, paused here and there, and then found a hollow and disappeared into its shadow.

'The light's fading,' Helen said.

'We should go. We'll never find our way—'

'What about them?'

'Papa said the Skulls have gone.'

'No, *them*. The scarred one, and the woman?'

Yes, what about them? Scott thought. And he knew that there were two possibilities. If they were of a vengeful frame of mind, they would kill him and Helen and leave their bodies down here to rot. No one would ever find them; this place barely existed. Or perhaps they had already gone, skimming back across the edge of the Wide and emerging somewhere else in the world.

Either way, there was little he could do to affect whatever was to come.

'I think they've gone,' he said. 'But I can't know for sure.' He coughed, dust harsh in his throat.

'I'm having some thoughts,' Helen said. 'Not sure…weird…'

'Me too,' Scott said. 'But we have to go.'

They climbed back up through the tunnels. Papa's timber chair lay broken on its side, the open pathway into the Wide closed. Now it was just another cave.

On the way back up, guided by a light that was fast fading, they found no immortals, and nothing of the Screaming Skulls.

Later, sunlight felt good on their skin.

Even as Scott and Helen walked from the valley and found themselves somewhere real again, they began to talk about their ideas.

Chapter Fifteen

in the blink of an eye

The last time Scott had seen a ghost it had been his grandfather, stretched agonisingly across reality and the unreality of the Wide. He had set Papa free and walked away, and he had not set eyes on another wraith since.

'You're no ghost,' he said.

'Of course not. I'm not dead.'

'Do you want to die?'

'Do you?'

'What do you think?'

Nina shrugged. It was a surprisingly familiar gesture, even though Scott had not seen it in over thirty years. 'I think you're looking old.'

'Ha! You can talk.'

'I don't look old, not like you.'

Scott smiled and lifted his hands to his wrinkled face. 'You should take a look in the mirror one day,' he said. 'Your skin's smooth and your hair's lustrous, but your eyes reveal your soul.'

They sat quietly for a while, taking in the late-afternoon sun. The garden was alive with a sunburst of flowers, the buzzing of insects, and birdsong. Between them a bottle of wine sat on the table, two glasses almost empty.

Scott sighed. 'I love this place,' he said. 'The house, the garden, the village, my wife. I love it all. And the thought of leaving it behind…'

'Awful,' Nina said.

'Awful,' Scott said. He fell silent again, looking down the garden towards the fields beyond, and the forest beyond that. 'But it's nature,' he said at last. 'The way things are.'

Nina snorted.

'What? You're beyond nature?'

'I can't say that, no.'

'Why are you here, Nina? Helen will be home soon, and I'd rather she didn't see you. She still has nightmares sometimes. Even with all we know, she still dreams bad dreams. So why are you here after all this time?'

'Time? It's the blink of an eye for me, Scott. Every day since then I've felt pain at what you did, but it's still the blink of an eye.'

'Where have you been?'

'Here and there.'

'Tigre?'

'Different heres, different theres. Places you've seen on the news.'

'So…'

Nina stood and walked to the edge of the lawn. She squatted down and ran her hand through the grass. It needed cutting, but Scott liked it the way it was. Wild. 'I've wondered,' she said. 'Since that time, I've wondered whether something like the Chord could ever really be destroyed.'

'You've been back?' Scott felt a brief chill even thinking about the House of Screaming Skulls. Not a good place to be. He and Helen had spent thirty years trying to forget. Though there were the dreams, of course, and the ideas. Yes, always them.

'I couldn't find it,' Nina said. 'None of us can. I'm not even sure it's there anymore.'

'So live with it.'

'I can't die, Scott,' she said. She stared at him, and in her aged eyes he saw the pain she had always been so loath to show.

'You didn't want to die,' he said. 'You lied to me about that. You wanted the book for everything else it contained. The "stuff", as you called it. More things. Whatever it was, *that's* what you wanted.'

'Then, yes. But things change.' She looked over the garden and into the fields.

'So why have you come to me? You think I may have lugged some of those slabs out with me?'

'No,' she said. 'I know you didn't. Tigre and I watched you all the way out of the valley.'

Scott guffawed, holding his side as the pain kicked in. A year, he'd been told, maybe less.

Helen had been sad, because she didn't want to be left on her own.

But they had both accepted it. It was the way of things.

'I don't know,' Nina said. 'I just thought maybe you'd kept some of it, somehow. A thing like that doesn't deserve to fade away.'

Scott thought of those rubbings, and the journals of dreams and ideas he and Helen had filled between then and now, ideas planted in them from inhaling the dust of the destroyed book. They wrote them down, then closed the books. Neither had been tempted to discover what they meant, and they had enjoyed growing old together.

'Maybe something like that should never have been written in the first place,' he said.

'Well...'

'Who spoke it, Nina? Who made you write it? When you and the others carved it all that time ago, who gave it to you?'

Nina smiled. 'So I guess we leave it at that,' she said.

'I suppose so.'

She nodded, smiled at Scott, and then walked down the length of his garden. She climbed the fence and strolled across the field, pausing for a few seconds at the old dead tree at its centre. Nina looked back and shielded her eyes, and he waved at her, laughing as he did so. *Waving her goodbye,* he thought. *Her poor damned soul, I'm waving her goodbye.* She turned away again and walked on, and after a few minutes she disappeared into the woods.

He never saw her again.

That night, after Helen had gone to bed, Scott opened some of their notebooks. He started to read, but he was quickly drawn to the window. He looked up at the moon and stars, knowing that he could never be their equal. The real world was out there, disturbed by street lights and the scar of human habitation, and he could not know it. Things Papa had told him came and went, and he shed a tear for the children and grandchildren he and Helen never had.

Eventually he went upstairs. He stood beside their bed for a very long time, looking down at his sleeping wife.

The next morning, sitting in the garden chair Nina had occupied just the afternoon before, Helen asked him something. 'Is there anywhere special you'd like to go, babe?' The implication was understood without ever being vocalised. *Anywhere special you'd like to go before you die?*

He pretended to think about it, scratching his chin and looking out at the oak tree in the field. It had been dead for a long time, but he had known it all his life.

He had not told Helen that Nina had come. There was no need.

'There is somewhere,' he said. 'Been thinking about this for a very long time. Think you have too. Somewhere to leave the sheets and our notebooks, with all those ideas in them.'

'Weird ideas,' Helen said.

'Weird,' he agreed, and a shiver went down his back. *So weird. Equations and poems, fractions and spells, songs and directions, a map and the way to elsewhere.*

'So?' she asked.

He blinked the ideas away. 'Edinburgh,' he said.

'You're sure you can find it again?' she asked quietly. She was so strong, so fit, and Scott was truly going to miss her.

'No,' he said. 'Not sure at all.'